DEAD FURY

A DETECTIVE JANE PHILLIPS NOVEL

OMJ RYAN

INKUBATOR
BOOKS

Published by Inkubator Books
www.inkubatorbooks.com

Copyright © 2024 by OMJ Ryan

OMJ Ryan has asserted his right to be identified as the author of this work.

ISBN (eBook): 978-1-83756-483-5
ISBN (Paperback): 978-1-83756-484-2

DEADLY FURY is a work of fiction. People, places, events, and situations are the product of the author's imagination. Any resemblance to actual persons, living or dead is entirely coincidental.

No part of this book may be reproduced, stored in any retrieval system, or transmitted by any means without the prior written permission of the publisher.

TRIGGER WARNING

This book deals with themes of child abuse and domestic violence. If you've been affected by any of the issues raised in this story these organizations can offer advice and support.

UK Resources:
   https://www.nationaldahelpline.org.uk/
   https://247sexualabusesupport.org.uk/
   https://rapecrisisscotland.org.uk/help-helpline/

US Resources:
   https://www.thehotline.org/
   https://rainn.org/resources

PROLOGUE

Her sister, Lesley, appeared almost childlike as she stood on the other side of the kitchen countertop, her eyes red and swollen from crying most of the afternoon. Despite being in her late thirties, you'd be forgiven for thinking she was the same frightened little girl whom she'd fought so hard to protect after their mum had died when they were just young kids.

'How could this be allowed to happen?' sobbed Lesley. 'He was supposed have been sentenced to twenty years! How did he get out three years early?'

'And you're *sure* he's out on licence?' she asked.

'That's what Sergeant Price told me, yes.'

She could feel her brow furrowing as she continued to chop carrots for the pot that had begun to bubble on the stove to her left. 'But I thought Price had retired *years* ago?'

Lesley nodded as she wiped her nose with a crumpled tissue. 'He did, but he's still got friends in the Sex Crimes team. One of them gave him the heads-up last night, and he came straight over to tell me today. He asked if I would let you know, seeing as you refuse to speak to him.'

'And for good reason,' she shot back. 'Everything that happened is in the past, and as far as I'm concerned, it can stay that way.'

Lesley's lip trembled. 'I'm scared sis. Of what Albert might do now he's out.'

Looking at the terrified woman standing in front of her, she really wished Sergeant Price had not been quite so diligent in his approach to supporting her sister. As the man responsible for catching and convicting their childhood abuser, she understood why he thought it would be in Lesley's best interests to warn her, but the problem was, thanks to the horrific events of their childhood, Lesley had spent most of her life crippled with serious mental health issues. Tragically, this news would only serve to make her state of mind even more fragile.

'Look,' she said softly, as she placed the knife down on the chopping block. 'If he's out on licence, then there's no way he'll risk going back inside by making contact with you.'

'How can you be so sure?' asked Lesley.

'Because Albert is the king of self-preservation, and he'll know that contacting *any* of his victims could see him going straight back to prison. And having read about what happens to sex offenders in Hawk Green, I doubt he'll ever want to go back in there.'

'But what if you're wrong? He knows where I live!'

'And whose fault is that?' The words escaped from her mouth before she could stop them.

'I wrote to him once,' Lesley spat back. '*Once*. And only because my therapist thought it might help give me closure.'

'I get that, but why did you have to put your return address on the letter?'

'Because I was out of my head on medication. I didn't know what the hell I was doing half the time.' The tears came again now.

'Look, I'm sorry, Lesley. I shouldn't have said that.' She stepped around the counter and drew her little sister into a tight hug. 'I'm just frustrated that they've actually let him out, that's all. I had always hoped they'd keep him locked up in there forever. Or better still, that he'd die behind bars.'

Lesley gripped her tightly in return. 'Me too,' she whispered as the tears continued to flow.

A few moments later, her attention was drawn to the sound of a key in the lock of the front door. 'Oh, God.' She sighed. 'Sounds like Des is home.'

Lesley released her grip and wiped her eyes. 'I'd better be going.'

'You don't have to,' she replied. 'You can stay for dinner if you like?'

'No, thanks.' Lesley shook her head. 'I don't think that's a good idea.'

The kitchen door opened now, and her husband, Des, stepped into the room. 'What's *she* doing here?' he slurred as he swayed slightly left and right, the heavy stench of alcohol suddenly filling the air.

'Lesley was just going, Des,' she said softly so as not to agitate him any more than necessary. He could be a mean man at the best of times, but nothing compared to his mood when he'd been drinking.

Des held her gaze for a few uncomfortable seconds, then turned his attention to Lesley. 'Off you go then,' he slurred once more as he made a walking motion with his fingers in front of Lesley's face.

Lesley didn't need telling twice, and a second later, she sidled past him and set off for the front door.

'I'll call you tomorrow, sis,' she shouted before the door slammed shut.

'What's wrong with her *this* time?' he asked.

'Nothing. She just had some bad news, that's all.'

Squinting hard, Des stared at his watch for a moment before glancing around the kitchen. 'And is that why my dinner's not on the table?'

'It won't be long,' she replied coldly. 'I'm just waiting on the carrots.'

Des sniffed loudly, then took a couple of shaky steps forward. 'I might as well have a beer, then.'

'Don't you think perhaps you've had enough?' She regretted saying those words as soon as they'd left her mouth.

'Who the fuck do you think you're talking to?' he growled. '*I'll* decide when I've had enough. Me. Not *you*.' After yanking open the fridge door, he pulled out a can of his usual high-strength lager, opening it with a noisy crack of the ring pull before taking a couple of slugs of the cold beer.

She dropped her chin to her chest and continued about her business in the vain hope he would leave her be.

Sadly he was in no mood to let it go. 'So what's this bad news, then?' he slurred again.

'What do you mean?'

'Little Miss Crybaby.' He took another slug of beer. 'What's wrong with her now?'

'It's not important, Des.'

'Oh really?' He raised his eyebrows. 'Then how come I'm still waiting on my dinner?'

'Honestly, Des, it's nothing,' she said, stirring the now boiling carrots on the hob, doing her best to avoid his gaze.

He slammed the can down on the countertop, causing her to jump with fright. 'I asked you a question, and I expect an answer, damn it!'

She swallowed hard before replying, knowing only too well what she was about to tell him would not be well received. 'She found out today that Albert got out of prison a few weeks ago and she came round here to tell me. Naturally she's upset.'

A snarl formed on his lips. 'I've told you before, you're never to speak of that man in this house. Never!' He threw the can across the room, and it landed with a loud crack as it smashed against one of the kitchen cupboards before dropping to the floor. 'I don't want to hear anything else about your sordid little affair with that nonce.'

'It wasn't a *"sordid little affair"*,' she yelled back. 'He raped me!'

Des's eyes bulged as he glared back at her. 'Who the hell do you think you are, raising your voice at me?'

She took a step backwards. 'I'm sorry, Des.' Her voice was laced with panic now.

'You will be,' he replied as he began to undo his belt. 'I think it's time I reminded you who's in charge in this house.'

'Please, Des. I said I'm sorry.'

He yanked at his belt before eventually pulling it free from his jeans. 'After everything I've done for you.'

'Des, please,' she begged. 'You don't need to do this.'

'Oh yes I do.' Wrapping the strap of the belt around his right hand so the buckle hung freely, he took another step forward, raising his arm in the air. 'I need to teach you some manners.'

In that split second and without knowing how, she stepped forward, grabbed the pan of boiling carrots and, in one fluid movement, threw the scalding contents directly into his face.

Screaming in agony, Des doubled over in pain, his hands clawing at his scorched skin.

Acting on instinct, she lifted the now empty pan high into the air before bringing it down on the back of his head shouting, 'I'll teach *you* some manners, you bastard!'

He went down heavily, hitting the ground face first, and a second later as he lay there groaning, she lifted the pan once more, smashing it down on his head a second time. Then a third, a fourth and for a fifth and final time.

Her heart raced, and adrenaline threatened to overwhelm her as she stared down at his now prostrate body. His battered and already swollen face was turned to the side – the eyes closed as dark red blood spread across the white kitchen tiles.

Suddenly, as if every sense in her body had been switched back on and in ultra-high definition, she was acutely aware of what had just happened. 'Oh my God,' she managed to whisper as she released her grip, and the pan dropped to the floor with a loud bang. 'Shit. Shit. Shit.'

Grabbing her phone, she dialled 999.

'What's your emergency?' the operator asked on the other end of the line.

'I need an ambulance…' She paused before continuing, 'I think I might have just killed my husband.'

1

Phillips knocked on the open door to Chief Superintendent Carter's office, located on the fifth floor of Ashton House, which served as the headquarters of the Greater Manchester Police. Her boss was sitting at his desk, his eyes locked on a raft of files in his hands. 'You wanted to see me, sir?'

Carter glanced up. 'Ah, Jane. Morning. Please have a seat.'

Phillips did as she was asked and sat patiently for the few moments it took for him to square away his paperwork.

'Thanks for coming in early. I wanted to talk to you about something of a slightly delicate nature before you heard it from anyone else.'

Phillips could feel her brow furrow. 'Oh. Really?'

Carter cleared his throat. 'Look, there's no easy way to say this, but last night I was informed by the new chief constable that Major Crimes is due to be investigated by Professional Standards.'

'You've got to be kidding me? What the *hell* for?'

'I'm afraid I had the same reaction.' Carter paused as he opened the top drawer of his desk and pulled out a folded-up newspaper. 'This is what it's all about,' he said flatly as he passed it across.

Phillips glanced at the copy of the *Manchester Evening News* in her hands. Her stomach turned instantly at seeing the story that had run just a few months ago, written by her one-time adversary and senior journalist at the *MEN*, Don Townsend. The front-page headline read TOP COP RETIRES TO AVOID ARREST. She swallowed hard as she turned her gaze back to Carter, trying her best to appear stoic. 'But this is old news, sir.'

'Indeed it is, but sadly the new boss fears that what happened to former Chief Constable Fox has tarnished the force as a whole. It seems he's adamant that whoever leaked this story to Townsend should be brought to heel.'

'And hung out to dry, no doubt.'

'I would think that's on the cards, yes,' said Carter.

'But everything Don wrote is true. Fox tampered with evidence to secure false convictions that aided her rise through the ranks, and when she was finally caught out, she retired rather than face the consequences.'

'That may be the case, Jane, but as the chief constable pointed out to me in no uncertain terms last night, the information contained in that story – as well as the other six he wrote in the week it broke – was confidential police business. And that means whoever gave it to Townsend broke ranks.'

Phillips's mind flashed back to her meeting with Don just a few months ago. During that brief liaison, she'd handed over every police file she could find that would implicate the former chief constable in a series of heinous miscarriages of justice: criminal activity that should have led to Fox spending several years in custody. Instead, under the orders of a Home Secretary keen to protect the reputation of the Greater Manchester Police, she had been pensioned off with her misdemeanours swiftly brushed under the carpet – meaning Fox had gotten away scot-free. Something Phillips simply could not countenance. Now, it appeared that her actions were potentially coming back to haunt her.

'Professional Standards will need to meet with everyone in the team within the next week,' Carter continued.

'Seriously?' Phillips protested, finding her voice once again. 'The former leader of the Greater Manchester Police, who was found to have planted evidence that led to a host of wrongful convictions gets off with just a slap on the wrist – and *my* team get a full-on internal investigation. Just because Don Townsend got his hands on some compromising files. For all we know, he could have found them on the bus – or in a taxi for that matter. It certainly wouldn't be the first time confidential documents have been misplaced.'

Carter looked her dead in the eye now. 'I think we both know that's not how he came by those documents, Jane.'

Phillips opened her mouth to speak, but the words seemed stuck in her throat.

'And besides,' Carter continued, 'as I understand it, Fox hasn't quite gotten away with it. From what I hear, she's been ostracised from her precious Cheshire-set glitterati whose approval she so desperately craved. There's also zero chance of her getting any of the lucrative non-exec roles she was banking on to boost her pension – *and* she lost out on her CBE in the New Year Honours List.'

'As I've always said, sir, if that's all that happened to her, she got off lightly.'

'I guess it depends on your point of view. If it were me or you in her position, I'm sure we'd be more than happy to keep a low profile and enjoy a peaceful retirement, but for someone like Fox, status means absolutely everything. So with her now being – for all intents and purposes – a complete nobody, well, that's got to hurt. And it'll smart even more knowing that everybody is fully aware of what she did. She's persona non grata, and there's absolutely nothing she can do to change that. She's out in the cold for the rest of her days.'

Phillips took a moment to process what he was saying, and she had to admit, he had a point.

Just then, Carter's PA, Diane, knocked on the door. 'Sorry to interrupt, but Viv from the chief constable's office has just been on the phone. He would like to speak to you as a matter of urgency.'

Carter nodded. 'Thank you, Di,' he replied, standing. 'I'll head straight along now.'

Phillips matched him. 'And I need to be getting back to my paperwork.'

'Actually, Jane,' Diane cut in, 'he'd like to speak to you both.'

Phillips recoiled slightly. 'He wants to speak to *me*?' She turned to Carter. 'But it's his first day in the job. Why would he want to talk to *me*?'

'I'll give you one guess,' he replied.

'What? Professional Standards?'

'Most likely, yes.'

Phillips felt her heart sink. 'Seriously. That's all I need.'

Carter walked round the desk and motioned with his arm in the direction of the door. 'Shall we?'

'If we really must,' muttered Phillips before leading them out.

2

'Have you spoken to him since you found out he was getting the top job?' Carter asked as they walked along the fifth-floor corridor.

'No, I haven't. In fact I've not spoken to him since he left Major Crimes, which must be coming up for five years now.'

'I remember you saying you guys didn't really get on when he was in charge.'

'That's putting it mildly,' Phillips scoffed.

Carter's brow furrowed. 'What was the issue between you two? You've never really told me why there was so much bad blood.'

Phillips felt her neck flush and suddenly felt awkward remembering when her issues with the new chief constable had begun, back when she was a young officer just starting out in the GMP. 'Er, let's just say it was a clash of personalities. I think it could be argued that we had very different views on policing.'

'Care to expand on that?'

Phillips offered a weak smile. 'I don't think now would be the right time,' she said as they approached their destination.

Carter nodded. 'Fair point,' he said before leading them into the outer office, where they were greeted by the new chief constable's executive assistant, Viv Hall.

Hall had been a recent recruit in what was her first role working within the public sector. Prior to joining the civilian ranks of the police, she had worked in London for a tech firm but had made the move north to Manchester to be with her fiancé, who had secured a playing contract for Stockport County Football Club. Phillips knew all this because Hall was a slim, attractive woman in her twenties with long blonde hair and killer dress sense who unsurprisingly had caught the attention of one of her team, DC Entwistle. Whistler – his nickname within the team – was well known for having an eye for the ladies. Phillips had smiled to herself as he had returned from the canteen one day last week, acting like a sulking teenager having just found out that the new girl from the chief constable's office had a boyfriend. Looking at her now, Phillips could understand why he had been so disappointed; she really was quite stunning and the total opposite of her predecessor, Ms Blair.

'Good morning,' said Hall brightly from behind her desk. 'Sorry, I'm still getting to know everybody. I'm assuming it's Chief Superintendent Carter and DCI Phillips?'

'That's us,' Carter replied more cheerfully than necessary.

Phillips allowed herself another smile. It seemed Entwistle wasn't the only one taken with Miss Hall.

'Can I get either of you a drink? Tea or coffee? Water, maybe?'

'Not for me, thank you,' said Carter.

'I'm fine, thanks.' Phillips had no intention of prolonging this meeting beyond what was absolutely necessary.

Hall offered a warm smile once more. 'In that case, please go straight in. Chief Constable Brown is expecting you.'

Phillips shuddered hearing the words *chief constable* and *Brown* in the same sentence. How, in just five short years, that little snake had made it all the way from DCI of the Major Crimes Unit to the highest office in the Greater Manchester Police, she would never know. More important and more pressing, however, was the question of how she was going to cope with having to report to him again.

Carter was first through the door. 'Good morning, sir,' he said brightly.

Phillips followed close behind to find Brown sitting at an imposing conference table he'd evidently had installed on the left-hand side of his large office, ready for his first day. The aroma of freshly brewed coffee hung in the air, and the office itself looked almost unrecognisable compared to when Fox had been its main occupant.

'Good morning indeed,' Brown said with a satisfied grin as he took a sip from the cup in front of him before gesturing to two chairs positioned opposite him. 'Please take a seat.'

Brown's Glasgow accent seemed to have softened since he and Phillips had last spoken. Probably his attempt at appearing less provincial, given that his previous role as acting chief constable of Thames Valley Police had seen him relocated to within a stone's throw of London.

'Welcome to Ashton House, sir.' Carter continued with the charm offensive. 'How are you finding your first day so far?'

Brown placed his cup on the saucer in front of him. 'Well, I won't lie; it does feel a bit surreal to be sitting here in this office. Especially given the amount of time I've spent on *that* side of the desk over the years, but I have to say I'm delighted to be back.'

Carter glanced across the room in the direction of the gleaming new desk and executive chair located near the window. 'You've really given the place a facelift, sir.'

Brown nodded. 'Long overdue. It was stuck in the past and needed bringing up to date.'

'Well, you've certainly done that,' Carter added.

'Thank you. I like to think this clean and fresh look is more reflective of the modern style of policing I'm looking to implement over time.'

Phillips felt her eyes roll, which evidently did not go unnoticed by the chief constable.

'You're very quiet, Jane,' Brown said coolly as he took another mouthful of coffee.

'Sorry, sir. I wasn't meaning to be,' she replied without feeling.

Brown allowed the room to fall silent for a moment before clearing his throat. 'Right, well, I'm sure you can both guess why I asked you to join me for this meeting.'

Carter sat forward slightly. 'Professional Standards, sir?'

'Professional Standards,' Brown repeated as he turned his gaze toward Phillips. 'Look, I'm sorry if it seems harsh of me to request the investigation so soon into my tenure, but I've been watching these events unfold over the last few months, and it was something I wanted to tackle as soon as I started.'

'We understand, sir,' said Carter.

Brown continued unabated. 'As I'm sure you're both aware, public trust in the police is at an all-time low thanks to Fox's abhorrent behaviour during her time in charge. And I felt it vitally important that as the new chief constable I set my stance out from the very beginning; there will be zero tolerance on police corruption, and that includes leaking confidential information to the press.'

Phillips curled her toes in her shoes in an attempt to keep her total disdain for the man from showing on her face. 'With respect, sir, given the fact the internal investigation is focused on MCU, are you saying you think the information printed by Townsend came from someone in my team?'

Brown waved her away. 'No. That's not what I'm saying, Jane. Not at all. But the fact of the matter is, confidential files containing information regarding historical Major Crimes investigations *was* leaked to the press—'

'Along with historical cases from the other departments she was involved with over the years,' Phillips cut in.

'True,' replied Brown, 'and in time we'll look at those teams as well. But we have to start somewhere, and the most recent case Townsend had access to that involved Fox was the Crowther case which was not that long ago and the responsibility of Major Crimes.'

Phillips opened her mouth to speak, but Carter beat her to it. 'We will, of course, cooperate with the Professional Standards team in any way we can.'

Brown nodded. 'That's the kind of attitude I was looking for. Like I said, this is a new era, and I'm the new broom that's going to clean up the image of the force across Manchester.'

Carter nodded as Phillips bit her tongue.

'To that end,' continued Brown, 'you should also know I'm due to deliver a press briefing this afternoon, announcing my plans for zero tolerance on police corruption. The public have every right to expect higher standards than were set by the old regime – and I want them to know I mean business from the off.'

Same old Brown, thought Phillips, a showboating, political animal if ever there was one.

Just then her phone began vibrating in her pocket. Pulling it out, she could see her second-in-command, DI Jones, was calling. She had no idea why, but it was all the excuse she needed to make her exit. 'I'm sorry, sir,' she said, turning her phone so Brown could see her screen. 'I've been expecting an urgent call from Jonesy. Do you mind if I take it outside?'

'Not at all, Jane. Do what you need to do.'

Phillips nodded as she answered, then headed for the door. 'Jonesy,' she said, louder than necessary, 'has that information I asked for come through yet?'

'You what, guv?' Jones sounded confused, his south London accent still as strong as ever, even after almost two decades living in Manchester.

Phillips remained silent as she strode past Hall in the outer office, finally speaking again when she was out in the corridor and well out of earshot. 'Sorry, Jonesy. That was for Brown's benefit.'

'Brown? Are you with him now?'

'I was, but your call just got me out of my first official meeting with him.'

'Oh, really? And how did that go?'

'I'll tell you later – the walls have ears in this place,' she replied. 'So what have you got for me?'

'Nothing really, guv. Just a guy found dead at the bottom of the stairs outside his apartment in Salford.'

'Doesn't sound like an MCU case. How come you got the call?'

'CSI think there's evidence to suggest he could have been pushed.'

'I see. Who's on scene?'

'Mac,' replied Jones, referring to the senior crime scene investigator Cormac O'Shea.

'Well, he knows his stuff, so if Mac thinks he was pushed, then it looks like we've just inherited a new case.' Phillips glanced back down the corridor towards Brown's office. 'Send me the address. I'll come over.'

'There's really no need, boss. I can cover it.'

'Trust me. If it's a choice between sticking around here and listening to more of Brown's bullshit, or spending the morning with you and Mac, it's no contest.'

Jones laughed. 'Well, when you put it like that.'

'I should be with you in half an hour.'

'No worries, guv. I'll send you the postcode now.'

With that, Phillips ended the call and set off back to her office in search of her car keys. With a bit of luck, she might end up out of the office for the rest of the day.

3

The weather had taken a turn for the worse by the time Phillips pulled her British racing green Mini Cooper into the car park of the block of flats where the body had been found – located less than a hundred metres from the water of Salford Quays. As she stepped out of the car, the rain was coming in sideways with the temperature close to freezing despite the fact it was mid-morning. *Classic February weather in Manchester*, she thought.

The red-brick apartment block was typical of the kind of development that had turned the previously derelict Quays into a salubrious, yuppie-filled space in the mid-nineties. Sadly, thirty years later, it now looked dated and in need of some serious TLC.

Pulling her collar up against the rain, she moved swiftly towards the main entrance of the block, where she could see a uniformed officer standing in front of the blue and white police tape used to cordon off the scene. Behind him she spotted Jones, just inside the front door to the building, standing on the other side of the glass.

Turning, he spotted her and opened the door. He was a man of slim build with the creased features of a formerly heavy smoker, the nicotine staining of days gone by evident on his teeth when he smiled. 'Good morning, guv,' he said cheerfully as she approached.

'Is it?' she replied as the officer lifted the tape, allowing her to step under it before moving inside and out of the rain.

Jones flashed a wry smile. 'Went that well with Brown, did it?'

Phillips exhaled loudly. 'It couldn't have gone any worse, to be honest.'

'Seriously, boss? It's only his first day. Even *he* couldn't be that much of an arsehole on day one, surely?'

'Oh, he could – and he *is* being.' Phillips pulled her wet dark hair into a short ponytail. 'Took him all of five minutes to announce that he's launching an official investigation into how Don Townsend got his hands on the police files that implicated Fox in the wrongful conviction of Archie Pearson – as well as all the other shit she pulled before we caught up with her. And the best news of all is that Major Crimes will be the main focus of that particular witch hunt.'

Jones was incredulous. 'You've got to be kidding me?'

'I'm not. Professional Standards will be questioning all of us over the next few weeks.'

'So he thinks one of *us* leaked that stuff?'

'Certainly looks that way.'

'But pretty much *everybody* hated Fox,' Jones protested. 'Why single MCU out?'

'Because the most recent investigation she tampered with was one of ours.'

'Which one?'

'The Crowther case,' said Phillips.

Jones shook his head in disbelief. 'This is bullshit.'

'I know it is. Total bullshit. Like we've not got enough to do as it is.'

'And does Carter know about this?'

'Yeah, he was with me in the meeting.'

'So what did he say?'

Phillips shrugged. 'What could he say? It was obvious that Brown has an agenda in play. It would seem that this is part of his strategy to be seen as the "Great White Saviour" of the Greater Manchester Police. "The man to rid the force of the tyranny of corruption".'

'He didn't actually say that, did he?'

'No, but he might as well have.'

Jones blew his lips. 'No wonder you wanted to get out of there, guv.'

'Exactly. Give me a crime scene over a boardroom table any day of the week. Speaking of which, you should see what he's done to Fox's old office. It's unrecognisable. Must have cost a small fortune.'

Jones let out a sardonic chuckle. 'No doubt we'll be paying for that when he cuts the overtime to balance the books.'

'You'd better believe it,' she replied.

'So, do Bov and Whistler know about this?' Jones asked, referring to the other two core members of the Major Crimes Unit.

'No, not yet. I got out of there as quickly as I could, so didn't get a chance to tell them.'

'Well, I'm sure they'll be as happy as you are to have the "mighty munchkin" back.'

Phillips laughed now. 'I forgot you guys used to call him that, you bugger. I won't be able to get that image out of my head next time I see him.'

'I take it he's still as diminutive as ever?'

'Like a ventriloquist's dummy in full police uniform.'

Jones laughed too.

Feeling slightly cheered up now, Phillips scanned the space around them. 'So where's our body?'

Jones thumbed over his shoulder towards a thick internal fire door. 'Through there.'

'Let's take a look, shall we?'

Jones nodded, then led the way through.

The scene that confronted them looked like something out of a movie, the crumpled body of a man Phillips guessed was in his thirties lying in a heap at the bottom of the concrete communal stairs, surrounded by people covered from head to toe in baggy white forensics overalls. Lights flashed, and the heavy-duty camera beeped as one of the crime scene investigation team leaned in to take photos.

'Any ID on the body?' Phillips asked.

'No, but I've sent the address through to Entwistle to check it against the council tax records.'

Phillips frowned. 'Do the neighbours not know who he is?'

Jones shook his head. 'It seems not. Kept himself to himself, according to the woman who found him.'

'And who was that?'

'Simone Hattersly, lives in the adjacent flat. She told us he lived alone, too.'

At that moment they were joined by the lead CSI, Mac,

carrying a large evidence bag in his gloved right hand. Even in his billowing white overalls, it was evident for all to see he was a tall man who spent a lot of time at the gym. 'Looks like a fatal head injury,' he said in his soft Dublin accent.

'What makes you think he was pushed?' asked Phillips.

'This.' Mac lifted the bag into the light. 'We found it in the utility cupboard on the landing above, which is full of cleaning gear. It's an old-school wooden broom, and the shape of the handle looks like a match for a bruise in the centre of his chest.'

'Can we see the mark?' said Phillips.

'Sure.' Mac turned and squatted in order to pull open the victim's shirt with a gloved finger on his left hand. 'Just here.'

Phillips remained silent for a moment as she inspected the circular bruise.

'We'll obviously check it for fingerprints,' Mac continued, 'but as it was found in a communal area, it might not yield any we can use.'

'Well, whatever you can get from it, we'll need it as quickly as you can.'

Mac stood again. 'So what else is new?'

Phillips ignored the playful jibe as she scanned the space. 'Any CCTV?'

'Nothing in here,' Jones replied. 'And as it's flats, no video doorbells internally either. But it looks like there is a camera pointing out above the front door.'

'Yeah, I spotted that on the way in,' said Phillips.

'Whether it works or not, given the age of the building, remains to be seen. I'll put a request into the management company as soon as we're done here.' Just then Jones's phone began to ring. 'It's Entwistle,' he said, switching it to speaker mode. 'Whistler, I'm here with the guv. Any luck with the ID?'

'Looks like the flat is registered to a Charlie Callus, at least that's the name on the council tax records, and based on the fact he's claiming the single-person discount, it seems he lives alone.'

'Any ideas on the next of kin?' Phillips asked.

'His wife, Heather Callus. Lives in Hathersage in the Peak District.'

'I thought the neighbour said he was single?' said Phillips.

'Could be divorced,' Jones replied.

'Yeah, maybe. Well, whatever, we need to speak to her and break the bad news.'

'I'm texting you the address now,' said Entwistle.

Phillips felt her phone beep as the message landed. 'While we're doing that, can you run a full background on Callus? See who he was and what kind of life he led.'

'I'll get straight onto it.'

'Great,' said Phillips.

'Keep us posted,' added Jones before ending the call.

'Right, then.' Phillips sighed. 'Looks like we're heading to the Peak District.'

Jones glanced at the torrential rain that was now bouncing off the concrete path outside. 'Driving on the Snake Pass in this weather? What a treat.'

4

With Jones taking the lead in the squad car, Phillips followed behind in her Mini. As her second-in-command had predicted, driving on the Snake Pass – the notoriously dangerous road that connected Manchester to the Peak District and South Yorkshire beyond – was proving treacherous, with dangerous amounts of surface water significantly reducing visibility in the tiny car. By the time they reached the small cottage in Hathersage, Phillips felt physically exhausted.

'Remind me to leave the Mini behind next time we drive in the rain, will you?' she said as they strode along the footpath towards the cottage.

'I thought you'd love driving it around those tight bends. Like being in the *Italian Job*.' Jones was of course referring to the ubiquitous Michael Caine movie.

'In the sunshine, yes,' she replied as they reached the front door. 'A monsoon, not so much.'

'Give me a warm squad car any day of the week,' he added before rapping his knuckles on the door.

The rain continued to fall as they waited.

'Why didn't we bring umbrellas?' she muttered, hopping from foot to foot.

Finally they could hear someone releasing the lock from the other side, and a moment later a blonde woman – whom Phillips placed in her thirties – with a notably swollen bottom lip, peeked out. 'Can I help you?' Her speech sounded slightly slurred.

'Heather Callus?'

'Yes.'

Phillips flashed her ID. 'I'm DCI Phillips, and this is DI Jones. Is your husband Charlie Callus?'

Heather frowned. 'Yes? Why?'

'Could we talk inside?' Phillips said softly. 'Out of the rain?'

'Sorry,' Heather said before opening the door and gesturing towards the back room. 'Please go through.'

Phillips headed inside with Jones following closely behind.

A moment later they found themselves in the small lounge, where the air was red hot thanks to a roaring open fire. Phillips noted the half-empty bottle of Chardonnay coupled with a large wine glass resting on the coffee table between them.

'Is Charlie OK?' Heather's words were laced with panic now.

'Do you mind if we sit down?' asked Phillips.

'Of course.'

Heather dropped slowly into the armchair immediately behind her as Phillips and Jones took seats side by side on the small leather sofa opposite.

'Does your husband live at flat 6, Osprey Court in Salford Quays?'

'He stays there, yes.' Heather swallowed hard. 'Look, what's this about?'

Phillips steadied herself. Even after almost twenty years of delivering this kind of news, she still found it incredibly difficult. 'A man was found dead this morning in the communal area outside that address. I'm sorry to tell you that a neighbour identified the body as being Charlie.'

'Oh my God!' Heather put her hand to her chest as her breathing increased rapidly. 'No. No. They must be mistaken. It can't be Charlie.'

'I'm afraid it is, Heather,' said Phillips gently.

'But how? How did he die?'

'We won't know until we get the results from the post-mortem, but we believe he may have fallen down the stairs and died from the resulting injuries.'

'This isn't happening.' The tears came now as Heather's body heaved, overwhelmed with shock.

Phillips stepped up and moved across to sit on the arm of the chair, wrapping her arm around Heather's shoulder. 'It's OK. We know this must have come as a terrible shock.'

Heather continued to sob like a wounded child.

Phillips glanced at Jones, who instinctively knew what she was thinking.

'I'll sort out some sweet tea,' he said.

Ten minutes later, with a steaming hot mug in her hand and a box of tissues in her lap, Heather was ready to talk again.

Phillips had retaken her seat on the sofa, with Jones sitting next to her, his notepad and pen at the ready. 'Can I ask when you last saw Charlie?' she asked.

Heather took a moment to answer. 'Yesterday morning, before he left for work.'

'He was here?'

'Yes.' Heather's voice was barely above a whisper.

'Sorry, but we got the impression he lived in Salford.'

'Just during the week. He's here—' She caught herself. 'I mean he *was* here on weekends.'

'Any particular reason why you lived apart during the week?' asked Phillips.

'His work.' Heather took a sip of tea. 'He rented it so he could stay there when he was working late – which seemed to be pretty much every night in the last few months.'

'And what did he do for a living?'

'He was a senior salesman at the Porsche dealership in Stockport. This is one of the busiest times of the year, apparently, because of the new registration plate coming out on the first of March.'

Jones scribbled in his notepad.

Phillips shifted in her seat slightly. 'I'm sorry to ask this, Heather, but what was your relationship like with your husband?'

Heather's face wrinkled. 'What do you mean?'

'Well, was it a happy marriage?'

'We had our ups and downs, but then doesn't every relationship?'

Phillips was reminded of her own recent challenges in that area with her partner, Adam, but immediately pushed those thoughts to the back of her mind as she changed tack. 'That looks like a nasty cut on your lip.'

Heather blushed as she gently touched her fingers to her face.

Phillips continued, 'How did you get that?'

'I fell into the bathroom door.' Heather's reply came almost too quickly. 'It's an old cottage, and I tripped on the uneven floor just as I was pulling the door towards me.'

'Really? Sounds painful.'

'It was.'

Phillips scrutinised her face to see if she was lying, and whilst she couldn't be certain, she was sure Heather was holding *something* back from them. Whatever it was, it would likely present itself in time, so she continued with her questions. 'Did your husband have any enemies who might have wanted to do him harm?'

'Enemies? I thought you said he fell down the stairs?'

'We're looking at all lines of enquiry at the moment. We can't rule out the fact he may have been pushed.'

'Charlie was murdered?' said Heather, her eyes wide.

'Like I said, we're looking at all lines of enquiry, just now.'

Heather stared silently into her cup, blinking rapidly.

Conscious of the fact she was likely suffering from shock, Phillips allowed her a moment to gather her thoughts before continuing. 'Could you tell us where you were this morning?'

'Me?' Heather recoiled. 'Why? You don't think I had anything to do with it, do you?'

'It's purely routine.'

'I was here,' she said flatly.

'All morning?'

Heather paused for a second before nodding.

'And can anyone verify that?'

'No. I was here on my own.'

Phillips turned her gaze to the wine bottle. 'Were you celebrating something?'

Heather glanced first at the empty wine glass and then back to Phillips. 'I've been quite stressed lately, that's all.'

Phillips offered a faint smile before changing tack once more. 'I know this will be very difficult, but we're going to need someone to officially identify Charlie. Would you feel up to doing that? Or is there someone else in the family who could step in?'

'No.' Heather wiped her nose with a tissue. 'I can do it.'

'Thank you,' said Phillips softly. 'Do you have anyone you can call to come and stay tonight?'

'My sister. She's not too far away. She can come over.'

'We'll also organise a family liaison officer for you,' Phillips added.

'I'll go and do that now,' said Jones as he pulled his phone from his pocket before jumping up from the sofa and heading out of the room.

'We'll do everything we can to make sure someone contacts you as soon as possible,' added Phillips. 'They'll be able to make the arrangements with the hospital regarding the identification.'

Heather stared into space once more, the tears not far from the surface.

'Is there anything else I can get you before we go?'

'No,' she managed to whisper.

Phillips stood now. 'I really am very sorry for your loss, Heather.'

Understandably, there was no response, so Phillips turned and made her way back to the front door, where Jones was finishing up his call.

'The FLO's all sorted, guv,' he said a minute later. 'Someone from the team will be calling round this afternoon.'

'Good.' Phillips nodded towards the front door. 'Let's talk outside.'

The rain had finally stopped as they walked back to their cars.

Jones touched his fingers to his mouth. 'What do you

make of the fat lip? I'd put money on the fact she didn't get that walking into a door.'

'My thoughts exactly,' said Phillips. 'And drinking wine so early in the day? That's a sign of a troubled mind if ever there was one. I definitely think we need to know a lot more about the grieving widow before we can discount her as a suspect.'

'Absolutely.'

Phillips glanced back to the house as she fished her car keys from her pocket. 'First things first, we need to find out what's really been going on behind closed doors. If Charlie had been knocking her about, well, that's a motive for murder right there.'

5

It was eight p.m. by the time Phillips parked up on the gravel drive outside the Victorian semi-detached house she shared with her partner, Adam. It was a palatial property they'd bought jointly just a couple of years ago in the leafy south Manchester suburb of Chorlton-cum-Hardy.

As she opened the front door, she was immediately met by her cream Ragdoll cat, Floss, who, as usual, snaked around her legs, meowing excitedly at her return.

'Wow, you're a sight for sore eyes,' she said as she scooped her up and headed for the kitchen. Finding it empty, she shouted for Adam. 'I'm home!' But there was no response.

Phillips felt a rush of adrenaline in her stomach, coupled with a sudden surge of panic as she stood there in the deafening silence. Two years ago Adam had almost died after being stabbed on the doorstep of the old house they shared – the attack perpetrated by a gangland henchman she had been investigating as part of a series of murders. And no matter how hard she tried, she still struggled to shake the fear it could one day happen again. With her panic rising, she set off at pace up the stairs and headed for the bedroom. Much to her relief, as she stepped inside, she could hear the shower running in the en suite on the other side of the room.

'Hello,' she said as she peeped round the door.

Adam was in the process of rinsing his hair under the thunderous jet of water from their rainfall shower.

She stepped closer and banged on the glass. 'Hello.'

Adam jumped out of his skin before turning to face her, his eyes wide. 'Bloody hell, Jane! You scared the shit out of me.'

She couldn't help but giggle. 'Sorry. I didn't mean to give you a fright.'

A second later he turned off the water and opened the shower door. 'You OK?' he asked as he leaned out and grabbed his towel from the heated rail. 'You look shattered.'

She sighed. 'I am. It's been quite the day.'

'How was your first day with the new gaffer?' he said as he wrapped the towel around his trim waist. Despite his demanding job as a helicopter emergency medical service – HEMS – doctor, and considering he was in his mid-forties, Adam had the tall, athletic physique of a man ten years his junior.

'Ugh!' She shook her head as she wandered back out to the bedroom. '*Shit* would be putting it mildly.'

'Really?' Adam followed her out. 'How so?'

Sitting down on the bed, she began removing her shoes. 'Brown called me and Carter into his office first thing to give us some good news.'

Adam's eyes narrowed. 'I can't tell if you're being sarcastic or not.'

She nodded. 'Oh, I am.'

'So what was the news?' he asked, rubbing his hair with the towel.

'He was super keen to tell us that Major Crimes is going to be investigated by Professional Standards.'

'For what?'

'In relation to the confidential files that proved Fox was bent that Don Townsend printed in the *MEN*.'

Adam stopped what he was doing and locked eyes with her. 'The files *you* gave him?'

She nodded sagely. 'Told you it was a shit day.'

'And do you think he knows you took them?'

She shrugged. 'I'm sure he suspects; otherwise why focus the investigation solely on my team? I mean, Fox was corrupt her entire career, not just when she was involved in MCU.'

'So what are you going to do?'

'Nothing. They'll have to prove I took the files first, and as only you and Don know I did, as long as I deny everything, I'm hoping it'll eventually go away.'

'And what if it doesn't? What if they can prove it was you?'

Phillips exhaled loudly. 'Well, with my track record for bending the rules, if that happens, it'll probably be game over.'

'As in you'll be fired?'

'I don't know for sure, but maybe, yeah.'

'Shit, Jane.' He shook his head now as he pulled on a pair of boxer shorts. 'I told you not to give that stuff to Townsend. It was never going to end well.'

'What was I supposed to do?' she shot back. 'Sit there and let Fox walk off into the sunset?'

'Yes! Exactly that, it wasn't your fight.'

'How can you say that? The woman built her career on decades of corruption. Innocent people went to prison just so she could climb the ladder. There was no way I could let her get away with that.'

'Jesus, Jane. The higher-ups always win. That's the way of the world.'

She jumped up from the bed. 'Well, it's not the way of my world. I did what I felt was right, and do you know what? I'd do it again if it meant another bent copper gets what's coming to them.'

Adam didn't respond but glared back at her instead.

'It would be nice to have your support,' she added.

'You do have my support, Janey, you know that. It's just hard to watch you play vigilante knowing it could seriously mess up your career.'

'A career isn't everything, Adam. Something you'd do well to realise.'

He rolled his eyes now. 'Oh, I wondered when this would be turned around on me.'

'Well, you do seem a lot more interested in playing with helicopters than you are in spending time with me at the moment.'

'I'm not playing with helicopters. I'm saving lives!'

'So you keep telling me.'

He opened his mouth to speak but seemed to think better of it as he glanced at the alarm clock on the bedside table. 'Look, I've got to go, or I'll be late for work.'

'And we wouldn't want that, now would we?' Her tone was sardonic.

Adam began pulling on his medical scrubs. 'Look, I

know I've been working a lot lately, but I'm on the day shift on Saturday and then off Sunday. Why don't we go out for lunch? We can sit down and talk about all this properly.'

She stared at him in silence for a long moment before replying, 'Yeah, OK.'

'I'll make a reservation.'

She nodded. 'I'm going to run a hot bath and see if I can wash off the day.'

'Sounds like a good idea.'

'Be safe,' she managed to muster before heading off towards the main bathroom and the sanctuary of a bubble-filled tub.

AFTER AN HOUR SOAKING in the candlelit bathroom, she climbed out of the water, wrapped herself in a thick towelling robe and wandered back to the bedroom. Switching on the flat-screen TV mounted on the wall opposite the bed, she grabbed a brush and stared into the mirror on the wall as she began to comb out the knots in her hair. A few moments later, the commercial break finished, and the local news returned for what was their final wrap of the day's stories.

The news anchor summed up what had previously been covered earlier in the program. 'Tonight's top stories, once again; the newly appointed head of the Greater Manchester Police has promised to clamp down on police corruption with his new zero-tolerance campaign.'

Phillips spun round to face the screen. Much to her horror, she found herself gawping at the diminutive figure of Chief Constable Brown standing in front of the press pack.

The announcer continued, 'Earlier today, Chief Constable Fraser Brown vowed to bring transparency and integrity back to the force after admitting the recent failings of his officers – most notably the disgraced former chief constable – had damaged the public's trust in the police.'

'God! Give me peace,' she growled before grabbing the remote and killing the TV.

Standing in the silence that filled the room, she felt a knot forming in her stomach. 'Why couldn't you let it lie with Fox, Jane?' she whispered to herself. And even though she knew the answer – that Fox *had* to be brought to bear no matter what the cost – it didn't make her any less worried about what lay ahead. She hoped to God Professional Standards would find nothing when they came looking, but the fact of the matter was, there was no way she could be certain of that outcome. Until the investigation was complete, she'd just have to hold her nerve and pray they came up empty-handed.

Just then Floss appeared at the bedroom door, meowing and staring up at Phillips in anticipation.

'Are you hungry, sweetheart?'

The cat continued to meow.

'Come on,' Phillips said as she headed out of the room. 'Let's get you something to eat – and me a very *large* glass of Pinot.'

6

She was aware that she was moving around the bedroom as she packed an overnight bag, but her mind was elsewhere. No matter how hard she tried, she couldn't shake the image of Charlie lying in a crumpled heap at the bottom of the stairs this morning, and the horrifying sound of his head cracking on the concrete played on repeat in her mind. She closed her eyes in an attempt to escape the sickening soundtrack, but it was no use; it was all-consuming.

Opening her eyes, she decided to switch on the TV to try to distract herself, and it worked for a short time as she caught the tail end of one of the soaps drawing to yet another dramatic conclusion before the closing credits began to run. With the infamous theme tune filling the room, she wandered into the en suite to round up enough toiletries to last her for the few days she expected she'd be staying at Lesley's place.

Her younger sister had not slept since she'd found out that Albert had been released from prison, and was really not coping very well at all. It was almost as if she'd regressed back to the broken, terrified little child who had suffered so much during all those years of abuse.

As she began filling her toiletry bag, she caught sight of her reflection in the mirror, and what she saw shocked her; she appeared to have aged ten years in the twelve hours since she had taken Charlie Callus's life. She hadn't planned to kill him, of course; it had just happened in the red-hot heat of their encounter – a moment in time when she had lost all self-control, and the demons that lived within her seemed to overpower her mind and body, just as they had when she'd rained down retribution on Des's skull. And that was what scared her the most, the fact her brutal acts of violence were becoming a habit she could not control.

Clenching her jaw tightly, she closed her eyes to escape her own reflection and took a long deep breath as she attempted to banish the sense of dread that threatened to overwhelm her. After a minute or so had passed, she opened them once more and headed back to the bedroom with her toiletries in hand.

As she placed the last few items into her overnight bag, the local news program began to play on the TV, and she suddenly found herself rooted to the spot. She stared now, in abject horror, at the sight of the female news reporter standing in front of the blue and white police tape surrounding the apartment block, where earlier that morning she had stepped over Charlie Callus's broken body before fleeing the scene as fast as her legs would carry her. Listening to the story unfold, her heart raced as the reporter relayed the fact that a body had been found in a communal area of the apartment block, and that the police were investigating the circumstances of the so far unidentified man's death. Resisting the urge to vomit, she dropped slowly onto the bed as she continued to watch the report play out until it finally came to a close and the program moved on to the next story.

Just then her mobile, which had been resting on the bed, began to ring, causing her to jump in fright, and for a split second she was consumed by panic. The police were onto her and calling to tell her they were on their way to arrest her. A totally irrational thought, of course; if they came for her, it would be without warning – she was pretty sure of that.

Summoning the courage to look at her phone screen, she could see – much to her considerable relief – it was Lesley calling. Grabbing the phone, she quickly hit the green answer icon. 'Hi, Lesley.'

'Where are you?' Lesley's voice was panicked.

She let out a silent sigh. This was all she needed right now. 'I'm just packing my bag.'

'How long are you going to be?'

'I'll be leaving here in the next ten minutes.'

'Somebody just rang the doorbell,' Lesley added, 'but when I went to answer it, there was nobody there.'

'Are you sure?' she replied. 'You didn't just imagine it?'

'I'm not crazy.'

'I'm not saying that. I just know how stressful all of this is for you, that's all.'

'I know what I heard. It was him. I know it was.'

'You don't know that, Lesley.'

'I'm telling you, it was Albert. I can feel him out there, watching me.'

She pursed her lips as she tried to figure out what to say for the best. Whilst she wanted to appear sympathetic to her sister's concerns, she certainly didn't want to add to her paranoia by feeding the narrative that their abuser had returned to their lives and was rekindling his reign of terror after all this time. In the end she opted for the most pragmatic approach. 'Look, just sit tight and keep the door locked. I'll be with you in fifteen minutes. OK?'

'OK,' said Lesley softly.

'I've got my key, so I'll let myself in.'

'Please hurry.'

'I will,' she said, then ended the call. Turning her attention back to the TV, she switched it off and tried her best to banish all thoughts of Charlie Callus from her mind. Something she knew would be easier said than done.

7

The next day, Phillips had risen early and decided to head to the office. Work had always been her sanctuary when life threatened to get on top of her, and she hoped that today it could once again provide the same comfort.

After leaving the house at 6 a.m., the little Mini Cooper made light work of the traffic as she navigated her way out of Chorlton and soon found herself cruising along a relatively free-flowing M60 – Manchester's outer ring road. Contentedly listening to Classic FM on the car's radio, her mind had finally quietened for a moment, and she was filled with renewed hope that things were actually going to be OK. But the peace wasn't to last long, as her phone began to ring through the in-car system just before 6.30.

Glancing down at the screen, she felt herself stiffen when she realised it was Don Townsend calling. With everything that was going on, he was the last person she wanted to speak to just now. That said, Townsend only ever called when he needed something, or – on the very rare occasion – he had something to share himself. Either way, she knew only too well that if she didn't answer, he would simply continue to call until she spoke to him. So it was with a certain amount of trepidation that she eventually flicked on the hands-free kit she'd had fitted to the classic Mini Cooper and answered it. 'Mr Townsend, I'm guessing this isn't a social call at this time in the morning?'

'Actually, in a way it is, Jane.'

Phillips felt her eyes narrow. 'Really? In what *way* exactly?'

'I hear you're being investigated by Professional Standards.'

She shook her head in disbelief. 'And where did you get that information from?'

'My editor, Clive, spoke to me about it last night.'

'And you didn't call me straight away? You're losing your touch, Don.' Her tone was laced with sarcasm.

'I must admit, I did think about it, but I was at a business dinner for the great and the good of Manchester when he told me over drinks in the bar. So I figured it was too late to reach out.'

'And where did your boss get this information from?'

'The new chief constable.'

Phillips was shocked into silence for a moment before eventually responding, 'As in *Brown* told him about the investigation?'

'Yep.'

'When? He only started yesterday, for heaven's sake.'

'Well, strictly speaking, Clive didn't hear it *directly* from Brown, but it came from one of his team who was attending the dinner. Apparently, you being under the spotlight was something Brown wanted people to know about. Thinks it makes him look like he's taking cleaning house seriously. Going after the "superstar detective" as he apparently put it.'

'Superstar detective?' Her jaw tightened as she accelerated into the outside lane. 'What a load of bollocks.'

'So is there any truth in it?'

Phillips let out an audible sigh. 'Don, do you *really* think I'm going to share confidential police information with you?'

'Why not? You've done it before.'

'Yeah, and look how that seems to be turning out.'

The car fell silent for a few seconds before Townsend spoke. 'Look, you might not believe this, Jane, but the reason I'm calling is to tell you that if it *is* true and you are up against Professional Standards because of the files you passed to me, you can rest assured I will not tell anyone where I got that information from. I have never revealed a source in my life, and I never will. You have my word on that.'

She was momentarily speechless again. She'd rarely seen this side of Townsend, and for the first time since the horrifying loss of his beloved, Victoria Carpenter – a woman whose murder Phillips had investigated some years ago – she actually believed that he cared about the consequences of his actions. 'Well, I must admit I'm a little surprised by that, Don. But I can't say I don't appreciate it.'

'Do they have anything that ties you definitively to those files?'

'I certainly hope not, because if they do, I'm well and truly screwed.'

'Well, like I say, they won't get anything from me.'

Phillips found herself nodding her appreciation as she indicated left before moving the car onto the exit ramp towards Failsworth and her ultimate destination, Ashton House.

'Right,' added Townsend. 'I've said my bit, so I'd better be going.'

'Thanks, Don. I appreciate the call.'

'Look after yourself, Jane,' he said before hanging up.

With the call ended, Phillips switched off the radio and drove the remainder of the journey in silence as she attempted to try to process what she'd just heard. She was well aware that Brown had not been her biggest fan the last time they had worked together, but she had hoped they could make a fresh start this time around. Evidently that was not the case. It was patently clear that she would have to watch her back and tread very carefully around her new boss. Fox had been an absolute nightmare to work for. Was Fraser Brown set to be even worse? 'Same shit, different day,' she muttered to herself before slowing down as she turned the car left into the car park and headed for her allocated space in front of the building.

8

She had lain awake for most of the night, staring at the ceiling above the bed in Lesley's spare room. Sadly, sleep was something hard to come by at the moment as she struggled to banish the images of Charlie Callus dead at the bottom of the stairs outside his apartment. And as if that wasn't enough to cause her current insomnia, thoughts of her husband, Des, were never far away either – lying as he was in an intensive care ward in Wythenshaw Hospital after she had beaten him half to death in their kitchen.

She was yet to visit him in hospital, of course; unwilling to witness the results of what she had done when she had finally had enough of his abuse. Speaking to a doctor over the phone in the immediate aftermath of the incident, it had been gently explained to her that her husband was very poorly, and that the next forty-eight hours from that point in time would be critical to his recovery. Those forty-eight hours had been and gone, yet he still remained locked in a medically induced coma as they attempted to reduce the swelling on his brain. She had tried to convince herself to be concerned for his welfare, but the truth was, she no longer cared what happened to him now. The stark reality was that whether Des lived or died, their marriage was over. There could be no going back to a man who had made her life a living hell for the last fifteen years, with both his physical and mental attacks.

Lying here now, thinking about the way he had treated her, she wondered how she had ended up with a man like him – especially given everything she'd been subjected to as a kid. But – as was often the case with so many children who experience abuse – in adult life she had found herself sucked into a series of toxic relationships, and none worse than her marriage to Des. A once charming man who had morphed over time into a spiteful, belligerent, abusive bully.

Glancing left now, she could see from the digital clock that the time was approaching 6.30 a.m., and it was with a deep sigh that she pulled back the duvet before swinging her legs out of bed. It was time to start the day.

After taking a long, hot shower, she pulled on her work uniform and, after checking on Lesley, who was snoring gently, made her way quietly downstairs so as not to wake her. Based on the noises she'd heard coming from the adjacent bedroom throughout most of the night, she guessed her sister had not had much sleep either.

With little appetite for food, she settled on a quick cup of instant coffee before slipping on her waterproof coat and heading out the door.

Soon after, she found herself trudging along the dark streets on another cold February morning as she made her way to work, and it was just before 8 a.m. when the train began slowing down as it pulled into the station. When it had finally stopped, she stepped inside the busy carriage and took her usual spot, grabbing one of the last remaining available seats. A few minutes later they were on the move again.

Like most of her fellow passengers, she passed the time by looking at her phone, doomscrolling through the latest social media posts the algorithms had decided she might like this morning. It was a well-worn routine that would normally allow her to zone out but, unsurprisingly, was just not working today. With an unshakeable sense that everybody knew what she had done, she looked up from the phone screen and glanced at the faces around her, her heart racing in anticipation of being identified as a killer. Thankfully, and much to her relief, all she found were the blank faces of her fellow commuters, lost in their own little worlds, their eyes locked on iPhones, ears plugged with headphones. Zombies of a digital age, swaying from side to side as the train trundled along towards the city centre.

Feeling a touch less anxious, she allowed her eyes to return to her phone and began clicking through the various news apps in search of any updates on what had happened to Callus, and who – if anyone – they might be looking for in connection with his death. Over the next five minutes she spotted a couple of different updates on the fact a body had been found in a Salford apartment block, but it seemed that the dead man had yet to be named, and at this point there was no new information on how he had died. Was that a good thing? she wondered.

Deciding that the best option to maintain her sanity right now was to push all thoughts of what she'd done to the back of her mind – something she'd learnt to do as a child – she switched her attention to her Facebook feed and the latest posts that had landed overnight.

A few minutes later, the train pulled into the next stop on the line, which was Flixton. The doors beeped before they opened automatically, and yet more passengers climbed aboard the already packed carriage, including a group of teenage schoolgirls, who huddled together just a few feet away. Unfortunately, a face she had come to recognise appeared just behind them. It belonged to a man well known to regular female travellers on this route as someone they should avoid.

Standing at around six feet, two inches tall with a large protruding belly and a leering expression, each morning he would jump on the same train at the same time and, for some unknown reason, focus all his energies on making the women around him feel incredibly uncomfortable. As was his wont in such an enclosed and busy space, he would push his large frame up against them, staring intently as the momentum of the train allowed him to bump and lean into them in a way that was entirely inappropriate. Sadly, as was often the case in today's world, most passengers pretended it simply wasn't happening, choosing instead to look anywhere else but at him and completely ignore how he was behaving.

This morning, wearing a long black coat and sporting a red Manchester United beanie, his behaviour would be no different, it would seem. As soon as the train began to move, he turned his attention to the group of teenage girls, placing himself within a couple of inches of one of them who was standing at the edge of the gang.

From her own position sitting in the seat opposite, she tried not to make it obvious she was watching what was going on, but unlike most days when she too had chosen to ignore him, today for some reason, she couldn't take her eyes off him.

As per usual, as the train built up speed, the man began to lean closer towards the girl stood in front of him, his belly inching into her back in time with the motion of the carriage. The young girl was either oblivious to his attention or pretending not to notice as his body pressed up against hers, and it wasn't long before a lecherous smile appeared on the man's face. He knew exactly what he was doing, and it was evident he was enjoying it too.

Watching him in action made her blood boil. How could he be allowed to get away with it? Why was nobody stepping in to protect these girls? Posters plastered all over the train urged people to report any antisocial behaviour or abuse to the British Transport Police via a confidential SMS number. Yet she'd never seen the slightest bit of evidence to suggest that anybody ever did. In that moment she contemplated giving the man a piece of her mind herself, but quickly thought better of it. The last thing she needed right now was any unwanted attention.

So it was with a growing sense of frustration that she continued to observe him from a distance over the next ten minutes as the train passed through several more stations and continued to fill up with yet more commuters. And each time it did, the overcrowded carriage allowed him to impose himself more and more on the young girl, who was by now looking increasingly uncomfortable trapped next to him.

Suddenly there was a deafening screech from the train's brakes, and a moment later the train came to a juddering halt.

A second later, the young girl yelled, 'Get off me, you fucking pervert!'

The lecherous man recoiled. 'What's your problem?'

'He just grabbed my arse,' the girl continued.

'Shut up, you little bitch,' the man sneered back.

Some of the other girls attempted to pull their friend away from the danger. 'You dirty old man,' one shouted.

'He's a disgusting pig,' yelled another.

At that moment, an older man – probably in his fifties – who had been stood close by, turned his attention to the melee. 'You need to step back, pal,' he said firmly in a thick Mancunian accent as he pointed at the accused.

'Piss off,' the lecherous man shot back. 'This is none of your business.'

'Actually, mate,' the older man replied. 'I've got a daughter their age, so it's very much my business, and you're bang out of order.'

As the conversation became more heated, the driver cut across them, announcing over the Tannoy the reason for their impromptu stop.

'Ladies and gentlemen, I'm sorry for the unscheduled delay to your journey this morning. I've just been informed we have a signalling issue at the next station, Urmston, and I've been asked to hold our position here until this can be rectified. At this stage I'm not sure how long that will take, but I will update you as soon as anything changes. I must apologise, I know the train is very busy this morning, and on behalf of North West Railways, I want to thank you for your patience and understanding during this delay.'

This impromptu stop only added to the increasingly tense atmosphere within the carriage, and things threatened to get out of hand as the two men attempted to square up to each other, albeit on opposite sides of the carriage, trapped as they were with several people between them.

The group of girls continued to throw insults at the man they had now collectively deemed a pervert.

Sitting in her position just a few feet away, she had seen

enough and decided it was time to act. Even if she couldn't actively get involved herself, she could at least report the lecherous man to British Transport Police – or BTP as they were labelled on the posters dotted around. Typing into her phone, she drafted a short message describing what the man had purportedly done, as well as what he looked like, along with the location of their carriage. A second later, she hit send.

For the next twenty minutes the train remained agonisingly motionless, and the argument between the lecherous man and the older man who had stepped in to defend the girls continued until finally the driver announced the signalling issue had been rectified and they would soon be on their way.

A few minutes later, after a further update from the driver, the train jolted forward and finally began to slowly creep towards the next station.

To her considerable relief, as they rolled into Urmston, she spotted two BTP officers standing on the platform, their hi-vis jackets protecting them against the pouring rain. It didn't take long for them to move in.

As the doors opened, the older man stepped out onto the platform, thumbing over his shoulder as he did. 'There's a bloke on there who's been touching up kids. It's the guy with the Man United beanie on.'

The leading officer nodded and moved inside the carriage. 'Excuse me, sir. Can we have a word?'

'What for?' The lecherous man stepped back. 'I haven't done anything.'

'He grabbed my arse,' the schoolgirl said, pointing at him.

'She's lying!'

Just then the driver returned over the Tannoy once

again. 'Ladies and gentlemen, I'm afraid there will be another slight delay here at Urmston as the British Transport Police deal with an incident on the train. We apologise for the delay and once again hope to have you back on your way as quickly as possible.'

By the time the announcement was complete, the BTP officer had moved to stand next to the man. 'If I can ask you to come with me, sir, I'm sure we can straighten this all out in no time.'

'But I didn't do anything.' The lecherous man continued to protest his innocence.

The BTP officer wasn't backing down. 'Please, sir. It won't take long.'

'She's making it up. I never touched her.'

'This way, sir.' The BTP officer motioned with his arm towards the platform.

Finally, the lecherous man relented. 'I want it known I'm doing this under protest,' he said before stepping out into the rain.

As the two officers began to speak to him on the platform, the doors beeped again and closed a second later before the train's engine revved, and it slowly began to move away.

Staring out through the window at the man protesting his innocence to the two officers, she wondered what purpose someone like him served to the planet. What possible reason had God made a human being like him, lecherous and intimidating and aroused by other people's fears? She had spent the majority of her childhood trying to escape someone just like him, and she shuddered as the memories she had fought so hard to lock away in the far recesses of her mind threatened to find their way to the surface.

9

With the time approaching 9 a.m. Phillips found herself sitting at the large rectangular table located in the conference room attached to the Major Crimes Unit office, ready to lead the morning briefing. Seated alongside her were the rest of the core team, her number two, DI Jones, and Detective Constables Bovalino and Entwistle – or Bov and Whistler as they were known within the team.

In spite of the fact Bovalino was sitting down, there was no hiding the sheer size of the man: tall and broad in equal measure with the swarthy looks of his Italian heritage. As ever, he was eating a large bacon roll and slurping from a steaming mug of tea, his favourite way to start the day.

Entwistle, on the other hand, was an entirely different-looking specimen. Whilst he was tall and muscular like Bov, he was at least ten years younger, in his late twenties. He was also blessed with chiselled features that appeared more suited to a catwalk model or superstar athlete than a police detective, and his light brown skin reflected his own heritage – a combination of his mother's West Indian as well as his father's Irish roots.

As was generally the case, with Entwistle considered the most tech-savvy of the group, it was his laptop that had been connected to the large TV fixed to the wall on the opposite side of the room, projecting a mirror image of his own screen.

With everyone settled and each of them ready to work, Phillips turned to Jones. 'Have you told them about the Standards investigation yet?'

He shook his head. 'I thought it best they hear it from you.'

Bovalino sat to attention now. 'What's up, boss?'

Phillips continued, 'I met with Chief Constable Brown yesterday, and I'm sorry to tell you he had some troubling news that affects everyone connected to Major Crimes.'

'Has this got anything to do with his press conference yesterday?' Entwistle asked.

Phillips nodded. 'I'm afraid it does. As part of his zero-tolerance campaign to stamp out police corruption, he's decided that Major Crimes is to be the subject of an investigation by Professional Standards.'

'You're shitting me,' snapped Bovalino.

'On what grounds?' Entwistle protested.

'He believes someone in this team passed confidential documents regarding Fox's misdemeanours over to Don Townsend.'

'What a load of bollocks,' added Entwistle.

'Why would any of us do that?' Bovalino chimed in. 'The guy's a snake.'

Phillips did her best to look unfazed by their reaction. 'Like it or not, we're all going to be questioned by the

Standards team, so do yourselves a favour and have a word with your Police Federation reps. You'll need them with you when the time comes.'

Bovalino shook his head in disbelief. 'Has Brown not got better things to worry about instead of investigating his own people?'

'I hear you, Bov,' said Phillips. 'But you know as well as I do that he's a politician first and a copper last.'

'I really hoped we'd seen the end of this kind of crap when Fox buggered off,' Jones cut in. 'But it seems like he's just the same as her, doesn't it?'

Phillips sighed. 'Looks that way.'

'Did you see him on TV last night?' Bovalino asked.

'I did, sadly,' she replied.

'He looked like a bloody hobbit stood in front of all those cameras,' the big man added.

Entwistle chuckled. 'He did look ridiculous, like. You could hardly see behind those microphones.'

Phillips felt herself smile for the first time in what seemed like an age. 'Anyway, like I say, talk to your fed reps and try not to worry. He's just a small man playing at being the big boss for the benefit of the media. I'm sure it'll all blow over in time,' she said with hope rather than certainty.

Each of the men nodded.

'So in other news. As you know, Jonesy and I met with Heather Callus yesterday.' She turned her attention to Entwistle. 'Did you have any luck finding anything in her or Charlie's backgrounds that might explain how she got that fat lip?'

Entwistle brought up a LinkedIn profile on his laptop that appeared on the big screen a split second later. 'Nothing much, really, although this confirms that Charlie was indeed a senior salesperson at the Porsche garage just off the M60 in Stockport.'

Phillips scrutinised the profile picture, which appeared incongruous compared to the crumpled, broken body she'd witnessed at the crime scene yesterday morning.

Entwistle continued as he switched over to Instagram now. 'The rest of his social media is pretty unremarkable and kind of what you'd expect from a bloke in his mid-thirties. Lots of pictures of nice cars, nights out with his mates and the odd photo of him and his wife on holiday together in various parts of Europe and the States. That said, though, none of the holiday pictures appear to have been posted in the last twelve months. The most recent looks to have been taken a couple of years back.'

Phillips folded her arms as she stared at the profile on the big screen. 'Which might suggest they weren't really a couple anymore. Especially given the fact they essentially lived in separate homes.'

Jones nodded along. 'She certainly wasn't telling us the whole truth when we spoke to her. She was hiding something.'

'I'll be doing a more detailed search on both of them today, including phones and finances. Digital Forensics should have a full download of his SIM this afternoon. Hopefully that might give us a bit more insight.'

Phillips turned to Jones. 'We should go and speak to his boss at the garage. See if they can shed any light on who Charlie Callus really was.'

'Sounds like a plan.'

'Is everything on track with the family liaison?'

'Pam Clement went to the house last night,' said Jones. 'I'm told an appointment has been made to identity his body for later this afternoon.'

'Which means his name will likely be released to the press by the end of the day or at the very latest first thing tomorrow,' Phillips added.

'Where are we at with CCTV from the scene?' asked Jones.

Bovalino sat forward. 'I've spoken to the management company, who are sending the footage over later today. I'll get stuck into it as soon as it arrives.'

Phillips nodded.

Just then, there was a knock on the conference room door, and a man she recognised only too well as her federation rep, Stuart Ash, opened the door and stuck his head inside. 'Sorry to interrupt, ma'am. Have you got a minute?'

'Sure,' said Phillips, feeling a sense of foreboding. 'We can go through to my office.'

Ash nodded, then turned and stepped back out.

Phillips locked eyes with Jones. 'This might take a while, so why don't you head over to the Porsche garage without me?'

'No problem, boss.'

'We can catch up when you get back.' With that she headed out after Ash.

A minute later as she followed him through the main office, she noted the sleeve tattoos on both wrists, visible for all to see thanks to his short-sleeve shirt, matched by several piercings in his left ear. Whilst she had met him on several occasions in the past, it never failed to amaze her how different his appearance was to most of his fellow police union reps.

Soon after, with her office door closed behind them, Phillips offered him the chair opposite her as she sat down at her desk.

Clutching his pen, Ash opened his leather-bound

notepad and wasted no time getting to the point. 'I take it you know why I'm here, ma'am?'

She exhaled loudly. 'Professional Standards are investigating who passed confidential files to the newspapers. The chief constable thinks it was me – or someone else on my team.'

Ash frowned. 'Has he actually *said* that?'

'Not in so many words, but I have it on good authority that's what he's thinking.'

'By whom?'

'I'm afraid that's confidential.'

Ash scribbled in his pad. 'Have you been made aware of the time of your first meeting with the Professional Standards team?'

'Not yet, no.'

'It should be in your inbox – sent this morning. I was cc'd on it.'

Phillips frowned as she unlocked her laptop screen. 'I haven't even logged in yet this morning.'

'We're scheduled to speak to them at three o'clock.'

'Today?' Phillips recoiled. 'Bloody hell, they're not wasting any time, are they?'

'No, ma'am,' he replied. 'And I suggest that neither should we.'

Phillips located the email invite and opened it up. It was indeed for 3 p.m. that afternoon. 'So how do you want to play this?'

'Well, I guess first things first, are you aware of anyone passing information to the press from within your team?'

Phillips took a moment to answer. 'The current team, no, but there was an issue with an affiliated member of staff who we found passing information across some time ago.'

Ash raised his eyebrows. 'Really? Can you tell me their name?'

'Am I allowed to say no?' asked Phillips.

He shrugged. 'Of course, ma'am, but if I'm going to help you defend yourself to the best of my ability, it makes sense for me to be armed with all the facts.'

Phillips shifted in her seat. 'Former senior CSI Andy Evans had a special relationship with Don Townsend at the *MEN*.'

'And what kind of information did he pass on?'

'Confidential intel regarding crime scenes he was managing.'

'And why did he do that? Was he taking money?'

'I'm afraid I don't know,' Phillips lied. 'He resigned as soon as I presented him with my suspicions, so I never got a chance to ask him about the details.'

'I see.' Ash made another note in his pad. 'So could he be the leak this time?'

'I very much doubt it. He left about a year before the stories made it into the papers.'

'Could he have sat on the files for a while?'

'To what end? I mean, what would be the point of that? He got away without being prosecuted last time. Knowing Andy and how panicked he was when we found out what was going on, I think he'll have been happy to keep a low profile. I really can't see him coming out of the woodwork a year later to get involved in all this.'

'So is there anyone else who you think might have had reason to leak those files to the media?'

Phillips flashed a wry smile. 'Did you ever meet Chief Constable Fox? Take your pick, Stuart. The woman made a lot of enemies over the years. Any one of them could have wanted to expose her for what she was.'

'Which was what in your opinion?'

Phillips looked him dead in the eye now. 'Nothing more than a crook hiding in plain sight.'

Ash nodded softly. 'Can I offer you some professional advice, ma'am?'

'Of course.'

'It might be best to avoid making statements like that in front of Professional Standards. The less invested you can appear in regard to Fox's previous behaviour, the better it looks for you.'

'I'll try to bear that in mind.' She sat forward, leaning her elbows on the desk. 'But is it not relevant to the investigation? I mean, the fact that Fox falsified DNA evidence that saw an innocent man spend the best part of his life in prison?'

'It may well be relevant, ma'am, but the one thing we need to avoid is having you looking like you had a grudge against the former chief constable.'

'You call it a grudge; I call it a desire for justice.'

'Of course, ma'am.' Ash checked his watch. 'We have three hours before we meet with them, and I understand it'll be DS Claire Healy leading the investigation.'

'Have you come across her before?'

'A few times.'

'What's she like?' asked Phillips.

'She's a shrewd operator. So we need to be prepared.'

'And how do we do that?'

'I thought we might do a bit of role-play.'

Phillips did a double take. 'Role-play? Seriously?'

'Yes, ma'am,' he replied. 'I'll ask you the kind of questions I think they'll come at you with. It'll help you formulate your answers.'

'Is that really necessary?'

'I certainly find it helps the other officers I work with. Professional Standards can be a tricky bunch to deal with, and that'll be made even harder if you go in cold.'

The last thing Phillips wanted to do was sit and play at being interrogated, but she knew he had a point. The way she was feeling in that moment, she was like a powder keg ready to explode with frustration, and that would not be a good look for her. So it was with a heavy heart she finally nodded her agreement. 'OK, then, Stuart. Do your worst.'

10

A couple of hours later with Ash away to grab some food before what could potentially be a long interview session, Phillips was sitting at her desk, updating the decision logs on the Callus case, when Entwistle knocked on the now open door. He was holding a notepad in his right hand.

'You got a sec for an update, guv?'

Phillips was glad of the distraction. 'What's up?'

Entwistle wandered in and stood in front of her desk. 'I've just run the finance checks on Charlie and Heather Callus and put a bit more meat on the bones.'

'Anything of note?'

'Nothing we didn't already know, to be honest.'

She reclined slightly in her chair. 'OK. So what are the headlines?'

'Looks like he earned good money at the dealership. In the last twelve months he took home close to eighty grand.'

'A tidy sum.'

'And it needed to be too. With the mortgage on the

Hathersage house and the rent on the Salford flat, plus two sets of council tax as well as utility bills, he was just about keeping his head above water.'

'What about her?'

He shrugged. 'From what I can make out, she didn't work but did receive a monthly payment from Charlie of six hundred pounds.'

'So he was paying her some sort of allowance?'

'I'd say so, guv. Most of which she appeared to spend either on Amazon purchases or in and around Hathersage at the local shops and supermarket. There are no other regular bills or direct debits that I can see.'

'Which would seem to suggest that Charlie was in charge of the finances,' said Phillips.

Entwistle nodded. 'Which is unusual by today's standards, but not unheard of.'

'Anything else of interest?'

'Not at the minute. That's the lot so far on the finances.'

Just then, Jones's number flashed up on her mobile. Switching on the hands-free function, she answered it. 'Jonesy, I've got you on speaker so Whistler can hear you. How did you get on with Callus's boss?'

'Nothing much to report, I'm afraid,' he replied. 'I spoke to the dealer principal, a guy called Spencer Peacock. He reckons Callus was a pretty decent salesman, by all accounts. Never missed a target and always made bonus.'

'Did he say anything about Charlie's relationship with Heather?'

'As far as Peacock could tell, things were OK at home, and if they weren't, Callus never mentioned anything about them having problems. That said, he was quite open about the fact Callus was a bit of a ladies' man, by all accounts.'

'Really? In what way?'

'Well, I think we can safely assume the flat in Salford was not just about reducing Charlie's commute. According to Peacock, it was an open secret around the guys in the dealership that he was using the flat to meet women he'd connected to on an online dating app.'

'And did you get the name of the app?'

'It's called Hooked,' said Jones.

Entwistle made a note in his pad.

Jones continued, 'I had a quick look online when I left the dealership, and it appears to be targeting men and women in long-term relationships who are looking to cheat on their partners. No strings attached.'

'How delightful,' Phillips said sarcastically. 'So if Callus was sleeping with other people's wives, we could well be looking at a jealous husband.'

'That's what I was thinking, yeah.'

Phillips turned her attention to Entwistle. 'Can you get me everything you can find on this Hooked app?'

'Of course, boss.'

'And get Digital Forensics to take a look at his profile on there. See who he met – and when – over the last few weeks.'

'I'll do that now.'

Just then, there was a knock on the door.

Glancing over Entwistle's shoulder, she could see that Ash had stepped inside her office, his leather-bound file in his hand once more.

'They're ready for us, ma'am.'

'Jonesy, I'm going to have to go. I'm due in with Professional Standards now.'

'Good luck with that,' he replied.

'Thanks. I'll see you when you get back.' Phillips ended the call.

'I hope it all goes well, guv,' said Entwistle with a sympathetic smile before making his way out of the room.

'You ready for this?' said Ash.

'As I'll ever be.' Phillips stood before pulling her hair into a ponytail. 'Right then, let's get this over with.'

11

It had been several years since Phillips had sat opposite Professional Standards, and the last time that had happened, she had been lucky to keep her job, the fallout for taking the law into her own hands. Given how close she had come to the premature end of her police career back then, she now found herself wondering how she had wound up here again – this time facing an interrogation by Professional Standards officers Detective Sergeant Claire Healy and Detective Constable Tammy Shaw.

DS Healy was a tall, dark-haired woman with angular features and long limbs. A large manila folder sat on the table next to her A4 notepad and pen. DC Shaw by contrast was short with tight, curly blonde hair and a round, elfin face. She too had a large A4 notepad in front of her.

The meeting had been scheduled to take place in one of the conference rooms on the fifth floor, just a few doors down from the chief constable's office. The space would normally be reserved for gatherings between the top brass but had been unofficially allocated to Professional Standards for the foreseeable future. Another statement of intent from Brown, thought Phillips.

Healy took the lead as she introduced herself and Shaw, and after explaining the fact that Phillips was not under caution and was therefore free to leave at any time, she got straight down to business. 'DCI Phillips, what can you tell us about how a collection of confidential files, including information specific to Major Crime investigations, got into the hands of the *Manchester Evening News*?'

'Nothing, I'm afraid,' said Phillips, determined to keep her answers short and succinct, just as she and Ash had rehearsed.

'So you don't know how they found their way to Don Townsend?'

'No. The first time I knew anything about them was when I read his articles in the paper.'

DC Shaw made a series of notes in her pad.

DS Healy continued, 'And is Mr Townsend an associate of yours?'

'We know each other to speak to, if that's what you mean.'

'So you're not friends?'

'No chance,' Phillips scoffed. 'Cops and reporters don't tend to make great bedfellows.'

Healy remained silent for a moment before moving on to her next question. 'So *you* didn't give those confidential files to him?'

Phillips curled her toes in her boots, a coping strategy she used when she could feel her anxiety building. 'No, I did not.'

'So how do you think he got hold of them?' Healy asked.

Phillips opened her mouth to speak, but Ash cut in before she could respond.

'Come on, DS Healy. DCI Phillips is here voluntarily, and as such we should really be sticking to specific questions on the facts in question, as opposed to going on a fishing trip regarding a rogue reporter.'

Healy moved her silent gaze to Ash for a long moment, then focused back on Phillips. 'What kind of relationship did you have with former Chief Constable Fox?'

'She was my gaffer for a time when she was the chief super of MCU, and like everyone else in this building, she was my overall boss when she took on the top job.'

'And did you get on?'

'Is that relevant?' Ash cut in again.

'Considering the impact the leaked files had on the former chief constable's reputation and her life outside of the force once they were printed, I'd say how DCI Phillips felt about Fox is relevant, yes.'

'It's no secret we didn't have a great relationship,' said Phillips, 'but then she was a very difficult woman to work for. Anyone who had regular dealings with her can testify to that.'

Healy nodded as she pulled out a file from the manila folder before scanning it for a few seconds. 'It's my understanding that you were the person responsible for uncovering Chief Constable Fox's inappropriate behaviour regarding the handling of DNA evidence in the Archie Pearson arson case. Is that right?'

Phillips took a sip of water from the plastic cup in front of her before responding, 'I think it's fair to say her "handling" – as you put it – of the Archie Pearson evidence was *illegal*, as opposed to inappropriate. She framed him.'

'And that bothered you, didn't it?'

'Yes. It bothered me. Just as it should any cop who cares about honesty and integrity on the job.'

DC Shaw continued in her note making.

'So,' said Healy, 'would I be right in saying that when the investigation into her behaviour resulted in no action being taken, you weren't happy about it?'

Phillips could feel a knot of frustration building in her stomach. 'Of course I wasn't. She broke the law, and she should have been held accountable for it.'

'I see.' Healy pulled out another document from the file. 'Just like *you* were when you broke the law in the Marty Michaels investigation?'

'I wondered when you were going to bring that up.' Phillips folded her arms against her chest. 'Didn't take long at all, did it?'

'Can you tell us what happened there?'

'I'm sure it's all in the file; you can read it for yourself.'

'I think it would be beneficial to hear it in your own words, Chief Inspector.'

Ash had warned her this would almost certainly come up, and they had prepared a short summary of the events in question, just in case. 'It's quite simple, really; an innocent man came to me looking for help, and based on the evidence presented at the time, I chose to help him get to the truth.'

'That innocent man being Marty Michaels?'

'That's correct.'

'And you helped him even though he was on the run from the authorities at the time?'

Phillips held Healy's gaze. 'Yes.'

'Do you consider *yourself* above the law, DCI Phillips?'

'No, I don't.'

'But yet you knowingly helped a fugitive evade capture, despite having every opportunity to turn him in.'

'I'm sorry,' Ash interrupted. 'Are we here to talk about the issue in the hand – i.e., the missing files – or are you on yet another fishing trip regarding DCI Phillips's previous actions? Which I must stress have already been dealt with by Professional Standards and resulted in her subsequent demotion at the time. I see no reason to go over old ground now.'

Healy appeared to take the hint and returned the document to the file.

All the time, Phillips was trying her best to appear stoic despite her overwhelming desire to get up and walk out. Something she knew would not look good for her.

'So how do you think the files from your office got into the hands of the press?'

'You're once again asking DCI Phillips to speculate on something she's told you she knows nothing about,' said Ash firmly.

'So you have no idea?' asked Healy.

'None whatsoever,' Phillips replied flatly.

'Who has access to the case files in Major Crimes, Chief Inspector?'

'Anyone with a departmental login.'

'And are those logins secure?' said Healy. 'Or can anyone get access to them?'

Phillips shrugged. 'Is any login secure these days? From what I see in the job every day, if you have the right kit, anyone can access any computer drive, given enough time.'

'So, what? Are you suggesting someone could have hacked into the Major Crimes case files and downloaded them?'

'It's certainly a possibility. Even someone as far removed from real police work as you, DS Healy, must know that.' It was a cheap shot. Ash had warned against such a jibe, but Phillips couldn't help herself.

Healy flashed a thin smile. 'Well, hopefully our own tech team are as good as those at the *sharp end*. Because we will of course be checking every login within the team to see if any of them accessed those files around the time they were leaked.'

Phillips attempted to quietly swallow the lump that suddenly appeared in her throat as her adrenaline spiked, causing her cheeks to redden.

Evidently the change in her complexion had not gone unnoticed by Healy. 'Are you feeling all right, DCI Phillips? You suddenly look a bit flush.'

'I'm fine,' she replied flatly as she reached for her water. 'It's just a bit hot in here.'

Healy's thin smile returned as she stared back at Phillips for a few uncomfortable seconds, before turning her attention back to DC Shaw. 'Have you got everything, Tammy?'

Shaw nodded as she continued to scribble on the pad. 'Yes. Everything I need.'

'Good,' said Healy. 'In that case, unless you have anything to add, we won't take up any more of your valuable time. We know how busy you must be on the *front line*.' Her tone was facetious.

Phillips ignored the jibe and remained silent as Ash stepped in.

'So are we done?' he asked.

'For now, Sergeant,' said Healy. 'But we may well need to talk to you again, Chief Inspector.'

'DCI Phillips will make herself available as required,'

said Ash. 'As I hope she's demonstrated, she fully intends to cooperate with the Professional Standards team in regard to this investigation.'

Healy began to square away her files. 'I'm glad to hear it.'

'If there's nothing, else, we'll leave you to it,' added Ash, standing.

Phillips matched him and a few seconds later followed him out of the room.

When they were finally out of earshot, Ash stopped so they could debrief. 'I think that went as was well as could be expected, don't you?'

Phillips glanced up and down the corridor to ensure they couldn't be overheard. 'Can they really check all the logins connected to Major Crimes?'

'I assume so, yeah.' Ash frowned. 'Is that a problem?'

'No,' Phillips replied, knowing the opposite to be true. 'Look, I've got a lot on, so I need to be getting back.'

'No worries. You know where I am if you need anything.'

'Sure,' Phillips replied absent-mindedly before setting off back down the corridor towards the MCU. As she walked, she cursed herself for not being more careful when she had downloaded those files earlier in the year. She could only hope Healy was bluffing and would not actually follow through on the threat, because if she did, there was every chance Phillips was in seriously deep shit.

12

Phillips was in no mood to talk to anyone after the showdown with Professional Standards and so decided to take a walk round the block to clear her head. It was no use, however, and her mind raced as she replayed the meeting with Healy and Shaw over in her head. And if that wasn't bad enough, she couldn't let go of what Townsend had told her – that Brown was actively trying to undermine her in public and seemed hell-bent on hanging her out to dry with the help of the Standards crew.

The dark clouds forming overhead perfectly matched her mood, and as the winter rain began to fall again, she decided it was time to head back inside.

Ten minutes later she wandered into her office.

Jones was standing next to her desk, holding a file in his right hand. 'The statement from Callus's boss, guv.' He laid it down.

'Thanks,' she said without feeling.

'So how did it go?'

Phillips exhaled loudly as she moved past him and took a seat behind her desk. 'Well, it wasn't great.'

'What happened?'

'Where do I start?'

Jones shrugged. 'Anywhere you like, boss.'

Phillips glanced out towards the office where Bov and Entwistle were hard at work at their respective desks, then checked her watch. 'I think I've had enough for one day. You fancy a drink?'

'I always fancy a drink,' Jones replied. 'Where you thinking?'

Phillips took a moment to consider their options. 'How about the Met in Didsbury? It's big enough for us to blend into the background. Plus it's not far from my house, and you can jump on the M60 from there.'

'Sounds like a plan.'

'Great. I've just got a couple of emails to send, and then we can go.'

Jones thumbed over his shoulder towards the office. 'Do you want me to invite the troops?'

'No, let's keep it to us for now. I've got just enough chat for one person. Any more than that and I think my head might explode.'

'I know what you mean,' said Jones.

ALMOST AN HOUR LATER, after leaving their cars in the large car park adjacent to the pub, Phillips and Jones strode through the large double-door entrance to the Metropolitan pub, located five miles south of the city centre in the salubrious suburb of West Didsbury. The time was just after six, and as was often the case most days, the bar was busy, the air filled with the sound of chatter and low-level music playing in the background.

'If you get a seat, I'll get the drinks,' said Jones. 'What do you want?'

'A small glass of Pinot, please.'

'Coming right up.'

Phillips offered a warm smile and set off in search of a quiet corner where they could download without being overheard. She found the perfect spot a few minutes later and dropped heavily onto the wooden bench wedged next to the far wall, in behind a long table.

Jones arrived soon after.

'That was quick.'

'I think the barmaid fancies me,' he said with a grin as he placed the drinks down on the table.

'She's only human,' Phillips replied, drawing her glass towards her.

'To be fair. It happens a lot.' He winked as he took his seat. 'I think it's the thinning hair.'

Phillips laughed before taking a long drink of her ice-cold wine. A few seconds later she felt herself relaxing for the first time since Carter had shared the news she was being investigated.

'So come on then, guv. Spill the beans. What happened with Standards?'

'You know, for a split second there, I'd almost forgotten about them.'

'I've heard Healy's a bit of a hard-ass.' Jones took a sip of lager.

'She certainly likes to think she is.'

'So have they got any idea who leaked the files?'

'I'm pretty sure they're convinced it was someone in the team.'

Jones placed his beer down on the table. 'And was it, guv?'

She recoiled slightly. 'What do you mean?'

Jones locked eyes with her. 'I think you know exactly what I mean.'

'What? You think *I* gave him the information on Fox?'

'Didn't you?'

Phillips felt a shot of adrenaline surge through her as her heart skipped a beat. 'Why would I do that?'

'Because you cannot tolerate injustice. Fox was about to get off scot-free after the Home Secretary stepped in – free to retire, off into the sunset with her gargantuan pension. How was that fair?'

Silence descended for a moment as Phillips took another mouthful of wine. 'How long have you known?'

Jones offered a wry smile. 'Since Townsend published the first story.'

'So why didn't you say anything?'

'Because it's none of my business,' he replied. 'And to be honest, until Brown stuck his oar in, I was glad you did it. Like I say, Fox had it coming to her after what she did to Pearson and all the others she stitched up over the years.'

'You can say that again.'

He scanned around the room now before leaning in a little closer. 'So is there any danger Healy will be able to pin it on you?'

'Worryingly, I think there is.'

'Really? How?'

'There's a good chance I could have left a digital trail on the system.'

Jones dropped his chin to his chest for a moment before looking up again. 'Tell me you didn't use your own login to download the files.'

'What else was I supposed to do? Use *yours*? Or Bov's or Whistler's? I wasn't about to stitch anybody up.'

'But you must have known they could trace it back to you, guv?'

'Of course I did, but if truth be told, at the time I didn't care. And to be honest, I didn't think anyone else would either. I kinda figured any new chief constable coming in would have their hands full sorting the fallout from Fox's demise, as opposed to looking for the source of the information.'

'But then *Brown* got the gig,' said Jones.

'Exactly. And if there was a chance he could finally get rid of me, he was always going to take it.'

Jones leaned back in his chair. 'Well, with a bit of luck, Healy might not go down the digital route.'

'Oh, she will. In fact, she told me that's exactly what she's planning.'

'Shit.' Jones rubbed his hand down his face, causing it to redden. 'What are you going to do?'

Phillips bit her lip before responding, 'At this moment in time, I really don't know.'

Silence descended for a few seconds before Jones spoke. 'So how did you explain the files going missing?'

'I said I didn't know how it happened.'

'And how did Healy react to that?'

'Kept trying to get me to speculate on how they ended up with Townsend, but then every time she did, Ash cut her off, saying I was there to deal in facts as opposed to trying to guess what had gone on.'

'Smart guy.'

'He was really good, actually. Especially when Healy started trying to bring up what happened when I helped Marty when he was on the run.'

'So, how did he handle that?' asked Jones.

'He told them it was old news that had been dealt with at the time, and nothing to do with their investigation.'

'Which is totally true.'

'Absolutely,' she replied. 'Healy tried her best, but in the end, she got nothing of note.'

'Which is a good thing, right?'

'Is it? I worry it'll just make her even more determined to focus on the digital trail.'

Jones took a sip of his drink. 'Brown's got a lot to bloody answer for. All our energy should be focused on closing our open cases, not worrying about being pinched by Professional fucking Standards.' He placed his glass back on the table. 'Does Carter know you gave the files to Townsend?'

'He hasn't said as much, but like you, I'm pretty sure he suspects it was me.'

'Well, even if he does, I'm sure he won't say anything to Healy.'

Phillips drained her own glass and set it down. 'No, I don't think he will.'

'I spoke to *my* fed rep today, Ray Bradley.'

'About the investigation?'

'Yeah. Told me he was on standby for my interview, which he thinks will be in the next few days.'

'So what will you tell them?' she asked. 'In light of what you now know.'

'The same as before,' he shot back. 'Absolutely sod all.'

Phillips let out a silent breath of relief.

Jones continued, 'I have absolutely no time for Healy and her crew – or anyone like them for that matter. Our job's hard enough without having to worry about being stitched up by one of our own. As far as I'm concerned, the files must have been left somewhere by mistake, and there's nothing else to say.'

'You don't have to lie on my account, Jonesy. This is my mess. I can deal with it.'

'It's not lying,' he said. 'It's simply omitting certain truths.'

'Well, I really appreciate it. You know that, don't you?'

He waved her away. 'I'm only doing what you'd do for me.'

Phillips flashed a faint smile.

'Right. It's probably time I was getting back.'

'Me too,' she replied as she stepped up from the chair.

Jones matched her and a moment later followed her out as they headed back to the cars.

'Anything planned for the evening?' she asked as they walked side by side across the car park.

'No. Some food and an early night, I think. I'm knackered. What about you?'

'Microwave meal for one and then catching up on all the paperwork I didn't get done today.'

'Sounds like fun.' Jones's tone was sarcastic.

'Adam's on nights again, so I've got nothing else to do. And besides, another one of Brown's new initiatives is to ensure we're up to date on all paperwork before the end of the financial year, which is just a few weeks away. So I've got a lot of catching up to do.'

Jones's indicators flashed as he deactivated the central locking on the car. 'Remind me what time Callus's postmortem is tomorrow.'

'9 a.m.,' she replied as she unlocked the Mini using the key.

'You want me to do it on my own?'

Phillips flinched slightly. 'But you hate PMs.'

'I know I do, but if it helps you get caught up on stuff, I'll take one for the team.'

'Really?'

'Yes. Really.'

'Well, yeah. I mean if you could, that would be great.'

'Consider it done,' said Jones as he opened the driver's door.

'Thanks, Jonesy. For everything.'

A broad smile appeared on his face. 'Anytime, guv. Anytime.'

13

Having struggled to sleep so much of late, she could only blame sheer mental exhaustion for the fact she had slept through her alarm this morning – after finally nodding off in the early hours.

Waking with a start now, she sat bolt upright in bed and checked the time on the digital clock: 6.54 a.m. Shit!

With no time for a shower, she dressed in haste, and after pulling her hair into a ponytail, rushed out of the house and onto the darkened street, in the hope of catching this morning's train, which was scheduled to depart at 7.30 sharp.

As she set off towards the train station, she wondered if the rain they had been experiencing in the last couple of weeks was ever going to stop. There certainly seemed to have been a torrential downpour every day so far this month, and this morning was once again no different. With the clock ticking down until her train arrived, she picked up the pace and pulled the hood up on her waterproof black jacket in an effort to stave off yet another soaking.

A couple of minutes later with the train station in sight, her mobile phone began to buzz in her pocket. Pressed for time as she was, she considered leaving whoever it was to their own devices, but in reality, no one ever rang at this time in the morning. Pulling it from her pocket, she could see it was Lesley, and if she was calling this early in the day, it wasn't likely to be good news. 'Is everything OK?' she asked as she answered.

'There's someone outside.' Lesley's tone was panicked, her voice a mere whisper.

The rain fell harder now against her face as she continued walking at pace. 'What do you mean there's someone outside? Where?'

'Out the back.'

'Are you sure?'

'I could hear them moving about near the bins.'

She checked her watch, 7.28. 'It's probably just a fox, Les, looking for food.'

'It's not a fox. It's *him*.'

As a result of her significant childhood trauma, Lesley had suffered from anxiety and depression her entire adult life, and from time to time – when she got really stressed – both those conditions could trigger bouts of paranoia. Until recently the paranoia had been quite well controlled, but that had changed abruptly in the last week since she was told Albert had been released from prison. This morning it seemed like it had returned in earnest.

'We've had this conversation before, Les, he's out on license. And like Sergeant Price told you, as a registered sex offender he'll be on a tag, which means he'll have a curfew and confined to whatever halfway house they've stuck him in. I doubt there's any way he could be hanging about in your garden at half seven in the morning.'

'He's out there. I'm telling you.'

In the distance she could hear a station announcement being made over the Tannoy. It sounded like her train was about to arrive, so she picked up the pace even more, almost jogging now. 'Have you actually seen anything?'

'No. All the curtains are closed.'

'And are all the doors and windows locked?'

'Yes.'

'OK. Well, there's nothing I can do from here, so just stay in the house, and I'll call you when I get to work and I can talk properly.'

'I'm frightened, sis. He's out there watching me. I can feel it.'

The train was visible now up ahead, pulling slowly into the station at the end of the road. 'Like I say, keep the doors locked and the curtains closed. I'll call you back as soon as I can, but I really have to go, or I'll miss my train.'

'You won't be long, will you?'

'I won't,' she replied before ending the call. A minute later she launched herself through the train doors just as the they began to beep closed. She'd made it, thank God.

After dropping into a seat in her usual spot in the carriage, she took a moment to catch her breath and allowed her racing pulse to return to normal. Staring down at her phone, she contemplated calling Lesley back, but the loud growl of the diesel engine coupled with the rhythmic banging of the wheels over the track would make any conversation nigh on impossible. Especially considering Lesley was currently incapable of talking on the phone at any level above a whisper. Plus the topic of their conversation was hardly something she wanted to broadcast in public. So she resigned herself to the fact she'd call her little sister as soon as she got to work and could find herself a quiet corner where she could talk properly.

Settling into her seat now, she unlocked the home screen on her phone. She'd had quite enough drama already for one morning, so decided against checking the news sites for any updates on Charlie Callus. No news was good news as far as she was concerned, and instead she decided to take her chances with the latest offering from Facebook. And so, for the next five minutes she scrolled through her feed, zipping past post after post without really taking anything in, her mind never far from the conversation she'd just had with Lesley. The noises that her sister had heard couldn't be Albert. Surely it was just her paranoia?

As the train began to slow, an automated voice announced that the next stop would be Flixton – home to the lecherous man who had caused so much bother yesterday morning. She hoped and prayed the police had arrested him and locked him up so he would no longer be an issue for every young woman using this train. Sadly, that was evidently not the case, and his sullen face was the first she laid eyes on through the window as the carriage came to a stop. After the doors beeped and opened, he stepped into the already busy carriage and took up a position just a few feet away. Once again he was dressed in a long black winter coat and wore the same red and yellow Manchester United beanie on his head. Standing holding the rail above his head, he glanced around the space as if waiting for someone to react to his presence, but his fellow passengers remained notably silent.

A moment later the doors beeped closed, and they moved off again.

As the train increased its speed, he was soon up to his old tricks, but with no women within touching distance, it appeared as if he had adopted a different strategy this morning, choosing to lock his gaze on any woman travelling in the carriage who dared to look in his direction. With a wicked grin fixed to his face and his brow tilted forward, he glared at every female in sight, staring intently at them until they averted their gaze in the hope of avoiding his special attention.

Why had the police not done anything about this man? After groping at least one teenage girl yesterday, how was he now free to return to the scene of the crime and continue with his well-practised intimidation tactics? It made her blood boil, and it was all she could do to not jump out of her seat and give him a piece of her mind. But she knew that was the last thing someone in her position should be doing right now. In light of what had happened to Charlie Callus, maintaining her anonymity was paramount at the moment.

Deciding it was best to try to block out what he was doing, she turned her attention back to her phone, switching her focus to Instagram in the hope that the feed might distract her more than Facebook had managed.

For the next few minutes the train trundled along. A squealing of brakes signalled it was slowing down, and it eventually made an unscheduled stop between stations.

Looking up from her phone, she looked out the window in the hope of finding out what had caused the delay, but there appeared to be no obvious reason for the stop.

Just then, the driver's voice boomed out over the Tannoy. *'Ladies and gentlemen, I do apologise for the delay to your journey this morning. It appears we have a fault with the electrical system on board, which means we'll need all passengers to switch to another train at the next station. On behalf of Northwest Railways, I'd like to thank for your patience as we look to get you moving as quickly as possible.'*

There was a collective groan from her fellow passengers as the news landed.

'This is all I need,' she whispered to herself.

After five long minutes where the train remained completely motionless, they finally started moving again, and a few moments later they arrived at Humphrey Park station, where everyone disembarked. Mercifully the rain had at least stopped by the time she stepped out onto the platform.

Another announcement followed, this time over the station PA.

'Ladies and gentlemen, the replacement service for Manchester Piccadilly will be arriving on platform two in approximately three minutes' time. As it's particularly busy this morning due to a number of late-running services at this station, can I please ask all passengers to use the full length of the platform wherever possible.'

With so many commuters brought together unexpectedly, the platform suddenly felt claustrophobic and dangerously overcrowded. Weaving through the sea of people around her, she managed to find some space further along towards the end of the platform before stopping in her tracks when she inadvertently found herself standing next to the lecherous man. Turning, she planned to go back the way she had just come from but realised her path was now blocked as even more people filed in behind her. She was stuck.

It was then she heard him utter the words that made her blood run cold.

'You're a pretty little thing, aren't you?' he said.

She spun back to see him leaning over yet another

young woman, this time standing on her own right on the edge of the platform, wearing what looked to be some kind of fast food uniform under her winter coat. With her head bowed, she was attempting to ignore his advances, casting her gaze anywhere but at him.

'Don't be shy.' He moved closer still now. 'I don't bite, you know.'

She could feel her fists clenching as she watched the girl squirm on the other side of his large frame. Why was nobody doing anything to stop this man? How was this being allowed to happen in such a crowded place? Again, her natural instinct was to step in and protect the girl, and it took every ounce of strength she had to stay quiet – to maintain her all-important anonymity.

The young girl had clearly had enough now as she attempted to get by him.

'Hey, where do you think you're going?' he said as he blocked her path.

At that moment the headlights of the replacement train appeared in the distance, followed by another announcement, this time in a staccato automated voice. *'The train now approaching platform two is the delayed 8.02 service to Manchester Piccadilly, calling at Trafford Park, Deansgate, Manchester Oxford Road and Manchester Piccadilly.'*

The man continued unabated. 'You smell nice.'

Her blood was boiling now as the train drew closer to the station.

'Leave me alone,' the girl finally said, stepping backwards as the sound of the train's brakes being activated filled the air.

'There's no need to be like that,' the man replied. 'Not you, not a *special* girl like you.'

Hearing the words *special girl* land, it was like she was

being driven by a motor – as if some other power was in total control of her body. Out of nowhere she found herself lurching forward, her arms raised in front of her, and as the train moved level with the platform, she threw all her bodyweight into the man's side, forcing him off the platform and onto the rails. A split second later he went under its wheels.

In that moment, everything around her seemed to be happening in slow motion, the sight and sounds distorted and distant. She was aware of people screaming and shouting as they attempted to get away, but she remained frozen to the spot.

And then a fraction of a second later, everything was thrust back in sharp focus. The melee that surrounded her was overwhelming, and the same crippling nausea she had felt standing over Charlie Callus was upon her. As people screamed and ran in all directions around her, she was acutely aware she had to get away immediately. With her heart pounding in her chest, she quickly scanned her surroundings, and then, after dropping her chin in an attempt to hide her face, slipped into the sea of people fleeing the platform, and headed for the exit to make her escape.

14

Standing at the entrance to the mortuary, Jones took a deep breath before pulling open the heavy door and stepping inside. The unique smell of the space hit him, and he was immediately reminded of why he hated attending post-mortems more than any other aspect of the job. The strange stench of powerful disinfectant combined with the sickly smell of a butcher's shop turned his stomach, and in that moment he had to remind himself why he had volunteered for the assignment: to try to reduce the mounting stress the guv was feeling. 'Come on, Jonesy. Time to put your big-boy pants on,' he muttered to himself before striding off down the corridor in search of the chief pathologist, Dr Tanvi Chakrabortty – or Tan as she was known to those close to her.

He found her just a minute later, walking out of her office dressed in pristine green surgical scrubs, her dark black hair pulled tightly into a bun. 'Jonesy,' she said, looking over his shoulder, 'is Jane not with you?'

'Nope.' He shook his head. 'I'm doing this one on my own.'

She raised her eyebrows. 'How come? I thought this would be the last place you'd want to be.'

'It is,' he replied. 'Just helping out the guv. She's got a lot on her plate at the moment.'

Chakrabortty offered a wry smile. 'I'd heard the new chief constable is keeping everyone on their toes.'

'Like bloody ballerinas, Tan,' he said sardonically.

She motioned down the corridor towards the examination rooms. 'Shall we?'

'If we must.'

'You'll be fine.' She placed her hand on his shoulder. 'I'll go easy on you, I promise.'

'It's not you I'm worried about.'

'We're flat out at the minute, so I had one of the team get started on the bloods and toxicology first thing. Hopefully we'll have the results by the time we're finished with Mr Callus.'

Five minutes later, wearing a plastic apron over his suit, Jones took up his position opposite Chakrabortty. The almost grey body of Charlie Callus was laid out on the surgical table between them.

'Right,' said Chakrabortty as she picked up a large scalpel in her gloved right hand. 'Let's get started.'

For the next hour and a half, Jones watched on as Tan methodically worked her way around the body, looking for clues as to what had killed him.

By the end of the usual thorough examination, Chakrabortty had come to several conclusions based on those findings. 'Considering the injuries to the back and right side of the head, I'd have to agree with the CSI team's initial assessment: it was the fall down the stairs that killed him, and he likely fell backwards. Based on the significant bruising sustained on the shoulders and upper back, it looks as if those areas took the brunt of the impact – along with a heavy blow to the back of the head, which caused a massive bleed on the brain. I estimate he would have died within a few minutes of the incident.'

'Any idea on time of death?'

'Between 7 and 9 a.m.'

'And you're sure he died where he was found?'

'Yes. The livor mortis indicates the body had not been moved post-mortem.' Chakrabortty pointed to the green and purple mark on the centre of Callus's torso. 'The bruising to this area here points to the fact he suffered a blow of some kind.'

'The CSI guys found a broom in the cupboard at the top of the stairs. Could that have caused it?'

Chakrabortty nodded. 'I had a chance to review Cormac's report last night, and looking at the diameter of the broom handle, I'd say it's almost a perfect fit.'

'So whoever killed him could have used the handle of the broom to knock him off balance?' asked Jones.

'Certainly looks that way, yes.'

'Was he drunk when he fell?'

'There's no way of telling just looking at the body, but hopefully the toxicology can give us a clear indication of his cognitive state at the time.'

For the next ten minutes Chakrabortty wrapped up the examination, and with their latex gloves and plastic aprons discarded in the bin, they made their way back to her office.

'Let's see if the toxicology report has arrived, shall we?' Chakrabortty sat down at her desk before logging on to her PC. 'Looks like it's landed,' she said a second later.

Jones waited patiently from his position in one of two

chairs opposite as she perused the digital file. 'Anything useful?' he asked eventually.

She nodded slowly, keeping her eyes on the screen. 'Well, it looks like there was *some* alcohol in his blood when he died, but at the level you'd find in someone who'd had a lot to drink the night before – as opposed to being intoxicated at the time of death.'

'Any drugs?'

Chakrabortty continued to read from the file. 'Apparently not.'

'So do you think it was likely he was compos mentis when he was attacked?'

'Hard to say for sure, but based on the absence of drugs and relatively low levels of alcohol in his system – plus the fact we found no additional injuries to the head – I think we can assume he was aware of what was going on when it happened.'

Jones took a moment to imagine the scene playing out in his mind.

She clicked through the file on-screen. 'That's interesting.'

'What is it?'

'Traces of saliva on his genitals.'

'Oh, wow.' Jones was momentarily taken aback. 'Enough for DNA?'

'Yes, so we'll run it through the system and see what comes back.'

'And how long will that take?'

'Based on the lab's current turnaround times, end of the day, I'd say.'

'Great.'

Chakrabortty's eyes narrowed as she continued to scrutinise the report. 'We also found traces of sodium benzoate, potassium sorbate, phenoxyethanol and methylisothiazolinone on his penis, testicles and anus.'

Jones frowned. 'And they are?'

'Cleaning agents.'

'What? Like bleach?'

'No, nothing that severe. They're the kind of mild chemicals you might find in products such as wet wipes.'

Jones took a beat to process what he was hearing. 'So what are we saying? Before he died he cleaned his balls with a wet wipe?'

She chuckled. 'I wouldn't have put it quite like that, but yes.'

Jones shook his head as he sat forward. 'So if I'm pulling all this together correctly, then the night before he's killed, our boy Charlie gets drunk, has intimate relations with somebody – as yet to be identified – and when he wakes up the following morning, cleans his bits with a wet wipe before heading onto the landing outside his flat – where someone pushes him backwards down the stairs with a broom handle.'

'As I always say, Jonesy, you're the detective, but I think that's it in a nutshell.'

He nodded. 'Right. So is there anything else we need to cover off?'

'Nope.' Chakrabortty reclined in her chair. 'That's your lot.'

'Brilliant.' Jones stood. 'In that case, I should definitely be getting back.'

'I saw Brown on the TV last night,' added Chakrabortty, folding her arms across her chest. 'Banging on about cleaning up the force.'

Jones sighed. 'We all thought we'd seen the end of the

political bullshit when Fox went, but I'm starting to think the wee Scotsman might be even worse.'

'How's Jane getting on with him? I remember she had real issues the last time they worked together.'

Jones retook his seat. 'Look, I know you guys are close, so I'm sure she won't mind me telling you…' He looked left to ensure there was no one within earshot outside the open office door.

'Go on,' urged Chakrabortty.

'Brown has instructed Professional Standards to investigate the guv, as well as the rest of us in MCU, on suspicion of sharing confidential police information with the press.'

Chakrabortty flinched. 'You're kidding?'

'I'm really not. He thinks it was one of us who passed all that stuff about Fox to Don Townsend.'

'Has Brown not got better things to do with his time?'

'Apparently not,' he replied.

'Why dig all that up? I mean, Townsend only put into words what a lot of us already suspected about Fox anyway.'

'Exactly right, but when it comes to Brown, there's no reasoning with him. And besides, like you said, last time they worked together, he and the guv didn't get on, and she continually stood up to him. Maybe this is his way of trying to get his own back.'

'But I don't get it.' Chakrabortty sat forward now. 'Jane is probably the sharpest detective on the entire force. Why would he want to marginalise her? I mean, she left once. If he makes life too difficult for her, she could do it again.'

Jones nodded. 'It's crazy, isn't it?'

Chakrabortty shook her head. 'Well, I really hope nothing comes of all this. I'd hate to think we might lose Jane.'

'Me too.' Jones glanced down at his watch. 'Look, I'd better be getting back. So you think we'll have the DNA results by the end play today?'

'Either that or first thing tomorrow morning. I have back-to-back PMs for most of the day, but I'll ask one of the team to keep an eye out for them.'

'Thanks, Tan.' He paused for a second. 'And you'll keep all this stuff about the guv to yourself, won't you?'

'Absolutely. But please let her know I was asking after her, won't you?'

'Of course.' Jones stood again now. 'I'm sure she'll appreciate it,' he added before heading for the door.

15

As soon as he arrived back at Ashton House, Jones brought the team up to speed on the details of the post-mortem.

When he was finished, Phillips turned her attention to Entwistle. 'Did the prints come back from the broom yet?'

'Yes, guv. Multiple prints, as you'd imagine with it being available to anyone – none of which are on the system.'

'Of course they aren't. That would be too straightforward, wouldn't it?'

'Sorry, guv.'

She continued, 'How about his phone records? Any joy with those?'

'Yeah.' He took a moment to open a file on his laptop. 'Turns out he had two phones. The one we found on the body and another CSI discovered in the flat.'

'Only drug dealers and people having affairs have two phones,' Bov chimed in.

'Yeah,' replied Entwistle. 'And from what I can see it looks like he was definitely the latter.'

'So what did you find?' Phillips asked.

'As I said, he had two phones. The first had all the standard numbers in the contact lists you'd expect, his wife, work, mum and dad, the doctors, etc. Now, according to the records attached to that phone, he lived a pretty average life with nothing remarkable to report. The second handset however, that tells a very different story.' He turned his laptop around so Phillips could see the screen. 'The only thing actively used on that phone was this app – the one his boss mentioned called Hooked. It's basically a place to meet people who want to cheat on their partners.'

'What kind of arsehole does that?' asked Bovalino. 'I mean, why stay married if you want to cheat all the time?'

Phillips stared intently at the app's landing page on the laptop screen, which was filled with a host of profile pictures of men and women in various stages of undress.

Entwistle continued, 'The app comes with a messaging service, which connects users directly, and based on Callus's inbox, he was a busy boy when it came to playing away from home.'

Phillips turned to Jones. 'Which backs up the theory that the killer could have been a jealous husband or boyfriend.'

'It would certainly make sense.'

'Yeah,' said Entwistle. 'Especially given he had a date with a woman called Trisha the night before he died. And looking at the messages between them, she seemed pretty excited to be going behind her husband's back.'

'Do we have any details on this Trisha?' Phillips asked.

'No, guv. It's first names only. But I have tracked down

the parent company for the app, which is based in Didsbury. They're called Mark One Enterprises and have offices on Didsbury Business Park. I spoke to their managing director, a guy called Kostas Panteli, this morning and asked for Trisha's details, but he wasn't very forthcoming. In fact, he said if we wanted any information about confidential client records, we would need to have a warrant.'

'Did he now?' Phillips turned her attention to Bovalino. 'How quickly can you get one sorted through your mate at the magistrate's court?'

The big man winced. 'Ordinarily a couple of hours, but he's on his honeymoon at the moment, so it'll take a bit longer. That said, he's introduced me to a couple of his colleagues, so I'm sure they can help expedite it.'

'What are we talking? Hours or days?'

'I reckon we could have one sorted by the end of the day, or at the very least first thing tomorrow.'

'OK,' she said. 'See if you can get one sorted by the end of the day, then Jonesy and I can pay this Kostas guy a visit first thing in the morning.'

Bovalino reached for the phone. 'I'll call the guys now.'

'And check the CCTV from the apartment again,' she added. 'I want to know what time Callus came home and whether or not he was alone. Based on the jealous-husband theory, we also need an ID on every male spotted on camera between 6 and 9.30 a.m. the morning he died.'

'On it,' said Bov.

Phillips stood up from the chair.

Jones matched her. 'Have you got a minute, boss?'

'Sure,' she replied. 'We can talk in my office.'

A minute later Jones pushed the door to.

She could feel her brow furrowing as she took her seat. 'Everything OK?'

'Yeah. It's just I mentioned something in passing to Tan this morning, and I'm not sure if I've overstepped the mark.'

'Which was what?'

'I told her about the Professional Standards investigation.'

Phillips smiled. 'Is that all?'

Jones recoiled slightly. 'You're not pissed off?'

'Why would I be? Tan is one of Major Crime's closest allies, and she's also a mate. I'd have told her myself if I'd have been there.'

Jones's posture visibly softened. 'Well, that's a relief.'

'In actual fact, I think it's a good thing she knows. I wouldn't put it past Healy and Shaw to try to drag her into all this in time. So you've done us a favour by giving her the heads-up sooner rather than later. What was her reaction?'

'Thinks it's utterly ridiculous and a total waste of time and resources.'

'Which of course it is,' replied Phillips. 'But when did that ever stop Brown from flexing his muscles?'

Just then Jones's phone beeped, indicating he'd received an SMS. He pulled it from his pocket and stared down at the screen for a moment.

'Everything all right?'

Jones looked up. 'It's from my fed rep, Ray Bradley. Looks like I'll be having my interview with Healy and Shaw at 1 p.m. tomorrow.'

Phillips nodded. 'How do you feel about that?'

Jones shrugged. 'What's to feel? It's just a couple of nosy bastards trying to make trouble.'

'I meant what I said the other day, you know. You don't have to lie to them on my account.'

'And *I* meant what I said, boss.' He grinned. 'It's not lying. I'm just being conservative with the truth.'

16

Mark One Enterprises was located in what appeared to be a recently constructed office block in Didsbury Business Park, hidden away in the South Manchester suburb of Didsbury. After pulling the Mini into one of the spaces allocated to visitors only, Phillips killed the engine and sat in silence as she waited for Jones to arrive. The clock on the dashboard indicated she was ten minutes early for their 9 a.m. meet.

It was another wet morning, and as the rain bounced off the small windscreen, she couldn't help but think about what lay ahead of her if the Professional Standards team managed to connect her to the leaked documents. Biting her bottom lip, she considered everything she'd put at risk – just to even the score with Fox. Should she have heeded Adam's advice to leave things well alone and just let it go? Or had she done the only thing available to her? They were questions that continued to plague her day and night, and it seemed only time would tell as to whether she'd made the right choice or not.

Thankfully, Jones pulled into the space next to her a moment later, saving her from any more self-flagellation than was absolutely necessary.

After nodding her acknowledgement through the window, she jumped out of the car, and together they rushed through the torrential rain and in through the revolving door at the front of the Mark One building.

'Almost two decades I've been living up here, and I still can't get my head round this bloody weather.' Jones ran his bony fingers through his prematurely thinning hair as they made their way into the main reception area.

'When it's coming down like this, I sometimes wish I'd stayed in Hong Kong,' she replied. She was of course referring to the country of her birth and the place she'd called home until the age of fifteen.

Taking in her surroundings, the whole place seemed to be well appointed, boasting a vast array of sharp lines, subtle lighting, and large, expensive-looking plants carefully placed to give the space a welcoming, almost homely feel.

Directly in front of them, a smartly dressed male receptionist, who Phillips figured was likely in his early twenties, looked up from his position sitting behind the long gleaming reception desk. The desk itself appeared to have been made from one large piece of moulded, shiny white plastic. 'Good morning,' he said, flashing perfect white teeth that matched his flawless skin and fashionably styled, thick black hair. 'Welcome to Mark One Enterprises. My name's Shane. How can I help you today?'

Phillips presented her ID as she approached the desk with Jones at her side. 'DCI Phillips and DI Jones from the Major Crimes Unit. We'd like to speak to Kostas Panteli, please.'

'Do you have an appointment?'

'Nope,' replied Phillips curtly. 'We're investigating a murder, so we don't need one.'

Shane's smile faltered now. 'I'll see if he's available,' he said as he picked up the phone on the desk.

Phillips and Jones watched on as he made the call, looking anywhere but at them.

'Hi, Jennie, it's Shane. The police are here to speak to Kostas.'

A beat passed as Jennie responded, and Phillips kept her eyes locked on the young receptionist.

'OK. I'll let them know,' said Shane before ending the call and turning his attention back to Phillips and Jones. 'Mr Panteli will be right with you.'

Phillips held his gaze. 'Thank you, Shane.'

A few minutes later a short, dark-skinned man wearing a crisp grey suit matched with a black shirt open at the neck walked across the polished concrete floor.

'Here he is now,' said Shane.

Panteli offered his hand as he approached. 'I'm Kostas. I understand you're from the police.'

Once again Phillips produced her ID. 'DCI Phillips and DI Jones from the Major Crimes Unit.'

'Major Crimes?' Panteli forced a smile. 'And how can I help?'

'Is there somewhere we can talk in private?' said Phillips.

Panteli frowned. 'Can I ask what this is about?'

'Like I said,' she replied, 'it'd be better if we can speak in private.'

Panteli turned to Shane. 'Is the conference room free?'

Shane glanced down at his desk for a second, then

nodded. 'Until ten, yes. Then the sales meeting is booked in there.'

'Please come with me,' said Panteli before striding off into the belly of the building.

With Jones at her back, Phillips followed him along the brightly lit corridor and into a large room, which appeared to be made almost entirely of glass. A long plastic table, similar in style to the reception desk, sat in the middle of the room, surrounded by a dozen or so leather and stainless-steel chairs.

As they stepped inside, Panteli flicked a switch next to the door, and the see-through walls suddenly turned opaque. 'Please have a seat,' he said, gesturing with his outstretched hand.

Phillips and Jones took the nearest seats to them as Panteli unbuttoned his suit jacket and dropped down into a chair opposite.

'So what's this all about?' he asked.

Jones pulled out his notepad and pen.

'We're investigating the death of one of your members,' replied Phillips. 'I believe one of my team, DC Entwistle, spoke to you about it yesterday on the phone.'

'Ah, yes, of course.' Panteli nodded slowly. 'And like I told your colleague, I'm afraid all our records are confidential.'

Phillips was keen to move the conversation along as quickly as possible. Reaching inside her coat, she pulled out the warrant, which she passed across the table. 'This grants me full access to all and any records you have on file regarding Charlie Callus and any other members he interacted with on your website, Hooked.'

Panteli examined the document for a second and sniffed before passing it back. 'It's an app, not a website.'

Phillips ignored the veiled jibe as she pulled out her mobile and took a moment to locate the screenshot she had previously saved to her photos. She turned the screen so he could see it now. 'We need to know the name and addresses of all the people Mr Callus interacted with on your platform, and in particular this woman, known as Trisha, who we believe he arranged to meet the night before he died.'

'That's not possible.' Panteli folded his arms across his chest as he sat back in his seat.

Phillips tapped the warrant on the table in front of her. 'This says different.'

'Oh, no. You misunderstand me. It's not a question of confidentiality. It's just we don't keep any address details on file. All our members need to sign up to the app is an email and a mobile number.'

'I see,' said Phillips, struggling to hide her frustration. 'Well, we'll just have to take those for Trisha, then, won't we?'

Panteli sat forward now, his voice a conspiratorial whisper. 'Look, can I be frank, Chief Inspector? If word got out that we were passing members' contact details to the police, well, it could be very bad for business. D'ya know what I'm saying?'

Phillips nodded silently for a moment before replying, 'And how do you think your business would fare if it got out that one of your members was found dead at his home – just a few hours after arranging to meet someone through your *app*? A death that we believe could be suspicious.'

Panteli straightened.

'I think that could be very, very bad for business. Don't you, DI Jones?'

Jones nodded. 'Absolutely, guv.'

'And it would appear that leaks to the press are

commonplace in the police these days.' Phillips presented the screenshot to him once more. 'So I'd suggest you talk to whoever you need to in this place to find me Trisha's details before anything *confidential* gets out.'

Panteli ran his hand through his thick black hair before reaching across to take a closer look at the phone. 'It could take some time to find her on the system.'

'Well, as you can imagine, this is an urgent matter, so we'd appreciate you getting the details as quickly as possible.'

'If you can just wait here.' Panteli stood up from the chair. 'I'll see what I can do.' A moment later he was gone.

Ten minutes passed before he returned with a printed sheet in his hand, which he passed to Phillips.

Examining it, she could see it contained the same profile picture of Trisha they'd found on the app, as well as an email and mobile number, plus a few other details such as age and sex, etc. 'Do you know the network for the number listed on file?' she asked.

'I'm afraid not, no,' said Panteli. 'Everything we have is on there.'

Phillips passed it to Jones, who glanced down at the details before taking a picture of them on his phone, then folded the sheet up and placed it in his notepad.

Panteli, who had remained standing, made a point of looking at his watch. 'I'm afraid this room is needed in a few minutes for the sales meeting. So if there's nothing else?'

'Looks like we have what we need for the time being.' Phillips stood up now, with Jones following her a split second later. 'But we may need to talk to you again as the investigation develops.'

'I'll look forward to it,' Panteli said without feeling as

he gestured with his right arm towards the door. 'I'll see you out.'

By the time they stepped outside a few minutes later, the rain had subsided sufficiently for Phillips to be able to call Entwistle without fear of getting soaked.

As ever, he answered promptly. 'Morning, boss,' he said cheerfully. 'How did you get on at Mark One?'

'We got some of Trisha's contact details but only an email and mobile phone number.'

'I can start with those,' he replied.

Phillips glanced at her second-in-command. 'Jonesy will send you a photo of what we have.'

Jones took a moment as he obliged.

'Got it,' Entwistle said a few seconds later. 'Do you know the network for the mobile?'

'We don't, no.'

Entwistle exhaled down the line. 'That will really slow us down, as I'll need to speak to each network individually to see who it belongs to. That's assuming it's actually registered and not a pay as you go.'

'How long will that take?' she asked, trying to keep the frustration out of her voice.

'Hard to say at this stage, guv. If we get lucky, a few hours, but if we need to speak to all the networks to find it, it could potentially take days.'

'Well, if it'll speed things up, get someone from the support team to help. We need to track Trisha down ASAP.'

'Will do,' he replied.

'Is Bov there?' Phillips asked.

'Yeah. I'll hand you over.'

She waited for the big man to come on the line.

'Guv?'

'Any news on the CCTV from Callus's place?'

'I've been going through it for the last few hours. Looking at the profile picture Trisha used on the Hooked app, I'm certain she was the woman who came home with him the night before he died. They arrived around 1 a.m., staggering in front of the camera and looking a little worse for wear.'

'Any sign of her leaving?'

'I'm still working through the footage,' he said. 'I'm about to start on the 6 a.m. hour next.'

'Well, let me know as soon as you find anything else.'

'Of course, boss. Oh, and I also spoke to the management company who look after the building. They're going to send me over a list of the key fobs used to access the building in the twenty-four hours surrounding Callus's death. Hopefully that might give us some insight as to who was out on that landing with him when he went down the stairs.'

'Great,' she replied. 'Jonesy and I are on our way back, so we'll see you in the next hour or so.' With that, she ended the call.

At that moment, Jones's phone beeped. Pulling it from his pocket, he shook his head. 'Aw, that's all I need.'

'What's up?' asked Phillips.

'It's my fed rep, Bradley. Says Healy and Shaw have moved my appointment forward to midday today.'

The knot in her stomach returned instantly. 'Well, at least you'll get it out of the way,' she said, trying her best to appear unfazed by this latest update.

'I know, but I have zero patience for all this shit. It's just a massive waste of everyone's time and energy.'

Phillips checked her watch. 'Well, we'd better be making tracks if you're going to get back in time. The roadworks on the M60 are brutal at the minute. I can't see it going down well with Professional Standards if you rock up late.'

'Maybe not.' Jones unlocked the squad car with an audible beep. 'But it'd go down well with *me*.'

'I'll race you back,' said Phillips with forced levity as she pulled the keys to her Mini from her pocket.

Thirty minutes later, as she followed Jones through the heavy traffic that was still causing havoc on the outer ring road, Phillips's phone sprang to life in the cradle on the dashboard of the tiny car. She could see from the screen it was Bovalino and immediately hit the green answer icon. 'Bov, what have you got?'

'Sorry to bother you, guv, but I've just had a call from Sergeant Hicks in the comms team. He's asking MCU to look into an alleged incident where a man's gone under a train at Humphrey Park station and died.'

'*Us?*' she replied, activating the windscreen wipers as the rain returned. 'We don't deal with suicides.'

'That's just it. They've had reports from the uniform team in attendance that the dead man may have been pushed.'

Phillips could feel her shoulders sag. With MCU's backlog of cases getting bigger by the day, another active case was all they needed right now. She sighed. 'Right, I'll take it.'

'Do you want me to call Jonesy and brief him too?'

'No, he's got his interview with Professional Standards at midday, so I'll have to do it on my own.'

'Well, if that's the case, I can meet you there, boss.'

'Don't worry about it. You've got enough to do.'

'That's true,' Bovalino replied. 'But from what Hicks said, it sounds like it's all a bit of a mess over there. Apparently the platform was mobbed when it happened. I think you might need the extra pair of hands.'

Phillips took a few seconds to consider the options. She really needed the big man's expertise focused on reviewing the CCTV from Callus's place, but the truth was she was starting to feel the mental strain of having so much on her plate at the moment. Having Bov with her at what was likely to be a very unpleasant scene felt like a good idea.

'OK. In that case, how soon can you get there?'

'It's not far from here, so probably about fifteen minutes.'

'Great. If the traffic holds, I think I should be there about the same time. I'll see you soon.'

'On my way,' he said.

'Thanks, Bov,' Phillips replied as she ended the call before pulling the car into the left-hand lane, ready to take the next exit.

17

After presenting her ID to the uniformed officer charged with guarding the entrance to Humphrey Park station, Phillips stepped under the blue and white police tape and made her way up the long ramp to the platforms above, where Bov was already waiting for her, dressed in white forensic overalls.

'Hi, guv,' he said as he passed her a matching disposable CSI suit. 'The body's just down there with Mac.'

Phillips followed his gaze and spotted senior CSI Cormac O'Shea moving around in the distance, the bottom half of his body concealed below the platform edge. 'Have you had a look at the damage?'

'Not yet, boss. I literally just got here and suited up myself.'

At that moment, the officer in charge of managing the scene, Sergeant Brooks, appeared. 'Good morning, ma'am,' he said as he approached.

'Brooks,' she replied, 'the comms team told us it looks like it could have been a homicide. Does that still stand?'

Brooks nodded. 'Yes, ma'am. We have an eyewitness who was standing next to the victim when he went over. She believes he was pushed off the platform just as the train pulled in.'

'Where is she?'

'In one of the tactical vehicles, having a cup of tea out of the weather. She was pretty shaken up, as you can imagine. PC Khalid is looking after her.'

'We'll need to talk to her once we've had a look at the body.'

'Of course,' he replied. 'She'll be ready whenever you are.'

'Any other witnesses?' Bovalino asked.

'We're speaking to everyone who was still here by the time we arrived, but to be honest, there weren't that many left.'

'Hardly surprising,' said the big man.

'We'll need to see all statements as soon as they're complete, OK?' Phillips zipped up her overalls.

'I'll make sure they're uploaded onto the system as a matter of urgency, ma'am,' said Brooks.

'Right.' Phillips turned her attention back towards Bovalino. 'Let's see if we can figure out what happened, shall we?'

A moment later she approached the edge of the platform with some trepidation, the big man at her back. Thankfully, from where they stood now, the body was hidden behind a large white screen erected to protect what was left of the deceased's dignity. 'How bad is it?' she asked Mac, who was standing just a few feet below her.

He turned to face her, pulling his mask down just enough so that she could see his face. 'Pretty grim, I'm afraid. The torso is in two parts, severed around the waist.'

Phillips took a deep breath before exhaling sharply. 'I guess we'd better take a look.'

Mac pointed just below her feet. 'Here, use the ladder. It's quite a drop.'

She followed his direction, once again with Bov at her back, and a few seconds later stepped down onto the oil-soaked track. The smell of diesel was pervasive.

'Be careful,' urged Mac. 'It's very slippery thanks to the oil and rain.'

He wasn't wrong, and it took a moment for Phillips to find her feet on the uneven surface.

'I hope you had a light breakfast,' Mac said before leading them towards the large screen.

The sight that greeted Phillips as she followed him round the temporary barrier stopped her in her tracks. 'Oh my God,' she managed to mutter, staring down at the two parts of the body, each surrounded by blood-stained gravel and covered with a dark blue plastic sheet.

Mac stepped next to the closest section of the body and crouched down before pulling back the sheet partway, exposing the man's mangled head and upper body. 'According to the driver's license we found in his wallet, this is Patrick Mahoney, aged forty-one and from Flixton. But as you can see, the face has been extensively damaged, so we'll need to identify him by either fingerprints or dental records.' He passed across a plastic evidence bag containing the licence.

Phillips felt sick to her stomach as she pulled out her phone and took a picture of it. 'Have you passed that information to uniform re next of kin?'

'Not yet, no. I've only just found it.' Mac replaced the sheet and moved to the next one, which he pulled back partially, exposing multiple open fractures to the legs. 'And so to the bottom portion of the body. Again, the damage is extensive.'

Bovalino winced. 'Bloody hell. I've never seen anything like it.'

'Sadly *I* have,' replied Mac. 'Back in Belfast, death by train was a real issue. Bored teenage kids with nothing better to do, playing chicken on the high-speed lines. The impact had an almost vaporising effect in some cases, which was quite surreal. Not quite the same with this one though, where the train was travelling at a relatively low speed. That said, I'm pretty confident death would have been almost instantaneous.'

'Let's hope so, for his sake,' said Phillips.

'There's a severed arm a little further along the line, too,' Mac added matter-of-factly as he pointed to another blue sheet up the track.

'Anything else you can tell us?' she asked.

'We're only just getting started, so no. It's a busy line that the network need reinstating ASAP, so we're going to move everything to the lab and do the examination there. Naturally I'll update you if and when we find anything of value. For now, you guys are free to go.'

'Great.' Phillips didn't need any encouragement and, after passing back the bag containing the licence, moved gingerly up the ladder and back onto the platform.

Bovalino followed her up. 'That has to be the worst thing I've ever seen in almost twenty years on the job.'

'Me too,' she said, unzipping her overalls. 'And that's saying something, given the horrors we've had the misfortune to have witnessed.'

The big man slipped his forensic suit off over his broad shoulders. 'Do you want to go and speak to the witness?'

'Sounds like a plan,' she replied. 'But before we do, can

you call Entwistle and see if we can get a next of kin sorted for Mr Mahoney?'

'No bother,' he replied.

A minute later, with their overalls bagged and tagged, she listened in as Bov relayed the details to Whistler on the other end of the phone.

'…that's all we have so far, name, age and the address on his licence.' Bovalino took a moment to listen to the response before signing off. 'As soon as you have anything, let us know. Cheers, buddy.'

'All sorted?' Phillips enquired.

'He's getting straight on it, so hopefully it shouldn't take long.'

'Good stuff. Right, let's see what our witness has to say,' she said before setting off back to the station entrance.

A few minutes later they found themselves heading back down the ramp from the platform towards the train station car park, where a multitude of police and emergency service vehicles were stationed. Spotting Brooks standing next to one of the large Tactical Unit vehicles, she strode across the wet ground towards him.

Seeing her and Bovalino approaching, he turned and pulled open a sliding door along the side of the vehicle, his voice audible as he spoke to the girl sitting inside. 'This is the senior officer I was telling you about,' he said, then turned to Phillips. 'Ma'am, this is Alison Breen.'

Phillips stepped next to the open door as the girl remained seated. 'I'm DCI Phillips, and this is DC Bovalino. We're from the Major Crimes Unit.'

The girl's wide eyes gave her a slightly startled appearance.

'Are you feeling up to answering a few questions about what happened?'

Alison nodded.

Phillips offered a sympathetic smile. 'Before we start, can I ask, did you know the victim at all?'

'No. I've never seen him before in my life.'

'OK,' said Phillips. 'So in your own words, why don't you tell us what happened?'

'Where do you want me to start?'

'You told officer Brooks you saw the man fall onto the track. What went on immediately prior to that?'

'Er, well.' Alison shifted on the seat. 'The guy was stood super close to me and really creeping me out.'

'In what way was he creeping you out?'

'He kept saying weird things to me.'

'Can you be more specific?' asked Phillips.

'He told me I smelt nice, that I was pretty and special.' She wrinkled her nose in disgust. 'He got really close to me and said I needn't be shy and that he didn't bite.'

'Did he touch you at all?'

'Not with his hands, no, but he kept pressing his fat belly into me, and he wouldn't let me get past him on the platform.'

'We were told the platform was full because of the broken-down train,' said Phillips. 'Could that be the reason he wouldn't let you by?'

Alison shook her head firmly. 'No. He was doing it on purpose. I tried not to look at him, but I could see in his face he was enjoying pushing up against me.'

Phillips waited a second before asking the next question. 'You told Sergeant Brooks that you think a woman pushed him off the platform.'

'Yes.'

'Are you sure she did it on purpose? Or could it have

been that because the platform was so busy she bumped into him by accident?'

'I can't be certain, but it looked to me like her arms were up in front of her, and she shoved him. Then again, it all happened so fast, I really don't know.'

Phillips shifted her stance. 'Do you think they knew each other? The woman and the victim?'

'I couldn't tell you.'

'Did the woman say anything to him? Use his name?'

'Not that I heard, but the train was making so much noise coming into the station, it was hard to hear anything.'

'I see,' said Phillips. 'Could you describe the woman? Or what she was wearing?'

'Again, it all happened so fast, but from what I saw, she had dark hair, and I remember she was wearing a black coat with something printed on the back.'

'Can you be more specific? Were there any letters or logos on it that you remember?'

'No.' The girl dropped her chin slightly. 'Sorry. I've not been much help, have I?'

'Don't be silly, you've done really well, Alison. Honestly, you saw a lot more than most people do, especially given the fact what you witnessed was so shocking.'

Alison produced a weak smile.

'Look, I think we've got what we need for now, so we'll leave you in the capable hands of Sergeant Brooks. He'll make sure you get checked out by a doctor. Events like these can affect us in ways that aren't always immediately apparent.' Phillips turned to Brooks. 'Make sure she's OK, will you?'

'Of course, ma'am.'

At that moment Bovalino's phone began to ring, and he stepped away to answer it.

Phillips turned her attention to Alison again. 'Thank you. You've been really helpful,' she said before heading over to find out what the call was about.

Seeing her approaching, Bovalino switched the phone to speaker. 'I've got the guv with me.'

'Hi, guv,' said Entwistle. 'I was just saying to Bov that the address you gave me is for a council flat on Lowry Gardens Estate, and the current address of one Patrick Mahoney according to council tax records. He claims the single-person discount, so it looks like he lives alone.'

'So no obvious next of kin,' said Bovalino.

''Fraid not.'

'Which means we'll need a tactical team to force entry,' said Phillips.

'Or,' Entwistle cut back in, 'as it's a council flat in a tower block, I can contact them and see if one of their caretakers can let us in. Properties that size usually have someone nearby during office hours.'

Phillips took a moment to consider the options. 'How long would that take?'

'Based on past experience, about an hour if the caretaker is on site or at least in the area.'

'OK,' she said. 'We can try that first, but if we get any resistance or delay, I want a tactical team over there within the hour. We'll head over that way now so we can be there as soon as access is made available.'

'No problem. I'll sort it straight away.'

'Thanks,' said Phillips.

Bovalino ended the call just as spots of rain began to appear in the air.

She patted the big man on the arm. 'Come on, let's get in the car before it starts chucking it down again. There's a McDonald's down the road. I'll buy lunch.'

He smiled. 'Now you're talking my language, boss.'

AFTER QUICKLY PICKING up a couple of burgers, they took seats in a booth by the window.

As ever, Bovalino wasted no time in getting stuck into his Big Mac meal. 'I wonder how Jonesy's getting on with Professional Standards,' he said through a mouthful of fries.

Phillips took a bite of her own burger. 'I'm sure he'll be fine,' she said, more in hope than certainty. 'He's smart enough to handle Healy.'

The big man loaded up on another handful of fries. 'My fed rep told me I'm due in with them in the next few days.'

'I did wonder when they'd get to you,' she said casually. 'How you feeling about it?'

He shrugged. 'All right, I think. I mean, I don't know anything about any leaked documents, and I've never spoken to Townsend in my life, so unless they try to stitch me up, I should be fine, I guess.'

'I'm sure they're not looking to stitch anybody up.' Phillips chewed her food in silence for a moment.

Bovalino glanced left and right before leaning in closer. 'Who do you think leaked those files, boss?'

'I haven't clue,' she said as nonchalantly as possible.

'Well, whoever it was deserves a medal as opposed to a bollocking as far as I'm concerned. What Fox did to Pearson was unforgivable, and God only knows how many other people she screwed over to get to the top of the greasy pole.'

'Yeah, maybe you're right,' she said before grabbing some fries of her own.

'And I have to say I don't miss her one little bit.'

'No. Me neither.' Thankfully at that moment and much to Phillips's relief, Entwistle's number flashed up on her phone which was resting on the table next to her food. She wasted no time in answering it. 'Whistler, where are we at with access to Mahoney's?'

'We're in luck. The maintenance team are on site today, doing some repairs to some of the neighbouring flats, so they'll be able to let you in as soon as you get there.'

'Excellent work,' she said.

Bovalino took a bite of his Big Mac as Entwistle continued. 'Just head straight to Mahoney's place. The site manager will be waiting for you.'

'Thanks, Whistler,' she said. 'I don't suppose Jonesy's there, is he?'

'No, boss. Said he was heading off to see Professional Standards.'

Phillips felt her stomach tighten at the thought. 'No worries. I'll catch up with him when we get back.'

'Do you need anything else from me, boss?'

'How are you getting on with finding Trisha's network?'

'Still working our way through them, but no luck as yet.'

'OK. Well, we'll let you get back to it.'

'No worries.'

Phillips ended the call as Bovalino chewed his last mouthful of burger and took a large slurp of Diet Coke.

'Well, as my old dad used to say, "If that's my lunch, I've had it."' He smiled as he closed his empty burger box.

She returned his smile as she placed her own empty cartons on a tray. 'Come on. It's time we were in Flixton.'

18

'The executive floor?' said Jones as he and Bradley made their way along the fifth-floor corridor to the conference room where Professional Standards lay in wait. 'All right for some.'

'Isn't it just,' said Bradley, nodding as they stopped outside the door. 'You ready?' he whispered.

Jones nodded. 'Yeah. I'm ready.'

Bradley knocked and, without waiting for an answer, stepped inside.

Jones followed him in.

DS Healy and DC Shaw were seated on one side of the large conference table, facing the door. Neither got up as their guests entered.

'Good afternoon, DI Jones,' said Healy as Shaw remained silent.

'If you say so,' replied Jones as he took a seat opposite her and alongside Bradley.

Healy took a moment to open her large A4 leather-bound notepad before laying her pen down on top. A small stack of files was piled up on the desk to her right.

Jones glanced across at Shaw, who was making notes in her own pad, attempting to read them upside down without success.

'As you'll be aware, you are not under caution, and therefore this meeting will not be recorded. However, DC Shaw will be taking notes.'

He nodded towards the detective constable. 'Looks like she's already started,' he said sardonically.

Healy appeared unfazed by his comment. 'I know officer Bradley has briefed you on why you're here, so I'll get started if that's OK?'

'Suits me.' He folded his arms across his chest. 'The sooner this is done with, the better.'

'So, DI Jones, what can you tell us about how a series of confidential documents, some coming directly from your department, found their way into the hands of the *Manchester Evening News* late last year.'

'Absolutely nothing,' he said flatly.

Healy's expression remained impassive. 'So you know nothing about how those files got into the hands of the press?'

'That's right.'

'Even though several of them came directly from MCU?'

'Correct.'

Healy's brow wrinkled. 'You seem very blasé about that fact.'

He shrugged. 'What do you want me to say? I'm merely answering your question.'

'Well, as a senior officer, I would have thought you'd

already started looking for the person responsible as soon as the stories hit the headlines.'

'And why would I do that? What was said about corruption in the force was true, especially so when it came to Fox.'

'If I didn't know better,' said Healy, 'I'd say you sound quite happy that those stories were printed.'

'Quite the opposite,' he shot back. 'The very fact they exposed our most senior officer as a liar and crook boils my piss, if I'm being perfectly honest. But that doesn't mean I have an axe to grind with the person who exposed her for what she was. Fox deserved more than an enforced retirement for what she did to people like Archie Pearson.'

'So you think the end justifies the means, do you?'

Jones looked her dead in the eye. 'I'm saying she got off lightly. There's no place in the force for bent coppers.'

'Does that include those who bend the rules, DI Jones?'

'I'm not following you,' he lied, as he had a pretty good idea of what might be coming next.

Healy began picking through the pile of files on the table next to her and made somewhat of a song and dance of locating whatever it was she was looking for. 'Ah, here it is,' she said finally.

Jones unfolded his arms and shifted in his seat.

Healy continued as she placed a mugshot of the radio and TV personality Marty Michaels on the table in front of him. 'Major Crimes was involved in this man's arrest. Is that correct?'

'You know it is,' he said, doing his best to hide his contempt for her.

'And yet, it was the head of Major Crimes, Detective Chief Inspector Phillips, who was later found guilty of aiding a fugitive when Mr Michaels went on the run.'

'And what has any of that got to do with this conversation?' Bradley cut in.

'Well,' said Healy, 'DI Jones said he can't stand bent coppers, yet he comes to work every day with a boss who broke the law. That doesn't quite stack up to me.'

Shaw continued to make frantic notes.

Jones folded his arms across his chest once more. 'DCI Phillips did what she had to to stop an innocent man from spending the rest of his life in prison. It was the right thing to do.'

'And you stand by that, do you?'

'I do.'

'Even though she broke the law? Something she took an oath to uphold.'

Jones felt his jaw clenching as he glared back at his interrogator.

'Sounds like double standards to me, DI Jones.'

Considering he was essentially in the meeting of his own volition, it took all of Jones's strength not to stand up and walk out, but he knew that would be a huge mistake and wouldn't help the guv one bit. So he bit his tongue and took a silent breath to help calm his racing pulse. Instead, he unbuttoned his left shirtsleeve and rolled it up so his severely scarred wrist was exposed. 'You want to talk about standards and oaths? Do you know how I got this?' He raised his arm in front of Healy's face.

'No, I don't,' she replied without feeling.

'I got this fending off a Triad assassin who was attempting to kill a witness in a murder investigation that DCI Phillips and I took the lead on. Nearly lost my arm in the process. That's the kind of shit *I've* faced to deliver on that oath you're talking about.' He pushed his arm closer to her. 'And this is nothing compared to what's happened to the guv in the line of duty.'

Healy stared back silently.

Jones dropped his arm back down on the desk. 'You can accuse us of many things, DS Healy, but don't ever question my or the boss's integrity – or anyone else in the team for that matter. We put ourselves in the firing line every day, come rain or shine. Every single day. Which is more than can be said for some.'

Healy nodded and flashed a thin smile before returning to the stack of files, where she pulled out another folder. Opening it, she examined the contents for a long moment before locking eyes with him once more. 'One of the files printed by the *MEN* relates to an investigation *you* were directly involved in, DI Jones, the Crowther case.'

He didn't respond.

'The master files for which are stored on the main drive in MCU.'

'So?'

Healy let out an involuntary chuckle. 'Oh come on, shouldn't *you*, as a senior officer in the department, be aware of *every* file that leaves that office?'

'A lot of people have access to the department drives. They're not exclusive to me or the team.'

'Really? Like who?'

Jones sat forward in his seat. 'Like IT, like the hundreds of support staff we second every year to help us trawl through ANPR footage, phone records and financials on suspects. The source of the stories could be any one of a hundred coppers. Not to mention hackers.'

Healy raised an eyebrow. 'Hackers?'

'Yes, hackers. I mean, has that even crossed your mind? While you're in here putting hard-working coppers through the wringer, the actual leak could easily have come from the outside.'

'You think someone hacked into the MCU main drive and took those files?'

'Why not?' said Jones. 'Data breaches happen all the time, and it's certainly more plausible than suggesting dedicated coppers like me or the guv had anything to do with it.'

'And how would these hackers know where to look?'

'Maybe they didn't. Maybe they were after something else and just got lucky with the shit they found implicating Fox.'

'Do you really think that's plausible?'

'Why not? It's no more outrageous than what you're accusing me or DCI Phillips of.'

'No one's accusing either of you of anything,' Healy shot back.

'Well, you could've fooled me.'

Healy fell silent as Shaw continued to scribble.

Jones turned to Bradley now. 'As I'm not under caution, I'm free to leave any time I want, aren't I?'

'Yes, you are,' he replied.

Jones returned his attention to Healy now. 'Well, in that case, I think I've wasted more than enough of my time and the taxpayers' money.' Pushing back the chair with his legs, he stood. 'I need to get back to some proper police work.'

Bradley stood too.

'We may need to speak to you again, DI Jones,' said Healy.

'Let's hope not, hey?' he replied before spinning on his heel and striding out of the room.

19

Patrick Mahoney's flat was located on the eleventh floor of the Trafford Park tower block on the outskirts of Flixton, just over ten miles west of the city centre. The block itself was an imposing structure built in the sixties that looked to have been refurbished sometime in the last five to ten years but was now starting to look a little tired once more.

After Bovalino parked the squad car in one of the few bays marked for visitors, they headed in through the front door and took the lift up to the eleventh floor, where Entwistle had assured them they would find the maintenance manager waiting for them outside Mahoney's flat. Stepping out onto the small, dimly lit landing, Phillips was pleased to see a tall, wiry man with thinning hair, wearing a hi-vis jacket over blue overalls, standing just inside the open front door of flat 11-3.

He turned to face them. 'You the police?'

Phillips nodded as she pulled her ID from her coat pocket. 'DCI Phillips and DC Bovalino.'

'I've been told to lock it up after you're done,' said the man. 'I'm on the next floor up with the team, doing some plastering. Just give me a shout when you're finished.'

'Will do,' said Phillips.

The man appeared keen to get back to his labour, and a moment later they had the place to themselves.

After each of them had pulled on latex gloves Phillips led the way along the narrow hall, past a small bedroom on the right, with a kitchen to the left, through to the compact lounge at the rear of the property. She stepped into the middle of the room and surveyed the space for a moment. It was fair to say the place was sparsely decorated with bare magnolia walls that were stained and scratched, sitting atop of worn grey carpets.

A small, brown fabric couch and matching armchair were positioned against the back wall, facing a relatively small, deep-backed TV that must have been close to thirty years old.

'Lovely spot,' said Bovalino sarcastically as he stepped to her shoulder.

'Yeah,' she replied absent-mindedly, spying something protruding from under the armchair. Taking a step forward, she squatted down to retrieve it.

'What is it, guv?' he asked.

'Looks like a laptop.' She stood back up, holding it in both hands. 'It's heavy, so I'm guessing it's quite an old one.'

'Want me to get it checked?'

'Yeah.' She passed it across. 'See if Digital Forensics can find anything on it that might tell us who he was.'

'Sure.'

With nothing much else to see in the lounge, Phillips decided to take a look in the kitchen. Wandering through, she found it be just as sparsely appointed with large spaces in the kitchen fittings where – based on the exposed piping and plumbing – the cooker and washing machine would normally have been positioned. An old kettle along with a small microwave that sat on the grubby countertop, alongside a standalone single-height fridge, were the only concessions in terms of appliances. There was a strong, putrid smell in the air as she stepped into the room, which she quickly traced to the open bin. Peering inside, she could see it was filled with takeaway boxes in various guises, and judging by the smell, Mahoney had not emptied it for quite a few days.

Spotting a pile of letters sitting on the windowsill, she moved across the room to see if they might hold any clues as to who Patrick Mahoney was. As she began to sift through them, it was evident someone – the same person judging by the handwriting – had been redirecting his mail from a previous address in Prestwich. At the bottom of the pile was an A4 envelope addressed directly to Mahoney, written in the same handwriting. Inside, she found two folded-up pieces of paper, which she pulled out and examined. The first was an uncashed cheque made out to Patrick Mahoney from a Mrs S. Atkins. The second was a handwritten note in the same handwriting as all the other letters. It read:

Hey little bro.

I hope you're OK, as I haven't heard from you in a while.

Sorry I didn't send this post sooner. I meant to, but things have been a bit manic here.

Anyway, it's probably best to get it redirected so you don't miss anything important, and I've included a cheque so you can sort it with the post office.

I know you don't like forms, so if you want me to come and help you do it, just let me know.

And give me a ring when you get a chance, it'd be good to know you're OK.

Lots of love, Shelly.

'I think we've got something,' Phillips shouted through to Bovalino, who had now moved on to inspecting the bedroom opposite.

He appeared in the doorway a second later, still carrying the old laptop under his left arm, now safely secured inside a large evidence bag.

She presented him with one of the letters. 'Looks like Mahoney has a sister who has been redirecting his mail.'

Bov's eyes narrowed as he inspected it.

She handed across the cheque. 'I'm guessing Shelly is the Mrs S Atkins on the cheque, and thanks to this little lot, we now know where she lives.'

'Nice work, boss.'

'Did you find anything of interest in the bedrooms?'

'No, nothing.'

'Well, in that case, we'd better go and break the news of what's happened to her brother.'

PHILLIPS LED the way up the path to the Victorian-built, semi-detached house set back from the road in the leafy suburb of Prestwich. The rain had subsided, but a cold wind was blowing as she pressed the bell fixed to the wall to the right of a front door.

A minute later the door opened, and a woman who appeared to be in her forties with thick, curly red hair looked out. 'Yes?'

'Shelly Aitken?'

The woman nodded. 'Can I help you?'

Phillips presented her credentials. 'I'm DCI Phillips, and this is DC Bovalino. Are you a relation of Patrick Mahoney?'

Aitken's shoulders appeared to sag. 'I'm Pat's sister. What's he done now?'

'Could we talk inside?' said Phillips, her voice soft and reassuring.

'Of course.' Shelly opened the door wide and moved to the side. 'Please come in.'

Phillips stepped inside with Bovalino close behind.

'Please go through to the kitchen at the back.'

'Thank you,' Phillips said as she led the way into what looked like an extension to the original property – a light and airy kitchen not dissimilar to the one she had in her old house.

'What's this about?' asked Shelly as she followed them into the space.

Phillips turned to face her and took a deep silent breath. 'I'm sorry to have to tell you this, Shelly, but I'm afraid a man died this morning when he was hit by a train at Humphrey Park station, and we believe that man was Patrick.'

Shelly let out an involuntary laugh, then stood motionless with her mouth open. It was something Phillips had seen many times in these situations, a common reaction as the next of kin's nervous system went haywire on hearing the shocking news.

'We know this will have come as a shock,' said Phillips.

Shelly's mouth opened and closed silently for a moment before she finally muttered, 'But that's not possible.'

'Maybe you should sit down.' Phillips nodded at Bovalino, who pulled a stool from the breakfast bar closer.

Shelly sat down, her eyes wide.

'I have a picture taken from a driving licence we found on the deceased.' Phillips fished her phone from her coat pocket. 'Would you feel up to looking at it to confirm whether it is in fact your brother?'

Shelly nodded nervously.

Phillips clicked onto the photo she'd taken of the identification card earlier and carefully held it at eye level. 'Is this Patrick?'

Shelly's gaze locked on the screen, and a split second later she burst into tears.

Instinctively Phillips moved in close and placed her arm lightly around her shoulders. 'I'm so sorry, Shelly.'

Bovalino stood motionless and appeared unsure of what to do for the best.

Phillips, conscious that her constable cut quite an imposing figure in moments such as these, caught his eye. 'Why don't you see if you can organise a FLO to come and speak to Shelly later today or tomorrow?'

'Of course,' he said, nodding enthusiastically before making himself scarce and heading out of earshot to make the call to the family liaison team.

Phillips, meanwhile, pulled out a second breakfast stool and positioned herself next to Shelly, sitting silently as the poor woman's tears flowed unabated. Keen to try to help in any way she could, she spotted a box of tissues on the kitchen counter and grabbed a handful, which she passed over.

Shelly took them in silence, then wiped her eyes and nose, which were now red and puffy. After a long moment she finally spoke. 'How did it happen?'

'We're not sure at this stage, but I have to tell you that we are investigating the circumstances surrounding his death.'

'What do you mean?' Shelly's eyes widened. 'Do you think he killed himself?'

'Like I say, we're looking at all the circumstances involved, and we can't rule it out. Is that something he might have considered?'

Shelly stared back blankly. 'Not that I know of.'

'I see.' Phillips cleared her throat. 'I must tell you that we're also looking at another possibility.'

'Oh?'

Phillips continued, 'We've spoken to someone this morning who thinks Patrick may have been pushed from the platform.'

'Pushed?' Shelly was incredulous. '*On purpose?*'

'It's one of the avenues we're investigating, yes.'

'But why would anyone want to hurt Pat?'

'At this stage, I'm afraid it's too early to say,' said Phillips.

'I don't believe this.' Her voice was barely a whisper.

'Look, I know this is the last thing you'll want to do right now,' said Phillips, 'but we're going to need your help to officially identify Patrick.'

Shelly stared at the floor as she gripped the ball of tissue tightly in her right hand.

Phillips continued cautiously considering what she was about to reveal. 'Because of the nature of his injuries, we won't be asking you to make a formal identification.'

Shelly blinked nervously. 'What do you mean by that?'

Phillips took another silent breath. This really was the worst part of the job. 'I'm afraid Patrick's body was very badly damaged when he died, so we're going to need another way of identifying him.'

'Like what?'

'Like DNA or fingerprints.'

'But how does that work now he's gone?'

'If you have anything still around that he might have touched, we could use that.' Phillips pulled Shelly's handwritten note from her pocket. 'I guessed from looking at this that he lived with you before he moved into the flat.'

Shelly nodded. 'For about three months when he came home after his accident.'

'What happened?'

'He was hit by a car a couple of years ago and ended up in hospital for pretty much the year that followed. Broke half the bones in his body and knocked a load of his front teeth out. He was in and out of surgery to sort out his legs and shoulders, which were pinned, and he ended up having implants and new teeth because his mouth was such a mess from the impact.'

'That sounds life changing for him.'

'It was, and not just physically.'

Phillips tilted her head to one side slightly. 'What do you mean by that?'

'He changed after the accident.' Shelly wiped her nose with the tissue. 'Mentally, I mean. He was different.'

'In what way?'

'I really don't want to say.'

'I know it's hard, Shelly, but it might be relevant in some way.'

Shelly exhaled deeply. 'I can't believe I'm telling you this about my own brother, but he developed a strange fixation with young women, well, more like girls, if I'm honest.'

'I see,' said Phillips. 'And what age of girl was he more interested in?'

'Schoolgirls mainly. Early teens.' She shuddered slightly. 'My husband, Thomas, walked into the bathroom one day to find him masturbating over a photo of one of our daughter's friends. Turns out he'd screenshot it from Facebook. She was only twelve, and that was the final straw for Thomas.'

'And when Patrick moved out?'

'Yes,' she replied. 'The doctors warned us after the accident that we would potentially see changes to his personality because parts of his brain were damaged when he hit his head. They did tell me which bit of the brain it was, but I've forgotten now.'

Phillips was familiar with the concept. A change in personality and behaviours – in particular sexual desires and appetites due to brain injury – had been a factor in several cases she'd worked on in the past.

'So how long had Patrick been living at the flat?'

'About six months, I guess.'

'And when was the last time you saw him?'

Shelly took a moment to think. 'It would have been late October, I'd say. I called round to see him, and I remember buying some Halloween-themed cookies at the bakery around the corner from his flat.'

Phillips changed tack now. 'Did Patrick work?'

'Not since the accident, no.'

'So would you have any idea where he would have been going on a commuter train at eight in the morning?'

Shelly dropped her chin to her chest momentarily before locking eyes with Phillips. 'Another fallout of the brain injury, I'm afraid. Pat used to work in a call centre in Castlefield until the accident. In fact, he was hit by the car when crossing Deansgate on his way to work. The driver jumped a red light at the junction by Liverpool Street and ploughed straight into him in the middle of the road.'

'I'm sorry to hear that.'

Shelly continued, 'He loved that job, and by all accounts, he was good at it. But he was away from work for so long after he got hurt that they had to let him go. It broke his heart, bless him, and he couldn't let go of the place.'

'And what does this have to do with him being on the train?'

'He took a lot of medication to try to regulate his behaviour, which worked fine when he actually took it. But if he was off it for more than a few days, he'd start having delusional episodes, and his memory would go all to pot. I lost track of the times I'd come down to breakfast and he'd be heading out the door to get the early train to the call centre. It was like he was being let go again every time I had to tell him he didn't work there anymore. If he was on the train to Deansgate at eight o'clock, then it sounds like he was off his meds again.'

At that moment, Bovalino stepped back into the room.

Phillips shifted on the stool towards him. 'How did you get on with the FLO?'

'They're sending someone over this afternoon to speak to Mrs Aitken,' he replied.

Phillips returned her focus back to Shelly. 'A FLO is what we call a family liaison officer. They can offer support to the families in situations such as these. They'll be able to give you any updates on the investigation into Patrick's death as soon as we have anything we can share.'

Shelly wiped her nose with the tissue once more.

'You've had quite a shock,' said Phillips. 'Is there anyone we can call to come and sit with you? Your husband or another relative?'

'I'll be fine,' Shelly replied. 'I'll call Thomas to let him know what's happened as soon as you guys have gone.'

'OK.' Phillips slipped off the stool. 'To save you having to look for anything of Patrick's, we can probably confirm his ID through his dental records. You wouldn't happen to know who his dentist was, would you?'

'Same as mine. Park View Dental Practice just off Bury New Road. We've been with them since we were kids.'

Bovalino took the initiative and typed it into his phone. 'I've got the number here, guv,' he said a few seconds later.

'Right, well, in that case, we can sort everything out with them.' Phillips paused. 'Are you sure you're going to be OK?'

Shelly nodded silently, the tears evidently not far away. 'I'll be fine.'

Phillips's heart went out to her as she pulled a business card from her pocket and passed it across. 'The FLO will do everything they can to help, but if you need anything else at all, my number's on there.'

'Thank you,' Shelly said in a low voice.

'I really am very sorry for your loss,' said Phillips before turning and gesturing for Bovalino to lead them back to the front door.

20

An hour later, Phillips and Bov strode into the main office of MCU, where they found Jones and Entwistle working quietly at their desks.

Jones looked up as they walked in, barely able to keep the scowl from hijacking his face.

'You all right, Jonesy?' asked Phillips. 'You look a bit pissed off.'

'Sorry. I'm still seething from my meeting with Healy and Shaw.'

Bovalino placed the evidence bag containing Mahoney's laptop on the desk before pulling out his chair.

Phillips dropped into the seat at the spare desk. 'Went that well, did it?'

'She claimed that she wasn't accusing any of us of passing those documents to Townsend,' he replied, 'but she had a funny way of showing it.'

'Why, what did she say?'

'It was more what she implied that pissed me off; that as a senior officer *I* should know where all department files are at all times, and that *you've* got form for breaking the rules based on the fact you helped Marty when he was on the run.'

Phillips folded her arms against her chest. 'She tried that shit with me as well. I guess it's to be expected. We'd probably put the same links together if we were in her shoes.'

'But that's just it, we would never be in her shoes because we're *proper* coppers.'

'Try not to let her get under your skin,' said Phillips. 'Because you know that's what she wants. To get inside your head.'

He sighed. 'Yeah, maybe.'

Phillips uncrossed her arms and sat forward now. 'Anyway, in other news, it looks like our jumper this morning may well have been pushed off the platform as suspected.'

'Yeah. Whistler told me you'd been looking into it.'

Entwistle stopped what he was doing and turned his attention to Phillips. 'How did you get on at Mahoney's flat, guv?'

'It didn't really tell us much about him other than you were right, he lives alone,' replied Phillips.

'But we did find this.' Bovalino passed the old laptop across the desk. 'We'll need Digital Forensics to have a look at it.'

Entwistle marvelled at it as he held the heavy machine in his hands. 'Wow. This is proper old school.'

Phillips continued, 'We also found an address for his next of kin, his sister, Shelly. So we did the death notification.'

'How did that go?' Jones asked.

'Unpleasant as ever, as you can imagine, but she did give us some insight into her brother, which might prove useful.'

Phillips shifted in her seat. 'Apparently Patrick was hit by a car and suffered a serious brain injury a few years back that she claims altered his behaviour quite significantly.'

Jones raised an eyebrow. 'In what way?'

'According to Shelly, after the accident, he started fixating on young girls – pre-teen and early teens mainly. They eventually had to throw him out because they caught him wanking over a photo he'd taken of one of their daughter's friends. She was only twelve at the time.'

'Bloody hell. So Mahoney was a paedo?' said Entwistle.

'Potentially, yes.' Phillips tapped the laptop in front of him. 'That's why we need to find out what's on there as quickly as possible. If someone did push him in front of a train, their motives may well be locked inside the hard drive.'

Entwistle nodded. 'I'll speak to the digital team as soon as we're done here.'

'Great.' For the next few minutes, Phillips shared the rest of the information they'd gleaned from Shelly about his issues with forgetting to take his medication on occasion and the subsequent delusions he suffered because of that.

When everyone was up to speed, her first question was aimed at Entwistle. 'How you getting on with tracking down Trisha?'

'Found her.' He flashed a broad grin, then pulled a printout from his notebook, which he passed across. 'Trisha Metcalfe, aged thirty-two and lives in Stretford. I've checked on the council tax records, and it seems she lives with a man called Steve Metcalfe.'

'Do we know if this Steve is her husband?'

'Nothing official, but a quick scan of her Facebook profile suggests he is.'

'So she and Callus were both potentially doing the dirty on their other halves,' Jones cut in.

Phillips's gaze remained locked on the printout containing Trisha's details for a moment before she finally looked up again. 'What a tangled web we weave.'

Bovalino tapped his pen against the computer screen. 'I've just spotted an email from the management company who run Callus's apartment complex. They've sent through the key fob records I requested, and it looks like there's bloody loads of entries to sift through.'

Phillips checked her watch. 'Well, time is ticking on, so do what you can for another hour or so, and then we can all probably call it a day. It's been a long week. I'm sure we'll all feel better after a weekend off and a fresh start on Monday.'

'Will do, boss,' replied the big man.

'What do you want to do about Trisha?' asked Jones.

She glanced down at Trisha's address once more. 'She's practically on my way home. I've got a few emails to send, and then I'll head off and see what she has to say for herself.'

'You want me to come with you?'

'No. I'm good. Save you the trouble of getting back afterwards. I have a feeling the traffic is going to be shitty tonight with the trains still causing issues.' Phillips stood now. 'Like I say, guys, finish up anything that can't wait and then get off home. We're not on call, so let's make the most of a couple of days off.'

A chorus of 'yes, guvs' filled the air as she headed back into her office.

A few minutes later as Phillips sat down to open her inbox, Sergeant Ash tapped on the door.

'Sorry to interrupt, ma'am, but I've just had a call from DS Healy.'

'Oh?' Phillips reclined in her seat slightly.

'Says she needs to see us both before we finish up for the day.'

'Did she say what it was about?'

'No. Just said it was important. She's in the same conference room as before.'

Phillips felt her whole body sag. The last thing she had the energy for now was another head-to-head with Professional Standards. 'Right,' she muttered as she stood up. 'We'd better go and see what she wants.'

21

Doing her best to appear unfazed by the sudden summons, she walked side by side with Ash towards the conference room.

'So, she didn't give you any clues as to what this is about, then?' asked Phillips, keeping her voice low so as not to be overheard.

'Nothing. Just that it was important and not to go home until we'd spoken to her.'

'That doesn't sound good.' Phillips felt the knot return to her stomach as they approached the door.

'I'm sure it's nothing to worry about,' he replied.

'Yeah,' she said without conviction as they stopped outside the conference room.

'You ready?'

She nodded silently, and a second later, Ash turned and stepped through the door.

As before, DS Healy was sitting on the far side of the large conference table with DC Shaw positioned to her left and a stack of files on the table to her right.

'Ah, DCI Phillips. Sergeant Ash.' Healy gestured to the chairs opposite. 'Please take a seat.'

As they followed the instruction, Phillips took a deep, silent breath, which she let out slowly in an attempt to slow her racing pulse.

Healy locked eyes with Phillips now. 'Thank you for coming so promptly, Chief Inspector.'

Phillips offered a faint nod, but said nothing, her stomach turning hoops.

'As you know, our digital forensics specialists have been looking into who could have downloaded the confidential files that were leaked.' Healy removed a file from the top of the stack and placed it on the table between them. 'I've asked you here to share the results of that search.'

Phillips glanced at the files momentarily, then back at Healy.

'It seems that someone did actually download *every* single file that was shared with the *MEN* news desk and subsequently printed by the paper.' Healy opened the manila folder, a satisfied grin threatening to hijack her face. 'And that person was *you*, DCI Phillips.'

In that instant, everything seemed to slow down as another shot of adrenaline surged through Phillips's body, and her neck flushed. She opened her mouth to speak, but no words would come out.

It seemed Healy must have sensed she had her opponent on the ropes and was keen to land the next blow. 'In fact, you downloaded all those files just four days before the first story was published by Don Townsend and the *MEN*.'

'That doesn't mean I gave them to him.' It was the only thing Phillips could think to say.

'Bit of a coincidence though, don't you think?' Healy shot back.

Phillips swallowed hard, her mouth now bone-dry.

'There's a big difference between a coincidence and proof.'

'That is true,' replied Healy. 'And after discussing the situation with Chief Constable Brown, we both believe that in light of this evidence, this investigation should be handed over to the IPCC. Something that will be happening as soon as this meeting is concluded.'

'The IPCC?' Phillips recoiled. 'Isn't that taking all this a bit far?'

Healy glared across the table. 'Confidential information pertaining to a series of high-profile investigations was leaked to the press by someone within the GMP. In doing so, that person brought the force into disrepute and damaged the public's trust in our officers. Chief Constable Brown takes that very seriously and is keen to see that whoever that officer was faces the consequences of their actions.'

'So what exactly is the end goal of the IPCC investigation?' Ash cut in.

'Well,' said Healy, 'they'll be looking to see if DCI Phillips is guilty of gross misconduct in a public office.'

'Is this really the best use of the taxpayers' money?' Phillips protested. 'Witch hunting hard-working coppers?'

'I can assure you there'll be no witch hunt.' Healy fixed her with an icy stare. 'The IPCC will conduct a thorough and detailed investigation. One that may lead to criminal charges being brought against you, Chief Inspector.'

Phillips did a double take. '*Criminal* charges?'

'Yes,' said Healy coldly. 'And you should know that if found guilty of those charges, the potential sentence you could face ranges from three years – to life in prison.'

22

'How are you feeling?' asked Ash as soon as they stepped back out into the corridor.

Phillips was lost for words, still processing what Healy had just told her. 'I need to get some air,' she managed to mumble before heading off down the corridor.

A few minutes later she stepped out through the main entrance of Ashton House into the cold February air and stumbled across the car park. As soon as she felt confident that she was out of earshot of any of her fellow officers, she pulled out her phone and dialled Adam. Frustratingly it went straight to voicemail. 'Where the hell is he?' she growled before trying him again but with the same result. After repeating the sequence three more times, she left a message telling him to call her ASAP and then dialled Carter's desk phone.

After several rings, a woman answered. 'Superintendent Carter's office.'

Phillips was momentarily taken aback. 'Sorry, Diane. I

think I must have called you by mistake instead of the boss.'

'Don't worry, he's been in a meeting all afternoon with the chief constable, so he diverted all his calls through to me.'

'When will he be free?' Phillips was struggling to keep the panic out of her voice.

'I couldn't say, to be honest. They're doing budgets and forecasting, and it may well run into the evening. Do you want to leave a message?'

'No. No, I don't.'

'Are you sure?'

'Yeah. I'm sure,' said Phillips. 'Look, I'd better go. Lots to do and all that.'

'No problem. I'll let him know you called when I speak to him.'

'Thanks, Di.' Phillips ended the call and took a deep breath as she tried to clear her head. What the hell was she going to do?

For the next couple of minutes, she tried over and over again to get through to Adam's phone but to no avail. Standing there now, all alone in the floodlit car park, she was filled with an overwhelming urge to jump in the Mini and get the hell out of there as fast as the little car could carry her. Much to her annoyance, however, she quickly realised she'd left her car keys on her desk. 'Damn it,' she whispered, her breath visible in front of her, before trudging back inside.

As she walked through the door to the main MCU office, she noted that Jones and Bovalino had already left for the night, and only Entwistle remained, still beavering away at his laptop. In no mood to talk, she avoided looking in his direction as she made a beeline for her office and the keys to her escape.

At that moment, her phone began to vibrate in her pocket. Pulling it out, she could see it was Adam. 'And about bloody time,' she muttered as she closed her office door before answering. 'Where the hell have you been?'

'Sorry. I was asleep,' he replied with a yawn. 'I'm on nights, remember?'

Phillips glanced back out towards the office to check if Entwistle was watching her, but his gaze remained fixed on the screen. 'I called you *six* times and just kept getting your voicemail.'

'I switched it off so I wouldn't be disturbed,' he replied. 'Anyway, what's so urgent?'

She lowered her voice. 'Healy just told me the Professional Standards investigation is being turned over to the IPCC.'

Adam took a moment to respond. 'What's the IPCC?'

'The Independent Police Complaints Commission.'

'So what does that mean?'

'It means that if they find me guilty of gross misconduct, I could face criminal charges and a potential custodial sentence.'

'What? For sharing a few files? That doesn't make sense.'

'I know, but there's precedence. A guy from West Midlands Police recently got ten years for passing information to an OCG.'

'What's an OCG?'

'Organised crime gang.'

'Well, it's hardly the same thing, Janey.'

'Maybe so, but if he got ten years, I could easily end up

with three. Can you imagine me in New Barn prison? I'd be a dead woman walking.'

'It's not going to come to that, babe. She's probably just trying to put the wind up you, that's all.'

'They've traced the file downloads to my login, Adam.'

'Oh shit,' he muttered. 'Tell me you didn't use your own.'

'Who else's was I gonna use?'

Adam fell silent on the other end.

'I'm scared, Adam. I'm really, bloody scared.'

'I know, Jane. But try not to worry. I'm sure it'll be fine.'

'How can you be so blasé about all this?' she shot back.

'I'm not being blasé. I just don't know what else you want me to say.'

At that moment, there was a tap on her closed door. Turning, Phillips could see it was Whistler wearing his coat and carrying his bag on his shoulder. 'Hang on a sec, Adam,' she said, before motioning for him to come in.

'Sorry to interrupt,' he said as he stepped inside. 'But I'm about to head off, and I wanted to double-check you're still OK going to Trisha's by yourself.'

With everything rolling round her mind after the revelation by Healy, she had totally forgotten the fact she'd promised to visit her on the way home. *Shit.*

She returned her attention to Adam. 'Look, I'm going to have to go.'

'OK,' he replied. 'I'm heading out to work in the next half an hour, but I'll call you later when I get a break.'

'Sure,' she said without feeling before ending the call.

Entwistle continued now. 'I don't have any plans tonight, so I'm happy to come with you if you'd like?'

It was a kind offer, and ordinarily she might have

accepted, but the last thing she wanted right now was company.

'No, honestly I'm fine.'

'You sure?'

'Yeah. You get yourself away.'

Entwistle nodded and handed across a yellow Post-it note. 'I dug out the postcode as well as the What3Words location for her address just in case. Hopefully it'll make it easier for you to find where she lives in this shitty weather.'

'Thanks, Whistler.'

'Right then,' he said with a flash of a smile. 'I'll leave you to it. Have a lovely weekend.'

'And you.' She watched him leave before exhaling loudly. In that moment, every fibre in her being wanted to tell Healy and Brown where they could stick the job, but that would mean they had won. And there was no way she was going to go down without a fight.

So after closing down her laptop and switching off the lights, she scooped up the keys to the Mini and marched out in the direction of the car park.

23

Today had passed by in a blur, and for obvious reasons she had struggled to maintain any level of focus or concentration at work. Being on and off the phone to Lesley across the day hadn't helped, either. Like a lot of people across Manchester this morning, she'd blamed her lateness to work on the chaos caused when one of the main commuter routes had shut for several hours due to a serious incident at Humphrey Park station. What none of her colleagues or clients could have known, though, was that *she* was directly responsible for that chaos, because *she* was the person who had pushed that man off the platform and under the train. She knew only too well what she had done was wrong – sinful even, given her upbringing – but at the same time she had felt compelled to do it, to rid the world of a vile predator hell-bent on abusing women – just as she had when she had pushed Charlie Callus down the stairs outside his apartment.

Still, no matter how justified she felt her actions had been in ridding the world of such a creature, it had not stopped her jumping out of her skin every time she heard a police siren through the office windows as they surged up and down Deansgate today – one of Manchester's busiest streets. In fact, she had been half expecting the police to turn up and arrest her at any moment. Mercifully, that had not happened, and she had made it through to the end of day a free woman.

Partly because the train network had yet to return to normal, with many trains cancelled or running a restricted service, and partly because she feared being recognised if she took her usual train back, this evening she opted to take the bus home. Frustratingly it would take almost twice as long as her usual journey time on the train, but she felt changing up her routine would be the right thing to do.

So, after making her way on foot through the rain, she arrived at the Piccadilly Gardens bus depot just after 6 p.m. It was a busy spot most days, but today it seemed especially crowded, as if everyone had had the same idea to ditch the train and hop on a bus home.

After waiting in line for about fifteen minutes, she eventually boarded the double-decker bus and grabbed a seat towards the back of the lower deck, attempting to make herself appear as insignificant as possible. Once again, anonymity was the word of the day.

Finally, after what was probably only five minutes – but felt like an hour – the bus doors closed, and the large vehicle backed away from the stand before eventually pulling off into the early evening traffic.

Still terrified that the police might rush onto the bus and drag her off at any moment, she kept her head down and prayed that the journey would be as swift as possible. Her heart raced every time someone pressed the bell, signalling they would be getting off at the next stop. The fear and anxiety she felt sitting trapped in her seat was unbearable, and all she wanted to do was get home so she could lock the world outside.

As the journey continued, her mind was never far from the events of that morning, and questions buzzed around her head like a swarm of worker bees. Had the lecherous man been fatally injured by the train? Did the police know what had happened to him? And were they already looking for the person who was responsible for it? Were they looking for *her*? Unable to think of anything else, she decided that finding answers to those questions was preferable to not knowing anything at all, so she made the bold move to take a look online. Careful not to draw any attention to herself, she slowly pulled her phone from her bag, and with the screen tilted towards her – and away from any of her fellow passengers' line of sight – she began searching through Google for any news of the man who went under the train.

Starting with the fairly generic search term *delayed trains in Manchester*, she was presented with a raft of links connecting her to timetables and route maps for the rail network across Manchester, hardly surprising given the circumstances of the day. But just a little further down the stack, she spotted a link that caused her adrenaline to spike as she clicked on it:

FATALITY AT HUMPHREY PARK STATION GROUNDS RAIL NETWORK TO A HALT.

After casually scanning her surroundings to ensure she wasn't being watched, she began reading the opening paragraph as her heart beat rapidly in her chest.

Manchester's rail network was thrown into chaos this morning when a commuter fell under a train at Humphrey Park station just after eight o'clock.

Her mouth dried in an instant as she read the next line.

The victim, a white male in his thirties who has not been named, was pronounced dead at the scene. Police are appealing for witnesses who may have seen what happened in the moments leading up to his death.

Placing the phone against her chest, she glanced out the window as she took a moment to catch the breath that had just been knocked out of her. As she'd watched him fall from the platform, she'd realised the man was unlikely to have survived the impact, but seeing it there in black and white suddenly made what she had done feel very, very real. The enormity of who she was and what she had become hit her like a hammer: a killer, not just once, but *twice* now.

Breathing deeply in an attempt to lower her heart rate, she turned her gaze back into the body of the bus, feeling dangerously exposed and anxious to get home as soon as possible. It was then that she spotted the man looking straight at her, standing as he was in the aisle that ran down the middle of the packed bus. Instinctively she looked away for a second before glancing back, only to find his eyes locked on hers. Once again her mind was awash with questions; was he undercover police? Were they onto her? Was she about to be arrested? Would she spend the rest of her life in prison? As panic began to surge through every cell in her body, it took every ounce of will power not to jump up from her seat and make a run for it. For all the good that would have done on a packed-out, moving vehicle.

Just then her phone began to vibrate in her hand, and as she glanced down at the screen, she could see it was her sister calling. Glad of the distraction, she hit the green answer icon. 'Hello?'

'He's been here again.' Lesley's words shot out in panic.

She felt her face wrinkle. 'Who has?' she said as quietly as possible so as not to be overheard by the passengers around her.

'Albert.'

'Albert has? What makes you say that?'

'He put a card through the door. It has a picture of a kitten on it, and it says "Sorry. Please forgive me" on the front.'

'Was there anything inside it?' she asked.

'No, it's blank, but I know it's from him. It has to be. He's trying to get inside my head again.'

Even though she was only too familiar with all the horrific events that had led to her sister's paranoia around Albert, yet more of her drama was the last thing she needed right now.

'Why is he doing this to me?' cried Lesley. 'Hasn't he hurt me enough?'

Hearing the fear and anxiety in her little sister's voice suddenly brought her to her senses. 'Look, I'm on the number 46 bus, which goes past your house. I'll jump off and come straight round.' She glanced at her watch. 'I should be there in about fifteen minutes. So just keep the door locked, and don't answer it to anyone but me, all right?'

'OK,' replied Lesley.

'I'll be there as quick as I can.' With that, she ended the call before allowing herself a surreptitious glance in the direction of the man who had previously been staring at her. Much to her relief, his attention appeared to be elsewhere now. Still, she couldn't say for sure who he was or why he had shown an interest in her, so she decided it would make sense to get off the bus sooner rather than later. Even though that would mean walking in the rain and would add another ten minutes to her journey, she figured it was better to be safe than sorry. So with that, she hit the bell to signal her intention to get off, then nudged the man next to her to get up. It was time to get the hell out of here.

24

As anticipated, the traffic this evening had been nose-to-tail pretty much all the way around the M60, and it was to Phillips's considerable relief that she finally spotted the exit for Stretford and pulled the Mini over to the left-hand lane as she headed for Trisha's address.

It was another ten minutes before she found the street she was looking for, and parked the car at the kerb outside of the narrow, new-build, semi-detached house set back from the street. With the weather showing no sign of improvement, Phillips pulled up her collar before jumping out and rushing to the front door located at the end of the short pathway. After rapping the large knocker fixed to it, she took a step back and waited.

A minute or so later, the door was answered by a tall, blonde woman who appeared to have been recently caught in the rain herself, her long wet hair sticking to the side of her face, the shoulders of her jumper darkened by the downpour. 'Yes?'

Phillips flashed her ID. 'DCI Phillips from the Major Crimes Unit. Are you Trisha Metcalfe?'

She frowned. 'I am. Why?'

'Could we talk inside?'

Trisha glanced left and right over Phillips's shoulder. 'What's this about?'

'I'm sure we'd both be more comfortable inside and out of the rain.'

'Sorry, yeah,' replied Trisha. 'Where are my manners. Please come in.'

Phillips stepped inside as Trisha closed the door behind her. A moment later they were both taking seats in the well-presented lounge at the back of the house. The central heating appeared to be on full blast, and the heat of the room made Phillips's cheeks tighten.

'So why am I getting a visit from the police?'

'Do you know a man named Charlie Callus?'

Trisha dropped her chin to her chest for a beat before looking up again. 'I knew I shouldn't have gone back to his flat.'

'So do you know him, then?'

She nodded.

'And are you aware of what happened to him after you spent the night together?'

'Yes,' said Trisha in a low voice. 'I saw the story on the news.'

Phillips felt her brow furrow. 'So why didn't you come forward? Any information you had about his last movements could be vital to the investigation.'

Trisha glanced towards the mantelpiece in the middle of the room.

Phillips followed her gaze and spotted the framed picture of Trisha in a wedding dress, a man of a similar age in a full morning suit smiling next to her. 'So you're married?'

'Yes.'

'And where is your husband now?'

'He's away at the moment.'

'And I take it he's not aware that you and Charlie were having an affair?'

'It wasn't an affair.' Trisha recoiled. 'It wasn't even a fling. It was just a one-night stand. It was only meant to be a bit of fun.'

Phillips scrutinised her face to see if she was lying, but there was no evidence to suggest she was. 'What time did you last see Charlie?'

'I got a taxi home about six thirty, I think.'

'On Tuesday morning?'

'Yes.'

'And how was Charlie when you left?'

'Fine as far as I could tell. He was flat out on the bed, sleeping off the booze from the night before.'

'Had he had a lot to drink?' Phillips asked.

'Oh yeah. He was hammered.'

'And did you guys sleep together that night?'

'How is that any of your business?' Trisha replied curtly.

'Because we found fluids and DNA on his body, and if you two were intimate, we'll likely match some of it to you. It'd certainly help us eliminate you from our enquiries if we know how it got there.'

Trisha folded her arms across her chest. 'We didn't sleep together because he was too drunk, but we did try a few *other* things.'

'I see,' said Phillips. 'So the saliva we found on his genitals, that was yours, was it?'

'Probably,' said Trisha before closing her eyes for a long moment.

'And you say Charlie was alive when you left at 6.30?'

'Yes.'

'How did you get home?'

'An Uber.'

'I'll need the details of your booking so we can verify it with the driver.'

Trisha pulled her phone from her pocket and took a moment to locate what she was looking for before passing it to Phillips.

She inspected the booking email for a moment before taking a picture of it on her own phone and handing it back. 'So did you see anyone else floating about at that time?'

'No, but then again, I really wasn't looking. I was still dressed in my clothes from the night before and just wanted to get the hell out of there.'

The walk of shame, thought Phillips before changing tack.

'When did you first meet Charlie?'

'Monday night.'

'So it really was a one-night stand?'

'Yes, it was.'

'And had you spoken to him before that, through the app?'

'Yeah, but just messaging,' said Trisha.

'For how long?'

'About a week, I guess.' Trisha sighed. 'Look, I'm not proud of what I did. I was stupid, and I never should have signed up for that bloody app, but I really didn't think it would come to anything. It was just meant to be a bit of fun and harmless flirting.'

'If that's the case, then how did you end up in bed with Charlie?'

Trisha shrugged. 'I honestly don't know. Steve and I have had a few problems recently, and I guess I just liked the attention I was getting. One thing led to another, and before I knew it, we were having drinks together.'

In a weird way, Phillips could relate to the unhappiness that had led to her behaviour. After all, things with her and Adam weren't great at the moment, and she knew only too well how complicated relationships could be.

'You won't tell Steve, will you?' Trisha's voice was brimming with panic.

Phillips shook her head. 'Your private life has nothing to do with me.'

Trisha's posture visibly softened.

'That said, though, as one of the last people to see Charlie alive, if this does end up in court, you could well be called as a witness. If that's the case, you may want to speak to your husband first about all this, because the press will have access to your full name and will be permitted to report on exactly how you came to be one of the last people to see Charlie alive. Including what time you left his apartment.'

'Oh God.' Trisha swallowed hard.

'I'm going to need you to come to the station to give us a DNA swab.' Phillips passed across her business card. 'For elimination purposes.'

Trisha stared down at it in her hand and muttered, 'What the hell have I done?'

'And once we've verified your booking with the cab firm, we hopefully won't need to speak to you again. But needless to say, I wouldn't be making any plans to leave town any time soon. OK?'

Trisha remained silent.

'Right, well, I'd better let you get on with your weekend.' Phillips stood up from the chair. 'Don't get up. I can see myself out.'

A few minutes later and back in the car, Phillips pulled out her phone and dialled Chakrabortty in her favourites.

'Jane, to what do I owe the pleasure at this time on a Friday night?'

'I was just wondering who's doing Patrick Mahoney's PM next week and when?'

'Give me a sec, and I'll check,' said Chakrabortty before going silent for a time.

Phillips waited patiently.

'Looks like it's been scheduled in for Monday at 9.30 with yours truly.'

'Good stuff. In that case, I'll see you then.'

'I'll look forward to it,' Chakrabortty replied. 'Will you be bringing Jonesy?'

Phillips let out an ironic chuckle. 'Not this time, no. Having seen the state of Mahoney's body at the scene, I think I'll spare him the experience of seeing that up close.'

'Might be wise given his weak stomach.'

'Yeah, exactly,' said Phillips. 'Right. Well, I'll leave you to it, Tan. Have a great weekend.'

'You too,' said Chakrabortty.

Phillips ended the call.

25

With Adam working on Saturday, Phillips was once again left to her own devices, and with thoughts of the IPCC investigation never far from her mind, she decided to bury herself in the backlog of paperwork that had built up after a busy week out in the field. She had also received an impromptu call from Carter, who was keen to know how she was feeling after hearing the news for himself that the investigation had been escalated to the IPCC. After reassuring him she was fine, and it was business as usual, she had got back to work and made a decent dent in the mountain of admin associated with the open cases she was managing at the moment.

So it was no surprise, then, that by the time Sunday came round, she was chomping at the bit to get out of the house and spend some time with Adam after he had been given what seemed to be a rare weekend day off.

As promised, he'd booked a late lunch for them at one of their favourite restaurants, Albertos Bar and Kitchen in West Didsbury. In Phillips's opinion, it offered the best

Sunday lunch anywhere in Manchester, and to ensure they made the most of their day, she'd even organised a taxi to and from the restaurant so they could both enjoy a drink with their meals.

Taking their seats in a leather-clad corner booth reminiscent of a Vegas nightspot, Phillips surveyed the room around them, which was brimming with excited diners, a mix of clientele from couples like her and Adam to families of varying sizes and mixes of generations.

'I love this place,' she said, trying her best to forget her troubles for one day as she picked up the menu.

Adam glanced around. 'Yeah, it's nice,' he said without feeling.

A few minutes later, their waiter, Franco, appeared. He was a short, wiry man with heavily gelled black hair and the dark skin of his Sicilian origins. '*Bonjourno*,' he said with a wide smile and a thick Italian accent as he approached. 'How are we today?'

'Very good,' said Phillips.

Adam nodded but remained silent.

For the next few minutes Franco talked them through the menu for the day as well as offering his own take on a couple of his favourites before taking their drinks orders. With the promise of a prompt return, he made himself scarce and left Phillips and Adam to enjoy some fresh bread with olive oil and balsamic vinegar.

'It feels like ages since we were last here,' said Adam before popping a piece of oil-soaked baguette into his mouth.

'That's because it is,' she replied. 'I checked the last booking I made on my phone and realised the last time we came here was September, for your birthday. We're in bloody February now.'

Adam raised his eyebrows. 'Wow. Where does the time go?'

'Work,' said Phillips.

They both fell silent as they studied the menu for the next few minutes until Franco reappeared holding a tray containing their drinks, which he placed down on the table in front of them. A large glass of pinot grigio for her, and a bottle of Morretti for him. 'Are you ready to order food?' Franco asked.

'I am,' said Phillips, who was so excited to be eating out for the first time in ages she'd already checked the menu online and knew exactly what she wanted.

Adam seemed less prepared. 'Er, you order yours, and I'll quickly figure out what I'm going to have.'

Phillips fixed her attention on their waiter. 'I'll have the calamari bruschetta to start, the mushroom risotto to follow, with a rocket and parmesan salad on the side, please.'

'Very good, madam,' Franco replied without writing anything down. 'And for you, sir?'

Adam's eyes were still fixed on the large menu. 'Erm, I'll just have the soup to start and the sirloin of beef for my main.'

'The sirloin is cooked pink, sir. Is that OK?' added Franco.

'Yeah, that's fine,' Adam replied, handing back the menu.

Franco flashed another wide smile before turning on his heel and striding off in the direction of the open-plan kitchen visible on the other side of the restaurant.

Phillips took a mouthful of the ice-cold wine and allowed herself to relax into the soft leather of the booth. 'This is more like it.'

Adam took a sip of his beer. 'Beats working for a change.'

'You can say that again.'

'We haven't had a chance to catch up on it,' said Adam as he placed his bottle down on the table, 'but I heard through the grapevine there was a bit of a mess to clear up at Humphrey Park station on Friday, and you were called in.'

Phillips shook her head. 'How does this stuff get out so quickly?'

Adam smiled. 'People love to talk in hospitals, babe. Gossip keeps the place running.'

'Sounds like Ashton House,' she said sardonically.

'So what happened?'

'A guy took a dive off the platform and under a train.'

Adam frowned. 'Jumpers don't normally come under MCU, do they?'

'That's just it. If the witness we spoke to is to be believed, our victim was pushed.'

'Bloody hell. That's no way to go.'

'It really isn't,' she replied. 'You should have seen the state of what was left of him.'

'I can imagine.'

As they each fell silent, Phillips took a moment to savour the busy atmosphere around her. The exciting chatter that filled the air was in stark contrast to the world of murder, mistrust and bureaucracy she had inhabited over the last week, and her mind was drawn back to Healy, Brown and the IPCC investigation, causing her stomach to flip. 'So how are things with your new boss, Terri?' she asked, attempting to distract herself.

'Pretty good, actually,' said Adam. 'She seems happy to let us get on with the job so far, which is great, and she said she's also looking to extend the team, meaning fewer weekend shifts going forward, which would be a bit of bonus.'

'Yeah, it would. I hardly see you at the moment.'

Adam lifted the bottle from the table. 'Er, last time I checked, you worked weekends too.'

'True, but not nearly as much as you. I do one in four; you seem to be working every other weekend at the moment.'

'I told you Olly being on honeymoon for a month was always going to mean more weekend shifts in Jan and Feb. It won't be quite as bad in March, and if Terri does come through with more staff, then we could end up with some decent time off in the summer.'

'Well, that would be good.'

Adam took a drink before putting the bottle back down. 'So how are you feeling about your conversation with Healy on Friday?'

'To be honest, I'd rather not talk about it. Not today, anyway. Let's just pretend there's no shit to deal with. Just for one day.'

He shrugged. 'If that's what you want.'

'It really is.' Phillips fell silent as she once again took in the room around her before casting her gaze to a poster fixed on the wall above the next booth. It proudly announced that the restaurant was fully booked for Valentine's Day – this coming Tuesday – and recommended trying Albertos delivery service if any customers had not been able to book in. Phillips had totally forgotten about the fact Valentine's Day was on the horizon. 'Are you on nights again this week?' she asked, turning her attention back to Adam.

'Yep. Another seven on, but then at least I get four days off.'

She found herself gently nodding before draining her glass and setting it down. It seemed Adam had no idea it was Valentine's Day this week either, which only added to her sense of sadness. What had happened to the energy and excitement they'd both felt in the early stages of their relationship? Where had their passion and mojo gone? Deep down, she knew the answer, but admitting it was a shared obsession with their work that was slowly eroding what they had was too terrifying to contemplate. Adam was unlikely to stop doing what he loved, and the way she was feeling at the moment, she was prepared to do whatever it took to hold on to her job too.

Just then, and much to her relief, Franco appeared with their starters, which he set down in front of them.

The aromas of garlic and basil filling the air were like smelling salts from the gods.

'Can I get you another pinot grigio?' Franco asked as he scooped up her empty glass.

'Yes, please,' said Phillips before catching herself. 'Actually, Franco, you'd better make it a bottle.'

26

'Someone looks like they had a big night last night,' said Chakrabortty as she passed Phillips a disposable apron.

Phillips winced. 'More like a big afternoon.'

'Special occasion, was it?'

'No. Just a rare Sunday off with a boyfriend who's never at home.'

'And how is the flying doctor? As dashing as ever?'

'Forever *dashing out* more like.' She sighed. 'He's always at work.'

'I know the feeling,' replied Chakrabortty.

'Sorry.' Phillips smiled. 'I sometimes forget you're a doctor.'

'As opposed to a butcher?'

Phillips laughed loudly now. 'That's not what I meant.'

'I know.' Chakrabortty chuckled too. 'I'm only teasing. Anyway, as time's ticking on, shall we go and have a look at our train victim?'

'Why not?' Phillips replied. 'Seeing a severed body up close is just what I need with a hangover.'

A few minutes later the two women stood on opposite sides of the surgical table that held the collection of parts that now made up Patrick Mahoney's body, all covered in a green surgical sheet.

'Dental records confirm this is Patrick Mahoney, as you initially suspected,' said Chakrabortty.

'Or what's left of him.'

'Quite.' Chakrabortty grabbed the sheet in her gloved hands. 'Right. Let's get started.'

Had Phillips been able to face breakfast this morning, she would surely have thrown it up right there and then, such was the grotesque sight that greeted her.

Chakrabortty had obviously noticed. 'You OK with this?'

'I'm fine,' she replied before placing the back of her hand to her nose and mouth. 'It's just a bit much for first thing on a Monday.'

'Sorry. I'm so used to it I sometimes forget how this stuff can affect people.'

Phillips took a deep breath in through her nose before exhaling sharply. 'I'm good. It's fine. Carry on.'

'You sure?'

'Yes,' said Phillips. 'Honestly, I am.'

Chakrabortty nodded, then began her dissection.

As she worked her way through the usual routine of a post-mortem, she explained in detail to Phillips how death had come about – aside from the obvious injuries to the body. And based on the impact required to sever it in two, it was likely that Mahoney would have known little to nothing about it. The doctor was sure he'd have died almost instantly, as witnessed by the damage inflicted to his liver, kidney, spleen and stomach.

As Phillips watched on, it really was awful to think that a human being could end their days in such a way.

'I spoke to his sister, who claims he never showed any signs of being suicidal, and we also have a witness who thinks he could have been pushed, but she can't be sure. Is there anything to suggest he might have been unsteady on his feet?'

'No alcohol or drugs in his blood.'

Phillips shook her head as she continued to stare down at the various body parts.

Chakrabortty continued, 'But then again, it's February. I guess he could have slipped on the icy platform and just gone straight under the train.'

'It's certainly a possibility,' said Phillips.

The remainder of the examination took about an hour, and by the time it was completed, Phillips had well and truly seen enough severed body parts and ruptured organs for one day.

'Jonesy mentioned you were having a spot of bother with Professional Standards,' said Chakrabortty as they wandered side by side back down the corridor.

Phillips stopped in her tracks. 'Actually, there's been a development there.'

'In what way?'

'It's been referred to the IPCC.'

Chakrabortty was incredulous. 'On what grounds?'

'Potential for gross misconduct.'

'That's insane.'

Phillips nodded sombrely.

'What has your fed rep said?'

'Not a lot.'

'I'm so sorry, Jane. I honestly can't believe they're doing this to you. You're the most dedicated officer I know.'

'Thank you. That means a lot.'

'Is there anything I can do to help?'

'Sadly not.' Phillips sighed. 'I've just got to sit tight and see where it goes.'

'Well, you know where I am if you ever need to talk about anything.'

'Thanks, Tan,' she replied. 'I really appreciate it.'

'Any time, you know that.'

27

'Morning, guv,' Jones said cheerfully as she strode back into the main office of MCU and over to the bank of four desks that housed Jones, Bovalino and Entwistle.

'How was the Mahoney PM?' Entwistle asked.

'Unpleasant.' She dropped onto the chair at the spare desk. 'But at least Chakrabortty was able to confirm the body was actually him. Dental records were a match.'

Jones sat to attention. 'Have you told the sister?'

'Shit, no. I meant to call her from the car on the way back, but I totally forgot.'

'I can do it,' said Jones.

'Thanks. That would be a real help.'

'Digital Forensics have shared the contents of Mahoney's laptop, guv,' said Entwistle.

'That was quick. Anything of interest?'

'Quite a lot, actually.' Entwistle turned his laptop so she could see the screen. 'The hard drive contained over five hundred images that are classed as indecent, including at least a hundred of naked girls under the age of thirteen. Plus, he had a pen drive with some links to porn sites dedicated to underage girls.'

'So he *was* a predator?' Jones cut in.

'Looking at this lot, most definitely.' Entwistle passed across a colour printout. 'I also found this profile on Hooked.'

'He was on Hooked? Well, that can't be a coincidence.' Phillips examined the sheet for a moment. 'Are you sure this is him? The Patrick Mahoney on here is eighteen, and the man in the profile picture bears no resemblance to the person I saw on the slab this morning.'

'I think it's a photo of when he was a lot younger. Mahoney wasn't on Facebook, but his sister is, and looking at some of her old family photos, that profile picture is a dead ringer for Patrick when he was a teenager.' Entwistle passed across another sheet. 'Some of these messages he sent to other members on the app are pretty explicit, and all to girls who claim to be eighteen and are looking for married sugar daddies, but appear a lot younger.'

'So he was potentially grooming them?' Phillips scanned down the page.

'Certainly reads that way, guv.'

'Well that could that be a motive for someone to want him dead, surely?' said Jones. 'An angry parent maybe, who found out what he was up to?'

'Maybe,' she said. 'Do we know if our eyewitness, Alison Breen, is on Hooked?'

'To be honest, I didn't think to look.'

'See if she is. For all we know, she could have arranged to meet him, thinking she was getting the eighteen-year-old version of Patrick Mahoney, and then reacted badly when the overweight predator turned up.'

'So you think she could have pushed him off the platform?' Bovalino added.

Phillips shrugged. 'It's a possibility, but probably quite unlikely. I mean, I'm not up on the dating rituals of teenagers these days, but I'm pretty sure meeting someone on a packed rush-hour train isn't a thing.'

Entwistle chuckled. 'No. I don't think it is.'

Bovalino sat forward now. 'I've found something on the PNC that backs up the theory of Mahoney being a predator, guv.'

He had her full attention now – intrigued as she was to know what he'd found on the Police National Computer.

'He was questioned by the British Transport Police only a few days ago when they got a tip-off about him touching up a teenage girl on a train. Whoever reported it sent a text to the passenger SOS number, which is advertised all over the trains.'

'So the girl he was accused of touching wasn't the one who made the complaint?' Phillips asked.

'Not initially, no. She backed it up when the BTP spoke to her, but the initial complaint came from another passenger.'

'Can we trace who sent it?'

'I'm not sure,' said Bovalino, 'but I can speak to the BTP officers involved and try.'

'Do that.' Phillips sat forward. 'If the person who sent it was a regular commuter, they may have also been around when Mahoney was killed.'

'I'll speak to them as soon as we're done.' Bovalino tapped his pen against his computer screen. 'I've also managed to get hold of the CCTV from Humphrey Park station, which I'll start working through this afternoon.'

'Great. And did you get anywhere with the management company and the key fob data from Callus's apartment block?'

'I was just coming to that.' He beckoned her over. 'Take a look at this.'

Phillips stepped up and moved to stand next to his shoulder, where she could see a CCTV still on his screen. 'What am I looking at?'

'I checked all the fobs that were used to enter or exit the building around the time of Callus's death. Everyone is accounted for and has already been spoken to by uniform apart from this woman.' He pointed at the still, which contained the back of a dark-haired woman's head pictured walking away from the camera.

'Any idea who she is?' Phillips asked.

'No. But she did use Callus's second fob to get in and out of the building.' He pulled up another still image, this time of her facing the camera.

Phillips scrutinised the image. 'What's that writing on her chest?'

He handed her a printout. 'I had to blow it up, but I'm pretty sure it says "Busy Bees Cleaning" or something similar. I figured she might be his cleaner.'

'It would explain why she has a fob.'

'That's what I thought, guv.'

'Track down Busy Bees and see if they can identify her. If she was in his apartment, she may be able to tell us if anyone else was knocking about at that time.'

'Will do.'

Phillips patted him on the shoulder. 'Good work, Bov.'

The big man produced a proud grin. 'Thanks, boss.'

Phillips returned to her office, and for the next thirty minutes she made further inroads into her decision logs and various other elements of paperwork, at which point Bovalino appeared at the door.

'Sorry to interrupt, but I've got a name and address for the Busy Bees woman.' Stepping inside, he handed her a yellow Post-it note. 'Her name's Paula Thomas, and according to her boss, she's regularly cleaned for Charlie Callus since he moved into the flat. She lives in Irlam, and based on the jobs she was booked in for, she should be finished at three today. If she goes straight home, I reckon she'd be back at her house by four.'

Phillips checked her watch. It was just approaching midday.

'Shall we pay her a visit later? I'm happy to drive.'

She took a moment to consider the options before eventually shaking her head. 'No. It's all right. We're all pretty stretched, so I can go on my own. You focus on speaking to the BTP crew. See what they can tell us about Mahoney and the alleged incident on the train.'

'Sure.'

'I'll head over to Paula's about five. It'll give her plenty of time to get back from work, and I'll be halfway home from there anyway.'

28

Considering she'd not seen him for almost twenty years, he hadn't changed all that much. He was a little plumper around the waist and neck now, and the once ginger hair had turned almost white, but she could tell it was him sitting on the bench in Alexandra Park, retired police sergeant Lionel Price. Many years ago now, he had been the man who had finally put an end to the hell she and Lesley had endured at the hands of Albert back when they were young, teenage girls.

'Hello, Lionel,' she said as she approached.

He looked up from his newspaper and took a moment to register her. 'Sorry, I almost didn't recognise you standing there. How you doing?'

'Oh, you know.' Her breath was visible in the cold air as she dropped onto the bench next to him. 'I'm still going, so that has to be something, right?'

'Absolutely.' Price folded his newspaper away. 'And how is Lesley doing since I spoke to her about Albert? She really didn't seem to take it very well on the day.'

'Lesley's not great, in all honesty.' She glanced around to ensure they were not being overheard. 'In fact, that's why I asked to meet you.'

'I must admit, I was curious as to why you wanted to speak to me after all these years.' His brow furrowed. 'Is everything OK?'

'No. It's not. She's a bit of a mess and not been sleeping since she found out about him getting out.'

'I did wonder if telling her was the right thing to do.' He shook his head. 'It was never my intention to upset her, but I figured she should know he'd been paroled.'

'Do you know where he is?' she asked, cutting to the chase.

'Albert? No, I don't. Why do you ask?'

'I need to talk to him.'

He recoiled slightly. 'Do you really think that's wise?'

'I don't honestly know, but I've got to do something.' She pulled the greetings card from her pocket and passed it across. 'This came through Lesley's door the other day.'

Holding it in both hands, he read the words on the front, '"Sorry, please forgive me",' before opening it and looking at the blank interior.

She continued, 'I think Albert sent it.'

'Albert?' said Price. 'Why would he do that? He's on license. He'll know he's not allowed anywhere near Lesley, or you or any of his victims for that matter.'

'That won't stop him.'

Price glanced back at the card. 'But there's no writing in it. What makes you think it's from him?'

'Because it's the sort of thing he would do.'

At that moment an elderly woman walking a white West Highland terrier shuffled along the path in front of them. 'Finally stopped raining,' she said as she passed by.

'You never know, I hear we might even get some sunshine tomorrow,' Price replied in a jovial voice.

'I won't hold my breath,' came the reply as she continued walking along the path.

When the old woman was far enough away, she continued, 'I've tried to play it down with Lesley because I don't want to worry her, but putting a blank card through the door is Albert all over. And it's not just the card. Someone rang the doorbell the other evening, and when she answered, there was no one there.'

'Could it have been a delivery guy who got the wrong house?' Price asked.

'That's what I thought initially, but when I saw that card, I knew she wasn't being paranoid. It was Albert. It's got him written all over it.'

Price took a moment to think. 'You said it was the other *evening*?'

'Yeah.'

'Do you know what time exactly?'

'Not for certain, but I think it was about eight o'clock.'

'But then it can't have been Albert. Like I said, he's on licence, and as a sex offender, he'll be on tag too, and that means he's not allowed out after seven o'clock at night.'

'That won't stop him.' She shrugged. 'It's him. I know it is. And that's why I need to talk to him.'

'So what will you say?'

'That he needs to leave Lesley alone.'

'And do you really think he'll listen?'

'I don't know, but I have to try.'

'But you were a victim too,' said Price. 'If it is him, aren't you worried that by seeing you again, he'll turn his attention to you?'

'Maybe, but the difference is *I* can handle him. Lesley

can't. And besides, Lesley was the one he obsessed over.'

She glanced around once more. 'Look, can you find him for me or not?'

'I'm sure I can, yeah.' He handed the greetings card back. 'I'm just not sure I should.'

'I need to know where he lives, Lionel.' She locked eyes with him. 'I need to put a stop to his stupid games.'

'And how exactly are you going to do that?'

'Make him see sense.'

'You're not going to do anything stupid, are you?'

'Of course not. Like I say, I'm just going to make him see sense.'

'I really don't think it's a good idea,' he said. 'Far better to let sleeping dogs lie.'

'I don't have a choice, Lionel. Unless I confront him, Albert will not stop. He'll keep playing these games, getting inside Lesley's head and eroding her sense of self until there's nothing left. Like I told you, she's not slept for days, and I'm really worried about what she might do if this continues.'

Price frowned. 'What do you mean, *what she might do*? You don't think she'll try to harm herself, do you?'

She nodded. 'She's tried it before. A few years ago when everything got too much.'

His eyes widened. 'God, I had no idea.'

'Albert broke her spirit once. I'm not going to let him do it again.'

Price chewed his bottom lip for a moment, evidently deep in thought. 'OK,' he said finally. 'I'll see what I can find out from the old team.'

'Thank you,' she said with a soft smile.

'I'll give you a call as soon as I hear back from them, but as it's a favour, it may take a day or two to sort.'

'That's fine.' She stood now. 'And thanks again, Lionel. It means a lot. To me *and* to Lesley.'

'Tell her I was asking after her, won't you?'

'I will,' she said before pulling up her collar against the cold and turning and walking away.

29

As Phillips had hoped, Paula Thomas was home by the time she knocked on the front door of her small, terraced house located in Irlam.

'Yes?' she said as she opened the door.

'Are you Paula Thomas?'

'I am.' She was a slight woman, no taller than five feet two, with dark brown hair. She wore a black T-shirt and matching leggings, finished off with Dr Martens boots.

Phillips presented her ID. 'DCI Phillips from the Major Crimes Unit. Can I speak with you inside?'

Paula's brow furrowed. 'Is this about what happened to Mr Callus?'

'Yes, I'm afraid it is.'

'Please come in.' Paula beckoned her in before leading the way down the narrow hallway and through the first door on the right, into the small kitchen. 'You're lucky you caught me. I've not long been in. Would you like a hot drink? I was just about to make myself a coffee.'

'No, thanks, I'm fine.'

As Paula busied herself at the sink, filling the kettle, Phillips spotted a dark blue fleece hanging on the chair next to the small kitchen table, replete with a white Busy Bees logo on the back.

'I couldn't believe it when Gavin told me about Mr Callus,' said Paula.

'Gavin?' Phillips asked.

Paula returned the kettle to its cradle and set it to boil, then turned to face her. 'He's my boss. He called to tell me about what had happened when he saw it on the news the other day. I was in total shock. I'd only seen Mr Callus that morning.'

'What time was that? When you saw him?'

'About eight o'clock, which in itself was a bit of a shock. He's never normally at home when I go in to clean. He's usually at the gym, which is why I was surprised to see him.'

'Really? How do you know that? About him being at the gym, I mean?'

'He told me the first day I cleaned for him. That's one of the reasons he picked Tuesday, so he wouldn't be around and I could start early.'

'And do you have any idea *why* he was at home last Tuesday?'

'I don't, but there was a woman there, and she was playing merry hell with him when I opened the door. I have a key, you see.'

Phillips nodded. 'Do you know who she was?'

'Never seen her before.'

'Did you happen to hear what they were arguing about?'

At that moment the kettle clicked off as it came to the boil, steam pouring out through the spout. Paula filled her mug. 'I don't, but as soon as she saw me, she went ballistic, asking him if I was one of his little sluts. I didn't know where to put myself.'

'What was his response?'

'He laughed and told her to stop being ridiculous.' Paula tipped a small amount of milk into her coffee, then stirred it before picking it up and taking a tentative sip.

'So you yourself never had a relationship with Mr Callus?'

'As in romantic? You're kidding, aren't you?' Paula scoffed. 'I'm a married woman, and besides, even if I weren't, I wouldn't go near him in a million years. Not wanting to speak ill of the dead or anything, but his personal hygiene left a lot to be desired.'

Phillips tilted her head to one side slightly. 'And how would you know that?'

'I cleaned his flat every two weeks. The place was a mess, used condom wrappers next to the bed, all manner of pubic hair all over the bathroom. It was disgusting.'

'So in your opinion, do you think he was quite active in a sexual sense?'

'Oh, yeah. Most definitely.' Paula took another drink. 'Based on the amount of different coloured hairs I fished out of his shower tray every week, I reckon he was a very busy boy indeed.'

'And you say you'd never seen the woman he was arguing with before?'

'No.'

'Could you describe her?' Phillips asked.

'Long blonde hair and about my height.' Paula tapped her bottom lip. 'She was bleeding at the mouth too.'

She had Phillips's full attention now. 'She was bleeding?'

'Yeah. I couldn't be sure, but it looked like he'd given her a slap.'

'Did he use her name at all?'

Paula's face wrinkled. 'Now you mention it, he did say it, but there was so much happening at once I didn't take it in. I *think* he called her Helen.'

'Helen?' Phillips repeated. 'Are you sure it wasn't Heather?'

'Actually, now you've said it, I think it might have been Heather.'

'And you say she was bleeding at the mouth when she left?'

'Most definitely.'

'But you didn't see him hit her?'

'No. In fact, I only saw her lip when she barged past me to get to the front door.'

'I see,' said Phillips. 'And you said that was about 8 a.m.'

'It would have been, yeah.' Paula cradled the mug in her hands. 'Do you know what happened to him? They never said how he died in the newspaper.'

'All I can say at this stage is he suffered fatal injuries from falling down the stairs.'

Paula's eyes widened. 'Oh my God. That's terrible.'

Phillips leaned back against the worktop behind her and folded her arms across her chest. 'Can you talk me through what Mr Callus did after the woman left?'

'Not really because he sent me home. Said he'd got his weeks mixed up so wasn't expecting me. Told me he needed to get ready for work and asked if I could come back next week. Given how awkward it was, I was glad to get out of there.'

'So what time did you leave?'

Paula sipped her coffee as she took a moment to think. 'I'd say about ten past, maybe quarter past eight.'

'And Mr Callus was still OK at that point?'

'Yeah.' Paula nodded vigorously. 'Totally.'

'What did you do then?'

'I went to grab a coffee and then on to my next job, which was in the city centre.'

Phillips took a moment to process the sequence of events in her mind before pulling a business card from her pocket and placing it on the countertop. 'OK. Well, I think that'll do me for now, but if you can think of anything else that might be useful, give me a call. My number's on there.'

Paula examined the card for a moment before turning her attention back to Phillips. 'I'm sorry, I don't really feel like I've been much use.'

'Don't be,' replied Phillips. 'You've been more helpful than you know.'

Paula smiled softly before placing the cup down. 'I'll show you out.'

A few minutes later, with Phillips back behind the wheel of the Mini, she called Jones's mobile.

'Guv,' he said, answering after a couple of rings.

'You'll never guess who the cleaner reckons was in Callus's flat the morning he died.'

'Who?'

'A blonde woman named Heather who ran out with a bloody lip.'

'You're kidding?'

'Nope,' Phillips replied. 'Having a right ding-dong with her husband, by all accounts. And, get this, she asked him if the cleaner was one of his little sluts.'

'So she knew about him playing away?'

'Certainly sounds like it.'

'What are you going to do?'

Phillips checked her watch. It was well after five. 'Guess I'll head over to Hathersage and see what the grieving widow has to say.'

'You want me to meet you there?'

'No. The traffic will be shocking at this time of day. No need for both of us to work late tonight.'

'As long as you're sure.'

'I am.' Phillips fired the engine. 'You get yourself home.'

'Keep me posted, won't you?'

'I will,' she replied before ending the call.

A moment later, she fired the engine, indicated and pulled the car away from the kerb and out into the rush-hour traffic.

30

'I'm sorry, I didn't mean to lie to you,' said Heather from her position sitting on the couch opposite Phillips.

'So why did you?' Phillips asked flatly.

Heather shrugged. 'I guess I was embarrassed and also didn't want you to think badly of Charlie.'

'So he was the one who gave you the fat lip?'

'Yes.'

'Had he done it before?'

She nodded sombrely. 'A couple of times, yes.'

'Recently?'

Heather nodded but remained silent.

'Look.' Phillips shifted in her seat. 'I'm sorry, but based on that, I have to ask, did you push your husband down the stairs?'

'No!' Heather recoiled. 'I ran out of there as soon as the cleaning woman turned up and came straight back here.'

'Can anyone vouch for that?'

Heather wrapped her cardigan tightly round her middle, as if it would somehow protect her from the questions. 'No. I was here on my own.'

Phillips took a moment to scrutinise her face to see if she was lying, but it appeared she wasn't. Knowing that Callus had brought Trisha home the night before he was killed, Phillips chose her next words carefully. 'What time did you arrive at the apartment?'

'Not long before the cleaner, actually.'

'And why were you visiting your husband at that particular time?'

Heather dropped her chin to her chest for a few seconds before looking up again. 'Do you really want to know?'

'Yes, I do.'

'I was trying to catch him in the act.'

'How do you mean?'

'I think he was cheating on me, so I went to confront him about it.'

Phillips did her best to hide what she already knew to be true. 'And what made you think he was cheating on you?'

'I found a condom in the pocket of his jeans when I was doing the washing on Monday night. We never used them because I'm on the pill.'

'I see. So what happened then?' Phillips asked.

'I tried calling him, but he wouldn't answer. I thought about driving over to the flat right there and then, but I'd already had half a bottle of wine, so I daren't risk it.'

'So you waited til the morning?'

'Yes.' Heather shifted in her seat. 'I kept calling his mobile into the early hours, but he wouldn't answer. So as soon as I was confident I could drive, I got in the car and went to confront him.'

'And what did he say?'

'Told me I was imagining it,' replied Heather. 'Said I had a screw loose and was totally paranoid. But I wasn't. I knew he was up to something, and I could smell it on him as soon as he opened the front door.'

'Smell what exactly?'

'Her. The little slut he'd been fucking. I told him as much, and that's when he slapped me in the mouth.'

'I'm sorry you had to go through that, Heather.'

Heather continued, 'And that's when the cleaner turned up. I got such a fright, and I was so embarrassed, I ran out of there.'

'And you didn't come back later?' said Phillips.

'No. I didn't.'

'Because we can check the CCTV at the front door to the apartment block.'

'I swear on my mother's life. I didn't go back.'

Phillips changed tack slightly. 'Can I ask how you got into the building?'

Heather did a double take. 'Why is that important?'

'Because every key fob is registered with the management company, and your husband's spare key was allocated to the cleaning firm.'

'Some guy let me in; he was on his way out.'

'Did you get a good look at him?'

'I guess so.'

'Can you describe him?'

Heather gazed up to the left, evidently trying to remember him. 'Tall, white guy with dark hair and a goatee.'

'Do you know how old he was?'

'I couldn't say, really. He was opening the door just as I arrived, and left it open for me. I was totally focused on what I was going to say to Charlie, so I wasn't really looking at him.'

'And you'd never seen him before.'

'No, but then I didn't go to the flat all that often. Hardly ever, in fact. Charlie didn't like me being there – and now I know why.'

Despite her obvious reasons for wanting to get back at her husband, Phillips didn't get a sense that Heather *was* his killer. And if what she said was true, the timing of her exit would likely exclude her from their list of suspects, and she would, of course, be able to confirm that through the CCTV. Still, it paid to be thorough. 'So what did you do after you got home that day? Before myself and DI Jones came to see you?'

'Stayed in and hit the wine until you guys showed up.'

Phillips nodded.

Heather stared straight at her now. 'I wouldn't ever have hurt him, you know. As mad as I was at him, I loved Charlie.'

'I'm sure you did.' Phillips knew this may well have been the case, but based on the number of homicides she'd investigated over the years by so-called lovers, it certainly didn't discount her as a suspect. 'The fact is you lied to us about where you were, and not long before your husband was killed, you were involved in a violent altercation with him. You can see how that looks.'

'Yeah. I can.' Heather's eyes began to glisten as her bottom lip started to tremble.

That was Phillips's cue to leave. 'Right, well, it's late, and I should be getting home.' She stood up from the chair and passed across her business card. 'I'll probably need to speak to you again, Heather. So I suggest you don't make any plans to go anywhere without telling us. My number's on there, OK?'

Heather took the card but remained silent.

'Look after yourself,' said Phillips, then headed for the door.

31

The following morning each of the team continued with their individual endeavours in their hunt for the people responsible for killing Callus and Mahoney. With Jones, Bovalino and Entwistle all hard at work, Phillips spent the first few hours of the day updating the decision logs with the information she'd gleaned from yesterday's PM with Chakrabortty, as well as her visits to Paula Thomas and Heather Callus respectively. And yet, thoughts of what was to come – knowing she was now being investigated by the IPCC – were never far from her mind. To say she was worried was an understatement.

As the time approached midday, she realised she was losing the battle to maintain her concentration and decided a break would do her good, so after stepping away from her desk, she wandered out into the main office to see if any of the troops were hungry.

Not surprisingly, her offer of a round of sandwiches and hot drinks was met with great enthusiasm, and so, glad of the distraction, she headed to the Ashton House canteen with a long list of requests.

Returning about twenty minutes later, she placed the cardboard drinks tray on the spare desk before handing out the steaming teas and coffees, along with the various sandwiches and snacks that had been ordered.

As each of the guys got stuck into their own food, Phillips took a bite of her cheese and pickle sandwich and revelled in the sound of contented eating all around her.

'God, I needed this,' said Bovalino, having inhaled almost half of his sandwich already.

'It's the only tasty thing you'll be getting today?' joked Entwistle.

'Hey,' Bovalino volleyed back whilst chewing his next mouthful, 'I'll have you know us Italians take Valentine's Day very seriously. It's the Latin lovers in us.'

'Poor Izzie, is all I can say.' Entwistle laughed.

'Got any plans for tonight, guv?' Jones cut in.

'No.' She shook her head. 'Adam's working, so probably just another microwave meal for one and a night on the sofa with the cat. How about you?'

'I've been married nearly twenty years, and I've got two teenage daughters.' Jones produced a wry smile. 'What do you think?'

Phillips laughed, then turned her attention to Entwistle. 'No doubt Ashton House's very own Casanova has plans, hey?'

He shrugged nonchalantly. 'I might be taking a certain someone out for dinner, yes.'

'And is that certain someone tall and blonde with legs to die for?' Phillips asked.

Entwistle recoiled slightly. 'Who told you about that?'

Phillips took a mouthful of coffee. 'I'm a detective, Whistler. I hear things.'

Entwistle chuckled.

'Speaking of hearing things,' Phillips continued, 'has anything come back from Heather's phone network regarding her movements the morning Charlie died?'

'Yep,' said Entwistle, resting his sandwich on the desk. 'I spoke to her phone provider just now, and they confirmed her SIM card pinged off the local mast at about 9.15 a.m. Tuesday and continued to ping off it for the remainder of the day. So it looks like she's telling the truth.'

'OK, I figured as much.' Phillips focused on Bovalino now. 'Any updates on Mahoney?'

The big man scrunched his now empty sandwich wrapper into a ball and tossed it in the wastebasket. 'I spoke to the British Transport Police about an hour ago. They confirmed the tip-off about Mahoney touching up passengers did come through their passenger text line. They've given me the number that sent the text, but again we don't know the network.'

'Well, let's see if we can track it down.'

'Will do, boss.' He clicked open a file on his computer. 'I also got my mate at Network Rail to send over the CCTV footage from Humphrey Park station. I've teed it up to show you.'

Phillips stepped up from the chair and moved to his shoulder.

'Starts just a few seconds before he goes off the platform.' The big man pressed play.

Jones and Entwistle joined them, and they all watched together as the footage rolled, showing the large crowd of people huddled together on the platform.

Bovalino tapped the top corner of the screen. 'This is Mahoney here.'

A second later, a woman appeared to rush towards him, making contact from behind, causing him to lose his balance and fall off the platform just as the train rolled into the frame.

Entwistle said, 'Oh my God. That's horrific.'

'Doesn't bear thinking about, does it?' Jones added.

Phillips stared at the screen. 'Play it again.'

Bovalino did as asked and rewound the footage before pressing play for a second time.

'Pause it there,' she cut in. 'Just after he falls onto the track.'

'What are we looking at, boss?' asked Entwistle.

'I'm not sure. Can we get it on the big screen in the conference room?'

'Email it over to me, Bov.' Entwistle moved to collect his laptop from his desk. 'I'll set it up.'

A few minutes later, they each took seats at the conference table as the footage played on the large TV monitor fixed to the wall.

'Pause it in the same place,' Phillips instructed.

Once again the footage was paused just after the train had hit Mahoney.

Phillips got out of the chair and moved to stand next to the large screen. 'Am I imagining it, or is that a bee on the back of the woman who made contact with Mahoney?'

'Might well be. No pun intended,' said Bovalino. 'They've always been a symbol of the people of Manchester and our worker bee mentality, so pretty ubiquitous around the city.'

Phillips continued to stare at the screen for a long moment.

'What you thinking, boss?' Jones asked.

She turned to face them now. 'You're going to think I'm crazy, but I feel like I've seen that logo once already this week.'

Jones sat forward. 'Where?'

'On the back of a jacket hanging on a chair in Paula Thomas's kitchen.'

'As in the cleaner Paula Thomas?' said Bovalino.

'Yeah. Paula from Busy Bees.'

'You think *Paula* pushed Mahoney off the platform?' Jones asked.

'Like I said, it's crazy, I know.' She focused on Entwistle. 'Can you pull up the CCTV footage of Paula leaving Callus's flat?'

'Sure. Just give me sec.'

A moment later they all watched as the video played and Paula could be seen exiting the building and walking away from the camera.

'Pause it there,' said Phillips.

Entwistle followed her instruction.

'Can we review the two images side by side?'

Once again Entwistle did as asked, presenting the two pictures on-screen at the same time.

Phillips moved closer, first pointing to the logo on the back of the woman captured in the station CCTV footage, and then at the logo on the back of Paula Thomas's coat. 'I'm no expert, but they look pretty similar to me.'

'Bloody hell, guv,' said Jones. 'I think you're right.'

Phillips turned back to face them again. 'Where did the train Mahoney was originally travelling on stop before they shipped everyone off at Humphrey Park station?'

Bovalino checked the logs in the BTP report. 'Looks

like it came through Urmston, Chassen Road, Flixton, which is where Mahoney had his flat, Irlam—'

'Irlam,' Phillips cut him off. 'That's where Paula Thomas lives.'

'So what?' Entwistle's brow furrowed. 'We're saying Paula Thomas is somehow connected to both Callus *and* Mahoney?'

'I don't know,' said Phillips. 'But we need to find out. I want everything we can dig up on her, and I want it yesterday.'

32

Some time later, the conference room door opened, and Carter stuck his head through. 'Have you got a minute, Jane?'

'Yes, sir,' she replied before following him out into the main office.

'I'm sorry to interrupt your meeting, but we're needed in Brown's office as a matter of urgency.'

Phillips felt her stomach flip with adrenaline. 'Do we know why?'

'His PA didn't say. Just that it was important.'

She exhaled sharply. 'Best not keep him waiting, then.'

Five minutes later they each took seats opposite Brown, who was sitting behind his sparkling new desk.

The chief inspector cleared his throat and, dispensing with any pleasantries, got straight to the point. 'I want to talk to you both about the IPCC investigation. I had hoped to speak to you yesterday, but I'm afraid my diary simply wouldn't allow it.'

Phillips's nerves jangled in anticipation of what was to come.

'If you're in agreement, I'd like this conversation to be without prejudice. Is that OK?'

'Of course, sir,' replied Carter.

Phillips simply nodded.

Brown continued, 'I thought you ought to know that it was me who authorised the escalation to the IPCC.'

Phillips curled her toes in her boots once again as she tried with all her might to stop her contempt for Brown from showing on her face.

'Given you were the last person to download the files, Jane – and just days before they were leaked – frankly I thought it warranted it.'

'I see, sir,' she said without feeling.

Brown's posture stiffened as he continued, 'And whilst I'm not necessarily accusing you of passing those documents to Townsend, I did want to give you the opportunity in this meeting to explain what you were doing with them – and perhaps get out in front of things.'

Phillips shrugged. 'I was just going through some old files, sir.'

'Why?'

'In all honesty, I was curious.'

Brown's eyes narrowed. 'Curious about what?'

'Well, sir' – Phillips shifted in her seat – 'given the fact that Chief Constable Fox appeared to have gotten away with breaking the law for most of her career, I wanted to try to understand how she was not held accountable for her actions by the Home Office. I thought maybe I might find the answers in those files.'

'And did you?'

'No.'

Brown stared back in silence.

'If I may, sir,' said Phillips, 'can I ask what you meant when you said you'd like to give me the chance to "get out in front of things".'

Brown pursed his lips for a long moment before replying, 'Well, as a chief inspector with over twenty years on the force, you have options in this situation that you might not have considered.'

Phillips knew exactly where this was headed, but refused to make it easy for him. 'And what options might they be, sir?'

Brown linked his fingers together on the desk as he sat forward. 'I'll get straight to the point, Jane.'

She wished he would.

'If you were to consider taking early retirement, I could quite easily make all of this go away.'

She nodded. 'And by all this, you mean the IPCC investigation.'

'Yes, I do.'

'Now hang on a minute,' Carter cut in. 'Since when did this become an option?'

Brown fixed him with an icy glare. 'I'll remind you who you're talking to, Chief Superintendent.'

'Sorry, I didn't mean to speak out of turn, sir,' said Carter. 'But with respect, why would we want to retire one of the GMP's most successful detectives?'

'Because it would send the right message to the rest of the force,' Brown snapped back. 'That nobody is above the law – no matter how many convictions they've made.'

Phillips was incredulous. 'So you *do* think I leaked those files?'

'Oh, come on, Jane,' said Brown. 'We all know you did, so let's stop pretending, shall we?'

Phillips remained silent or risked saying what was really going through her mind, which would only land her in even more trouble.

Brown continued, 'This whole thing with Townsend has been very damaging to the reputation of the GMP.'

Phillips knew Brown well enough to know it was his own reputation he was really agitating about.

'If we were seen to be making a somewhat significant change in personnel with your retirement, it would go some way to rectifying the damage done and mean any investigation by the IPCC could be closed.'

'With respect, sir, I think we're being a bit premature here,' said Carter.

Phillips remained silent.

At that moment, there was a knock on Brown's office door.

'Come in,' he said in a loud voice.

Phillips could hear his assistant step inside the room behind her, but her gaze remained fixed on the chief constable.

'Sorry to interrupt, but your car's outside, sir,' said Viv.

Brown checked his watch. 'God, is that the time?'

Viv continued, 'You're due at the town hall in forty-five minutes.'

'Thank you, Vivienne,' said Brown. 'Tell the driver I'll be down shortly.'

'Of course,' she replied before stepping out of the room.

Brown turned his attention back to Phillips. 'I don't expect you to make a decision right away, but think about what I'm offering here, Jane. A way out of this mess with your reputation and pension intact.'

Phillips didn't react.

'Right.' Brown stood up. 'I think that covers everything, so I'll let you both get back to your work.'

Phillips was out of her own chair in a flash, striding out of the office with Carter falling in behind.

A minute later, back on the fifth-floor corridor and well out of earshot, she stopped and turned to Carter. 'The nerve of that guy,' she raged.

'Well, I must admit I wasn't expecting that when he called us in.'

Phillips paced back and forth as she tried to process what Brown had just said. 'He won't stop until he gets me out. You know that, don't you?'

Carter raised his palms in defence. 'Try not to go to the worst-case scenario, Jane. I think he's just feeling you out on this. Like he said, it's just *one* option here.'

'Yeah, and the other option could see me behind bars.'

'You don't really think it'll come to that, do you?'

'But what if it does?' Phillips stopped pacing. 'I wouldn't last five minutes in New Barn prison.'

'Honestly, I can't see that happening,' replied Carter. 'And for all his big talk in there, the IPCC would still have to prove you guilty of gross misconduct and *then* find enough evidence to warrant criminal proceedings. I just don't see it coming to that.'

Phillips felt her shoulders sag as the reality of her current situation hit home. 'Maybe he's right. Maybe early retirement is the best option here.'

Carter shook his head. 'Not as far as I'm concerned. That's the last thing I want.'

'Thank you, sir,' she said with a faint smile. 'But the reality is, I just don't know if I've got any fight left in me. I really don't.'

PHILLIPS'S HEAD was still spinning by the time she walked back into MCU. Thankfully, she was quickly brought back into the moment as Bovalino beckoned her over.

'Guv, come and have a look at this.'

She walked over to stand at his shoulder again.

'My mate at Northwest Railways has sent me over the travel card logs for Humphrey Park station from the morning Mahoney was killed.' The big man pointed to his computer screen. 'Luckily, every card is registered in the name of the person it belongs to.'

Phillips leaned in to get a closer look.

'Look here, logging out of the station at 8.17 a.m.'

'Paula Thomas,' said Phillips triumphantly. 'Well, I never.'

Jones and Entwistle stopped what they were doing and listened in.

'I found something else that's interesting too.' Bovalino moved on to a different spreadsheet.

'Looking at her travel card activity over a typical month, every Thursday and Friday she always logged in to the system at Irlam, and off again at either Piccadilly on a Thursday or Oxford Road on a Friday. However, last Friday morning – quite out of character based on the previous two months' logs – she logged out at Humphrey Park station.'

'Well, that's suspicious in itself,' said Entwistle. 'Breaking with her normal routine.'

'True,' replied Jones, 'but given what she may well have just witnessed, it could be argued she was just trying to get away because she was traumatised.' to

'Jonesy's right.' Phillips nodded. 'Just because she logged out at a different station doesn't mean she's guilty of pushing Mahoney off the platform. That said, it does look like the person who did is a dead ringer for Paula. We need definitive evidence that proves that the woman with the Bee logo on her back *is* actually Paula Thomas. And we also need to be able to prove that she was actively involved in pushing Mahoney under the train.'

'So how do we do that?' Bovalino asked.

'Check every camera they have at Humphrey Park station. We need CCTV footage that shows the woman's face as well as anything else that either confirms or at least suggests she deliberately shoved him in the back. There may be angles we've missed that could give us better pictures.'

Bov picked up his phone. 'I'll call my mate at Network Rail now.'

'Great,' said Phillips, feeling the same rush of excitement she always got when a case began to open up in front of them. 'Time is of the essence on this one, guys. So let's get cracking.'

33

'He's living in a veterans' refuge?' she asked as she stared down at the address on the yellow Post-it note in her hand.

'It's supported living as opposed to a refuge.' Price was sitting next to her on the same park bench where they'd met just yesterday.

'I didn't even know Albert had been in the military. He certainly never mentioned it.'

'Jason, the guy in sex crimes I used to work with, gave me a bit of insight on that, actually,' he said. 'Turns out he did about three weeks of basic training when he was in his late teens before being medically discharged. Something to do with shin splints, by the looks of it.'

'And that entitles him to be classed as a veteran, does it?'

Price nodded. 'Apparently so. The armed forces are very strong on that, by all accounts. Serve just one day and you can access all the benefits that come with being a soldier. And from what Jason said, Harry Gregg House is quite an upgrade on the usual halfway houses used by the probation service. Self-contained apartments with twenty-four seven support and not far from the city. As opposed to a bedsit in the middle of nowhere.'

'Sounds like Albert. Always finding a way to game the system.' She slipped the Post-it note into her coat pocket. 'You managed to get this back pretty quickly.'

'Yeah. I was surprised myself, actually. I thought it would've taken longer, but Jason had been looking at Albert's file quite recently so had the information to hand.'

'And why was he doing that? Looking into Albert's file, I mean.'

'Jason worked the case with me back when he was just starting out. He was very junior, so you wouldn't have met him, but he played an integral part in pulling the evidence together that convicted Albert. Given the magnitude of the case, he has kept a distant eye on Albert while he's been in Hawk Green and built something of a dossier on him over the years, including knowing exactly where he would be staying when he was released, so he had it all pretty much ready.'

'Well, I'm very grateful he did,' she replied. 'Please thank him for me.'

He shook his head. 'I didn't tell him it was for you. I figured it was best not to.'

She flashed a faint smile.

Price continued, 'I did have a good look through the dossier though, and I thought you might want to know that it looks like Albert had quite a hard time of it in Hawk Green.'

'In what way?'

'Well, even though he was in protective custody, it seems as though he was attacked by other inmates on several occasions, including one incident a few years ago when he was hospitalised with two broken legs.'

'Karma,' she said flatly.

'I have to admit, that was my thought too.' Price scanned his surroundings for a moment before continuing, 'I also asked Jason about Albert being on tag.'

'And what did he say?'

'That he is, which means he's on curfew and can't leave Harry Greg House between 7 p.m. and 7 a.m. each day. So he couldn't have been the person who knocked on Lesley's door that night. It's electronically monitored, so probation would know if he was to ever break his curfew.'

She took a second to process what he was saying. 'And there's no way to cheat the system?'

He shrugged. 'There's never one hundred per cent guarantees when it comes to dealing with criminals, but as far as I'm aware, the tags aren't easy to tamper with.'

'But it's not impossible that it could have been?'

'Not impossible, no,' said Price. 'But highly unlikely.'

'And that's why I need to talk to him, because like I said before, Albert is the king of gaming the system. If anyone can find a workaround to the tag monitoring, it's him.'

'I still think it's a bad idea to go and see him.'

'I know you do, Lionel. But I promised Lesley I'd find a way to make him stop.'

'If it is him playing games, do you really think he'll listen?'

'I honestly don't know. But I have to at least try.'

'Well, if you're going to insist on doing this, I think I should come with you.'

'No.' She exhaled sharply. 'This is between me and Albert. I have to do this on my own.'

'I really don't think that's wise.'

'Maybe not, but I can't sit by and do nothing while Lesley slowly loses her mind.'

'I understand,' said Price. 'But please promise me you won't do anything reckless.'

'And how am I going to do that when it sounds like he's monitored twenty-four seven?'

'I suppose you have a point there,' Price conceded. 'And on that, Jason said Harry Gregg has a pretty strict curfew of its own, and visitors aren't allowed into the building after 7 p.m. So you'll need to go there during the day, which, for my money, is not a bad thing at all. More people around to step in if things get out of hand.'

She turned to face him again. 'I appreciate you're just looking out for me, but trust me, I'm not going to do anything stupid.'

He smiled softly. 'I get that, I just worry about you, that's all.'

'I know you do.' She stood up from the bench now. 'Thanks for this, Lionel. I owe you one.'

'Just please promise me you'll be careful, will you?'

'I will,' she replied, then turned and headed off towards the main road and out of the park.

34

Phillips had spent the last couple of hours trying to focus on updating her growing pile of paperwork, but with Brown's words about her taking early retirement still rolling around her mind, she'd struggled to make any real progress and was feeling more than a little frustrated.

'Can I borrow you, guv?' said Bov as he tapped on her open door. 'I've found something of interest on the CCTV.'

Glad of the distraction, she jumped out of the chair and followed him back out into the main office, where the big man sat back down at his computer.

'Where's Jonesy?' she asked, spying his empty chair.

'Dunno,' Entwistle replied from his seat next to her. 'Said he needed to run an errand.'

She nodded, then turned her attention back to Bovalino.

'This is from a camera positioned at the exit to Humphrey Park station, captured a few minutes after Mahoney was killed,' he said before clicking play on-screen.

She watched the footage roll for a few seconds before a woman she recognised walked into shot. 'Paula Thomas.'

'Yes, boss.' He tapped on the screen with his pen. 'And look at the logo on the front of her coat.'

Phillips leant in closer. 'It looks like the exact same bee that we saw on the woman who shoved Mahoney off the platform.'

'It is. I checked,' he said as he passed across a printout taken from the previous footage.

She stared down at the sheet in her hands and felt a surge of excitement. 'It's identical.'

Just then the door to MCU opened, and Jones strode in carrying a large file. 'I've got something you need to see,' he said.

'So have we,' Phillips replied, pointing to Bov's screen. 'Clear footage of Paula Thomas from the front, leaving the station.'

Jones stepped next to her and eyed the paused CCTV. 'Hey, that's the same logo we saw on the back of the pusher.'

'It has to be her,' said Phillips.

'Or one helluva coincidence,' added Jones.

'And we all know how you feel about those, boss,' said Bovalino.

She flashed a knowing grin. 'And if she was capable of pushing Mahoney under a train, then it's not a long walk to think she could have pushed Callus down the stairs too.'

'So do we have enough to arrest her, boss?' Entwistle asked.

'For Callus, definitely not. We simply don't have the evidence. As for Mahoney, we have footage that points to her as the killer, but I still don't think we have enough for a conviction at this stage. Without motive, we'll struggle to prove intent to a jury.'

Jones raised the file in his hand. 'That's where I might be able to help.'

Phillips felt her brow furrow.

He passed it across. 'I was running a few background checks on Paula, and her name popped up on a domestic incident reported about a month back. I've just been to see the Domestic team, namely DS Ellington, who dealt with it, and he shared some interesting information about Mrs Thomas.'

Phillips opened the file and began leafing through the contents.

Jones continued, 'Specifically, that she was arrested but then later released on police bail after she put her husband in intensive care. Hit him with a hot pan multiple times, according to Ellington.'

'And she wasn't charged?' Phillips asked.

'She claimed it was self-defence, and as you'll see from the file, there's a long history of domestics at the Thomas household – and scanning through the reports, it seems Paula invariably came off worse each time.'

'So she's a battered wife,' Bovalino cut in.

'Sounds like it,' said Phillips. 'Which could give her motive to go for Callus – seeing his wife bleeding after he hit her in the mouth.'

'So what are we saying?' asked Entwistle. 'Paula was somehow triggered by what happened between Charlie and Heather?'

'Potentially, yeah. Especially if Paula herself had suffered ongoing abuse at the hands of her husband.'

'But then why go after Mahoney?' Entwistle added.

'I might have something that could explain that,' said

Bovalino as he clicked out of the CCTV footage and into an Excel spreadsheet. 'It was the next thing I wanted to update you on, boss.'

'What have you got?' she asked.

The big man continued, 'I've been going through Paula's travel card data and realised that in the back end of each file, each card is attached to an email and mobile number. Out of interest I cross-referenced her number against the British Transport Police's passenger tip line.'

Phillips could feel her eyes widen. 'Tell me the tip-off about Mahoney came from Paula.'

Bovalino nodded. 'Yup. She was on the same train when he was allegedly acting inappropriately with young girls the day before he died.'

'So Paula saw him doing it,' Jones ventured.

'Yeah,' Phillips replied.

'And if they both travelled on the same train every day,' said Entwistle, 'she'd probably seen Mahoney at it many times before.'

Phillips nodded. 'Which explains why she killed him – and the same for Charlie Callus – because they were abusive men. Just like her husband.'

35

'So have you spoken to the CPS about your suspicions?' asked Carter, sitting at his desk.

'Yes,' replied Phillips from the chair opposite his desk. 'And as I suspected, we still don't have enough to charge her.'

'What do they want? Blood?' Carter shook his head. 'We can place her at both scenes, *and* we have her on video pushing one of the victims off the platform.'

'According to Simms in the CPS, it's not clear from the footage we have that she actually pushed him.'

'It looks pretty damn clear to me,' Carter shot back.

'And to me, but Simms isn't having it.'

He sighed. 'We can still arrest her though, can't we?'

'We can, sir, but my worry is that by going after her without concrete evidence, any half-decent solicitor will advise her to go no comment and run down the custody clock – which means we'll have nothing more than we have right now. My preferred strategy would be to go through her digital footprint and see if we can find anything in her call logs and messages that proves she was involved in either murder, or ideally both.'

Carter frowned. 'Isn't that a bit of a risk? If she did kill them both – or even just one of them, for that matter – couldn't she do it again?'

'I'll admit it is a risk, sir, and I'm not suggesting we leave her to her own devices indefinitely. I just need time to check her phone and to do a bit more digging into the CCTV at Humphrey Park station to find the additional evidence the CPS need that proves she was involved.'

'And how long will that take?'

'We've already put the request in with Digital Forensics, so twenty-four hours tops,' she replied. 'If we haven't got anything new, we'll bring her in regardless and just have to take our chances that we can crack her in interview.'

'I'm not convinced this is the right way to go, Jane. Feels a bit of a risk to leave her out there.' Carter bit his bottom lip. 'But I trust your judgement, and obviously I'll back whatever you want to do.'

'Thank you.'

Carter sat forward as he linked his fingers on the desk. 'That said, we both know the spotlight is on MCU right now, and I don't need to tell you what's at stake here.'

Phillips could feel the pressure to get a result enveloping her, as if it were a living thing weighing heavy on her shoulders. 'I know, and I won't let you down, sir.'

'I know that, Jane.' Carter produced a faint smile. 'And with that in mind, I'd better let you crack on.'

She didn't need telling twice and was out of the chair in a flash, striding down the fifth-floor corridor just a few moments later.

'You OK, boss?' Jones asked soon after, as she took up

her usual position at the spare desk on the bank of four. 'You look a bit stressed.'

'Just got a lot on my mind,' she replied before turning her attention Entwistle. 'Where are we at with tracking Paula's phone?'

'I spoke to Will Heslop in the digital team, and he reckons he'll have a full download back with us by the morning. He's on the early shift tomorrow, so he's going to send everything through as soon as he comes in.'

'What time will that be?'

'About seven.'

'OK. In that case, I'll need you all in at that time too.' She glanced at each of them in turn. 'Is that OK?'

'Of course,' Entwistle replied.

Jones nodded.

'Fine by me,' said Bovalino.

She locked eyes with the big man. 'Any updates on the CCTV from Humphrey Park station?'

'I'm working my way through the additional cameras just now,' he said. 'There's eight of them in total, covering both platforms – as well as the exits and car park – so quite a lot to get through.'

'Well, I've got nothing to do tonight,' she replied. 'So I can have a look at a couple for you.'

'Me too,' said Jones. 'Sarah's out with the girls.'

'Great.' Bovalino's posture seemed to visibly soften. 'That would certainly speed things up.'

Phillips checked her watch; it was approaching 6 p.m. 'The canteen shuts in half an hour, so I'll go and get us some drinks and a few sandwiches to keep us going. I have a feeling we could be in for a late night.'

It was approaching midnight by the time Phillips unlocked her front door and stepped inside the darkened house. Floss, as usual, snaked around her legs a moment later. Bending down, she scooped up the little Ragdoll cat and carried her through to the kitchen, where she switched on the light. 'What a day,' she sighed as she listened to the rhythmic purring of the little bundle of fur in her arms.

After a few minutes of cuddling, Phillips gently returned Floss to the floor before grabbing some dry food and filling her bowl. Once the cat was sorted, she moved across to the fridge in search of cold wine. Right now, it seemed like the only thing that could help her unwind. It had been a tough day, and her mind was refusing to quieten down. Thankfully she'd had the foresight to put a bottle of pinot grigio in the fridge before she left for work that morning, and as she touched her fingers against it, she was delighted to feel it was almost ice cold to the touch. *Perfect.* Pulling it out, she unscrewed the top before grabbing a glass from the hanging rack located above the island in the middle of the kitchen. It was then that she spotted the red envelope that had been left propped up against the kettle. Taking a step closer, she could see her name scrawled on the front in Adam's handwriting. 'Oh shit,' she mumbled as she picked it up and ripped it open. 'Valentine's; I totally forgot.'

The card itself was handmade and a simple design: a red, 3D heart fixed to the front with a white background and the words *Love You* across the top. Inside was blank but for a handwritten message from Adam.

I know I don't say it enough, but I really do love you, Janey.

Thank you for putting up with me and my ridiculous hours at the moment.

I'm really looking forward to spending a lot more quality time together very, very soon.

Happy Valentine's. All my love, always.

A xxx

Phillips felt a pang of guilt as she stared down at the message. Even when the guys had been joking about it being Valentine's in the office that morning, it had not occurred to her that she needed to buy a card for Adam. Considering the current state of their relationship, she had assumed sending cards was not high on either of their agendas.

Glancing at her watch, she could see it was now well after midnight. 'Sod it,' she said as she screwed the top back on the wine before putting it back in the fridge. Grabbing her keys from the side, she strode purposefully back towards the front door. There was bound to be a twenty-four-hour petrol station open somewhere nearby. Even the naffest of cards for Adam to come home to in the morning was better than no card at all right now.

36

'There you go,' she said as she passed a mug of steaming hot tea to Lesley. 'You look like you need it.'

'Thanks, sis.' Lesley cradled it in her hands. 'I'm just not sleeping at all since I found out Albert got out.'

She took the armchair opposite her sister, who had taken up a position on the couch adjacent to the window that looked out to the front of the house. 'So where's the card?'

'I'll have to go and get it.' Lesley placed her tea on the coffee table between them before standing up and heading out of the room, returning a minute later. 'It came in the post yesterday,' she said as she retook her seat. 'The postmark on the envelope is Manchester Central.'

She stared down at the gaudy pink Valentine's card in her hand before reading the message on the front aloud. 'To my special lady.' Opening it, she could see it had not been written in, the message inside simply stating, *Always my number one girl.* 'You don't know it's from Albert,' she said without conviction.

'That's what he used to call me.' Tears welled in Lesley's eyes. 'His number one girl.'

She desperately wanted to provide comfort to her little sister, but the truth was she knew in her heart that Albert most likely *had* sent the card. It was exactly the kind of thing he would do, a ploy to get inside Lesley's head. To break her down until she was close to losing her mind, at which point he would attempt to sweep in and pick up where he left off all those years ago – inflicting even more mental abuse on her.

'We need to go to the police,' said Lesley as a tear escaped down her cheek.

'And say what?'

'That he's stalking me.'

'We don't have any evidence, Les.'

'But what about when he knocked on the door? And that card makes it two that he's sent since he got out.'

'But we can't prove that he actually sent them.'

'Well, what about the phone calls? We can talk to them about those too.'

'They won't listen, Les,' she replied. 'They never do. They'll just think you're being paranoid.'

'Because that's what you think, isn't it? That I'm being paranoid.'

She dropped her chin to her chest and sighed loudly before locking eyes with her sister again. 'That's not what I think at all.'

'So why won't you do anything to help me?' Lesley's tears flowed in earnest now.

Seeing her sister at breaking point was killing her. Moving off the chair, she took a seat next to her, wrapping a protective arm around her shoulder as she wept. 'Ssh, ssh. It's OK, let it out, Les. Let it out.'

'I can't take it anymore, I can't,' Lesley mumbled in between her tears. 'Knowing he's out there, watching me. It's driving me mad.'

She rested her chin on the top of her sister's head. 'I know. I know.'

'We need to tell the police.'

Going to the police would not make any difference. She knew that only too well. Albert was a very smart and devious man who knew exactly how to play the system. With no proof that he had been stalking Lesley, there was little chance the police would (A) believe them, and (B) be able to do anything about it even if they did. It was Lesley's word against his, and even though he was a convicted paedophile, he was still a very charming man to the uninitiated. She was under no illusions; he could likely talk his way into making the police believe he was innocent of any wrongdoing. No, the only way he was going to stop was if *she* stopped him. And that was exactly what she was going to do. 'Can I borrow your car today?'

Lesley pulled away and locked her big sad eyes on her. 'Please don't leave me on my own.'

'I have to work, sis,' she protested.

'Can't you call in sick? Just this once?'

'No,' she shot back. 'I've got back-to-back clients all morning, and my boss will go mad if I don't turn in. And besides, I don't get paid if I'm off, and with Des still in hospital and not working, I need the money.'

'But I don't want you to go. I'm scared. What if he turns up at the house?'

'He won't, but even if he did, if you lock the door, there's no way he can get it in.' She stood up from the sofa now. 'And if he did turn up here, that's when you *can* call the police.'

'Please don't go,' Lesley pleaded. 'I can't cope on my own.'

It broke her heart to see her sister in so much pain, but staying at home and hiding behind the blinds wasn't going to fix this. She needed to take action to put an end to this once and for all. 'You'll be fine,' she replied. 'And if I take your car, I can come back and check on you at lunchtime. In the meantime just keep the doors locked and the blinds closed. I'll have my phone on me, so you call me if you need to, OK?'

Lesley's bottom lip trembled as she nodded silently.

'Try not to worry, sis.' She offered a faint smile. 'I'll get this sorted. I promise.' With that, she turned on her heel and headed for the front door.

37

As Phillips had hoped, first thing that morning, Will Heslop from the Digital Forensics team had provided Entwistle with a full history of Paula Thomas's call records. And since then, she and Entwistle had been interrogating the data, huddled together at the conference table, checking everything on the big screen. Meanwhile, Bovalino was sitting at his computer in the main office, working through yet more CCTV, whilst Jones was away from his desk, running a full background check on their number one suspect.

With the time approaching 9.30, Carter wandered into the conference room with his hands in his trouser pockets, his normally erect posture looking unusually subdued this morning. 'Morning,' he said, sounding unconvinced by his own words.

'Morning, sir,' she replied.

Entwistle nodded. 'Sir.'

'You guys look hard at it,' Carter continued.

Phillips glanced towards the big screen. 'Just going through Paula's phone records.'

'Oh really?' He raised an eyebrow. 'Anything of interest?'

'There is, actually.' She turned to Entwistle. 'Pull up the call logs around the times of Callus's and Mahoney's deaths, will you?'

He did as requested, and a few seconds later two Excel spreadsheets appeared on the screen. 'As expected, we've been able to geolocate her phone to both Callus's building around the time when Chakrabortty suggests he died, and to Humphrey Park train station when we know Mahoney was killed.'

Carter's brow furrowed as he stared at the data.

Phillips continued to narrate what he was seeing. 'What's interesting is that most days – and by that I mean almost every day – she rarely switched her phone off during the week we've been looking at. And when she did switch it off, it was for a matter of minutes. Digital Forensics suggest switching it on and off in that manner was likely to be her rebooting the phone. Something most of us would do when our handsets are unresponsive.'

Carter folded his arms across his chest.

'But,' Phillips added, 'in the immediate aftermath of our killings, Paula switched it off for a couple of hours each time.'

'She was attempting to hide her digital footprint,' Carter muttered.

'That's what we were thinking, sir.'

'It still amazes me that people think the only way we can track them is by tracing their phones,' added Entwistle. 'Especially when there's cameras everywhere, and even travel passes carry personal data.'

'I know,' said Phillips. 'Big Brother is definitely watching. That's for sure.'

Carter turned to face them both. 'So with this information and the CCTV and travel logs from the station, do we now have enough to arrest her?'

Phillips felt her face wrinkle. 'Not quite. I still think we need a proper motive to make it all stick.'

'But you said you thought she was doing this as retribution against abusive men. Surely that's all the motive you need.'

'For us, yes,' she replied. 'But for the CPS I think we need more.'

Carter nodded silently as he glanced back at the screen and then returned his gaze to Phillips, his brow furrowed. 'Can we have a word in your office?'

'Of course, sir,' she said before standing and following him out.

A few minutes later she closed her office door behind him. They both remained standing. 'Is everything OK?'

Carter's shoulders sagged. 'Look, with all that you've got going on, I've deliberately kept this away from your desk. But it's getting to the point where I really think I need to share something with you.'

'Oh?' She felt her stomach tighten.

'I have it on good authority that our new chief constable is under pressure from the Home Office to reduce the budget deficit going into the new financial year.'

'Right.'

Carter continued, 'From what I understand, he's seriously considering a series of radical cost-cutting measures that will directly impact MCU.'

Phillips folded her arms across her chest. 'What kind of measures?'

He sighed. 'He's talking about merging Major Crimes and Serious Crimes together.'

She rolled her eyes. 'That old chestnut's doing the rounds again, is it? Fox was talking about that for years, but it never happened. Even with *her* obsession for cutting costs, she knew it would be a logistical nightmare to implement. Thankfully it never got past the discussion phase each time.'

'True, but as we know, Brown is a political animal like no other. Saving a million quid from the annual salary and pension pots will do his reputation with the Home Secretary the world of good.'

'As well as his chances of becoming the next commissioner of the Met Police,' added Phillips.

'Quite.'

'No wonder he was so keen to see me retire.'

'Like you've always said, Jane, his ambition knows no bounds. Even though it weakens the force overall, he'll happily sanction it if it makes him look good.'

She shook her head. 'This is all we need at the moment.'

'I know, and with the IPCC investigation hanging over you, I really didn't want to worry you. But it seems the plans to merge MCU and SCU are gathering pace.'

'Where are you getting this info from?'

He smiled thinly. 'Let's just say I have a friend in the finance department who has been asked to model the different options. And the main takeaway from all of the options is that he's planning to have one DCI running the new team.'

'Which would be between me and Cleverly in SCU?'

'Yes,' said Carter sombrely. 'And no chief supers across

the service at all. Superintendent will be the highest rank under Brown.'

Phillips felt her eyes widen. 'So he wants *you* out as well?'

'Looks that way. Or at the very least, he wants me demoted and on a lower salary.'

'But he can't do that,' she protested.

'He can, and he will.' Carter sighed loudly. 'That's why we need a result on the Callus and Mahoney cases ASAP. Charging Paula Thomas for their murders would be very handy for Major Crimes right now.'

'I know, sir. And I don't think we're far away at all. I really don't. I just need to be able to prove her motive to make it stick.'

'So do we have an updated timescale in mind?'

'It's hard to say, but if you can give me another twenty-four hours, hopefully we can find what we need.'

He nodded. 'I know you guys will do everything you can, Jane.'

'We will, sir. You can be sure of that.'

He nodded sagely. 'I just hope it's enough.'

38

The door buzzed, signalling the automatic lock had been deactivated. Pushing it open, she stepped cautiously into the reception area of the veterans' housing scheme where Albert Stone was currently a resident. Scanning the space, she noted one door marked 'Residents' and a second marked with the banner 'Office'.

The office door opened a split second later, and a smiling, middle-aged woman with shoulder-length blonde hair appeared. 'Can I help you?' The lanyard around her neck suggested she was called Amy.

'I was hoping to speak to Albert Stone if at all possible.'

'Is he expecting you?'

'No,' she replied.

'In that case, he might not be in. If you can give me your name, I'll call his flat and check for you.'

Her stomach churned as she cleared her throat. 'Just tell him Lina's here. He'll know who I am.'

Amy smiled and returned to the office, leaving the door

slightly ajar as she made the call. Evidently Albert was in, based on the one side of the conversation that was filtering through the gap.

Knowing he was somewhere in the building made her feel physically sick, and for a split second she was tempted to make a run for it, but she was here for one reason and one reason only – to get him to leave Lesley alone. She was determined not to let her little sister down again.

As soon as the short call was concluded, Amy peeped out once more. 'Albert's on his way down. He won't be long.'

'Thank you,' she replied before Amy pushed the office door shut once more.

The reception area fell silent aside from the sound of her heart beating wildly in her chest as she waited for him to appear.

A few minutes later the residents door opened, and the man who had ruined so much of her life appeared.

Her adrenaline spiked seeing him in the flesh again after all these years. He hadn't changed much. Sure, he was nearly two decades older, and the thin, lank hair was now almost white, but his long skinny frame appeared as grotesquely familiar as it always had. His skin, grey and waxy just as she remembered it.

'Hello, stranger,' he said with a lopsided grin that exposed his tobacco-stained teeth. 'This is an unexpected surprise.'

'I need to talk to you,' she said, attempting to remain stoic despite her racing pulse.

He thumbed over his shoulder, his grin even wider now. 'Would you like to come up?'

'We can talk outside,' she said flatly before spinning on her heel and heading back to the front door.

A moment later she found herself back on the street just as the rain began to fall.

The door opened behind her, and Albert followed her out.

'Over here,' she said, making her way under the cover of an empty bus shelter located just a few feet away.

She noted for the first time that he now walked with somewhat of a limp as he made his way over to her. 'Get that in prison, did you?' she asked, glancing at his wayward left leg.

Ignoring her question, he placed a rolled-up cigarette between his lips before lighting it with a Zippo and taking a long drag. 'So what do you want to talk about, Lina?' he asked finally.

She pulled the Valentine's card that had been sent to Lesley from her coat pocket. 'This shit has got to stop.'

He glanced down at the card as smoked billowed from his nostrils, and shrugged. 'I don't know what you mean.'

'Oh, cut the crap, Albert. I know you sent this to Lesley.' She held it in front of his face now so he could see the front clearly. 'You always called her your number one girl.'

A wicked smile crept across his face as his eyes glistened. 'Did she like it?'

'Of course she bloody didn't,' she snapped back. 'She's scared half to death.'

He recoiled. 'Of what?'

'*You.*'

'But I'm her dad.'

'You're a fucking paedophile is what you are! You ruined her life.'

'It was an illness,' he replied calmly. 'And I'm not like that anymore.'

'Bullshit. Once a monster, always a monster.'

He tilted his head forward slightly as a snarl threatened to spread across his top lip. 'I am her father, and I have a right to communicate with her.'

'Oh, and sneaking around in the shadows at night, not to mention ringing the doorbell and running away, is communicating with her, is it?'

His posture relaxed slightly as he took another long drag. 'I have to admit, that was unfortunate. I lost my nerve at the last minute.'

'So it *was* you?'

'I just wanted to see my little girl,' he said, exhaling more smoke into the cold morning air.

'But how did you get to the house at night? I thought you were on tag?'

'There are ways around everything in life. You just have to know where to look and who to ask.'

She took a moment to process what he was saying before nodding in the direction of his accommodation. 'I was surprised to see you in a place like this. Ex-military don't often take kindly to someone with your record.'

He took another long drag with smoke once again billowing from his nose a moment later as he replied, 'Most of these places are filled with Iraq and Afghanistan veterans suffering with severe mental health issues. Trust me, those kind of guys keep themselves to themselves.'

'Thought of everything, haven't you?' She was struggling to hide her utter contempt for the man she had once called her father.

He smiled smugly as he flicked his cigarette to the ground. 'I know people, Lina. It was my business for over twenty years, after all.'

She felt her jaw clenching as she locked eyes with him.

'So what's it going to take for you to leave Lesley alone, Albert?'

'I just want to talk to her.' He glared back now. *'Face to face.'*

'Never gonna happen. Not in a million years.'

'Well then, I'll just have to keep sending her more gifts, won't I?'

'Do that and I'll go to the police.'

He chuckled. 'And say what?'

'That you're stalking Lesley.'

'And where's your evidence?'

'This!' She held the card up in front of him again.

'I wore gloves when I bought that, and the same every time I handled it afterwards.'

'Well, I'll tell them about you sneaking around the house.'

'Really?' He laughed again. 'Like you said, I'm on tag. There's no way I could have been at the house when you claim I was, and the tracking report will prove it.'

'In that case, I'll tell them you tampered with it.'

He shrugged. 'And how do you propose to prove that?'

She could feel her hatred for the man surging through every fibre of her being. 'You really have got it all figured out, haven't you?'

'I've been away a long time.' He folded his arms across his chest. 'And I've had a lot of time to think about what I was going to do once I got out.'

She stared directly into his dark, soulless eyes, and her heart sank. It was evident that Albert would not back down and would not stop harassing Lesley until he got what he wanted: to see her face to face. It was clear in her mind now what she had to do, and she swallowed hard, knowing what lay ahead. 'Have you got a mobile?'

'I do.'

'Is it registered?'

'No. Pay as you go.'

'OK. I'll speak to Lesley and see if she'll agree to speak to you.'

Albert's crooked grin returned.

She held up her index finger. 'But it's a one-time deal. You get to say your piece, and then you leave her alone for good. Understood?'

He stared back at her for a moment, evidently considering the offer. 'OK,' he said finally.

'But I mean it, Albert. After this, neither I nor Lesley will ever see or hear from you again. *Ever.* Do we have a deal?'

Albert remained silent for a few seconds before responding, 'Yes. We have a deal.'

She pulled out her phone. 'I'll need your mobile number.'

He nodded as he fished his phone from his trouser pocket. 'I don't remember it off the top of my head.'

When he had eventually found what he was looking for, she typed the number into her own handset as he dictated it to her.

'When will I hear from you?'

'Sooner the better, as far as I'm concerned,' she replied. 'I want you out of our lives as quickly as possible.'

He stared back in silence as he pulled a pouch of rolling tobacco from his pocket.

'I'll text you with a time and a place.'

'I'll be ready,' he said as he began pulling tobacco onto a large cigarette paper. 'I'm not going anywhere for a while.'

She gave him one last cursory look before turning away and heading back to the car.

A couple of minutes later, as she approached the spot where she'd parked, she reached into her handbag in search of the keys. Spotting a bunch sitting inside to the left, she pulled them out, but as she held them in her hands, she realised they were Des's house keys. In her rush to visit Lesley that morning, she must have grabbed his instead of her own keys by mistake. Seeing her husband's keys, she was reminded that she had still not made any attempt to visit him in hospital. Yet she felt no guilt and no concern for his welfare. Those days were long gone now. Plus, she had far more pressing matters to attend to.

Then, as she glanced back at the keys in her hand, she spotted something on one of the links that gave her an idea. Des, for once, might actually hold the solution to all her problems.

39

With the pressure to prove Paula Thomas had motive to kill both Callus and Mahoney now almost crippling, Phillips was struggling to clear her mind as she returned to the conference room, where Bovalino and Entwistle were still hard at work, sifting through their prime suspect's phone records displayed on the big screen – mirrored from Entwistle's laptop.

'Any news from Jonesy on the background check?' she asked as she took a seat.

'Not yet,' Bovalino replied.

'And what about her phone records?' She asked attempting to keep the overwhelming pressure she was feeling out of her tone. 'Anything we can use?'

'We've confirmed her phone pinged off the local phone masts in Salford in and around the time of Callus's murder, and the same for the location and time of Mahoney's death, but nothing in her call records that appears out of the ordinary.'

'Other than the fact she switched the handset off immediately after both murders, no,' said Bovalino.

'Which we already knew.' Phillips sighed. 'And goes no way to proving motive.'

The big man shook his head.

'Sorry, guv,' said Entwistle.

Just then the conference room door opened, and Jones stepped in carrying a manila folder.

Phillips sat to attention. 'Please tell me you've found something in the background check that proves motive.'

Jones grinned as he pulled a pen drive from his pocket. 'I think I might have, actually.'

'What is it?' Phillips felt her pulse quicken.

Jones passed the pen drive to Entwistle. 'Open up the file labelled Albert Stone, will you?'

'Albert Stone? Why do I know that name?' asked Bovalino.

'It rings a bell with me too,' Phillips added.

Jones took a seat at the conference table as Entwistle opened up the file on the big screen. 'He was the child psychologist who was done for abusing the children in his care in 1997.'

'Oh, I remember him,' said Bovalino. 'Happened in the nineties, but he wasn't caught until the late 2000s.'

'2007.' Jones turned to Entwistle. 'Open the mug shot, will you?'

Once again Entwistle did as he was asked, and a second later Albert Stone's gaunt, angular face appeared on the big screen.

Bovalino sat forward in the chair. 'That's him. A right nasty piece of work.'

'Yeah,' Jones continued. 'Got twenty years for multiple

counts of rape and sexual assault of children over the age of thirteen.'

'Pure evil,' spat Bovalino. 'He was supposed to be protecting those kids, not bloody preying on them.'

Phillips stared at the middle-aged man on-screen, pictured in one of the ubiquitous grey sweatshirts given to prisoners in custody. 'So what does Albert Stone have to do with Paula Thomas?'

Jones opened the manila folder on the conference table. 'Stone had two daughters, who were fifteen and thirteen at the time the assaults took place in 1997. Paulina and Lesley.'

Phillips locked eyes with him now. 'Paulina, as in Paula?'

He nodded. 'Or Paulina Stone as she was at the time. Looks like she started going by Paula from around the time she turned eighteen.'

Phillips nodded along silently.

Jones continued. 'Now according to the file, Albert was accused of molesting them both, but Lesley refused to testify against her father. Paula, on the other hand, stood in the dock and claimed he raped her multiple times when she was in her early teens.'

It was all starting to make sense to Phillips now. 'So Paula Thomas was not only abused by her husband, she was also abused by her dad.'

'I'm afraid so, yeah.' Jones pulled a document from the file and passed it across. 'And this is his official parole paperwork. He was released four weeks ago after serving sixteen of the twenty-year tariff.'

Phillips stared down at the document in her hand.

'He's currently living in Harry Gregg House in Longsight,' Jones added.

'Harry Gregg?' Bovalino chimed in. 'Didn't he play for Man United – one of the Busby Babes?'

'Yeah. The facility was named after him,' said Jones. 'It's a supported living scheme for veterans.'

Phillips looked up from the file. 'Stone was in the military?'

'According to his file, he did three weeks of basic training before being medically discharged. It doesn't say what for, but it does mean he's entitled to stay at Harry Gregg House – which, by the sounds of it, is a damn sight nicer than your typical parolee halfway house.'

'Having seen some of those places used by probation, I'm sure you're right.' Phillips fell silent again as she attempted to process this new information before turning her attention to Bovalino. 'Remind me, when was Paula arrested for the assault on her husband?'

The big man's brow furrowed. 'Let me check.' He began sifting through the files in front of him for a minute or so until he found what he was looking for. 'Looks like it was Tuesday, 30th of January.'

She took a second to review the parole paperwork in her hands. 'And Albert Stone was released two weeks prior to that.'

'What you thinking, guv?' said Entwistle.

Jones frowned. 'That the two are connected?'

'Exactly.' Phillips sat to attention now. 'Picture this. Two weeks after Paula Thomas's childhood abuser gets out of prison, our girl is severely triggered and – after years of being treated like a punch bag – finally snaps and turns the tables on her violent husband, beating him into a coma.'

'For the first time in her life *she* has control,' Jones cut in.

'She's fighting back,' Phillips continued. 'And once the

genie's out of the bottle, it can't be put back in. So when she saw Heather Callus taking a beating from Charlie, there was no way she could let him off the hook, and in the moment – just as was we suspect was the case when she attacked her husband – she took back control. Likely the same thing happened when she pushed Mahoney off the platform too. She'd seen him at it before, even reported him for it, yet there he was, let off by the police and free to continue abusing young girls to his heart's content. She couldn't let that happen, so she used the cover of a packed platform to push him under the train.'

'We studied a case like this at uni,' Entwistle cut in. 'Where a victim's traumatic past triggered their violent present.'

'Wouldn't be the first time we've seen it happen,' said Jones.

'Which means Albert Stone could potentially be in danger.' Phillips pushed her chair back and stood up. 'And like it or not, despite his past crimes, it's our job to protect him. Come on, Jonesy. I think it's time to bring her in.'

40

Jones was at the wheel as they drove at speed for the thirty-minute journey from Ashton House in Failsworth to Paula's home in Irlam. It was approaching midday by the time they pulled up outside the well-appointed red-brick end-of-terrace house, featuring a large bay window on the ground floor – likely built in the early 1900s.

Parking the squad car on the road directly outside the property, they jumped out in unison, and a moment later Phillips led them up the path to stand in front of the large ornate front door, painted olive green. With Jones at her shoulder, she rapped the heavy knocker fixed to it, then took a step back and waited.

With no immediate response forthcoming, she tried again with the same frustrating result. 'I was worried she might not be at home,' she muttered as she took a step back to take in the whole house.

'All the curtains upstairs are closed, boss,' said Jones. 'Maybe she's in bed?'

'At midday?'

'She could be sick?' he replied. 'Or been working nights?'

Phillips took a moment to consider his suggestions.

Just then the front door to the adjoining house to the left opened, and a petite, elderly lady, whom Phillips believed to be in her eighties, stepped out. She was wearing a long blue winter coat, and her head was protected against the looming clouds by a plastic rain bonnet, the kind of attire rarely seen these days on anyone under the age of seventy. She was pulling a small tartan trolley bag in her right hand.

'Excuse me,' said Phillips.

The old lady looked across.

'I don't suppose you know where Paula is, do you?' Phillips kept her tone deliberately light, almost jovial.

The older lady eyed her and Jones suspiciously.

'Sorry.' Phillips pulled out her credentials. 'We're from the police.'

'Is this about what happened to her husband?' the neighbour asked.

'Kind of, yeah.'

'Bad business, that, but then I wasn't surprised. I could hear him through the walls, you know. Shouted at her at all hours of the day and night, he did.'

'Happened a lot, did it?' Jones asked.

She nodded. 'Oh, yes. It's been a blessed relief him being in hospital the last few weeks. I can finally watch my television programs in peace.'

'When was the last time you spoke to Paula?' said Phillips.

'Ooh, it'll be a while ago now. But I hear her coming and going every now and again when she opens and closes the front door. The sound comes through my walls, you see.'

'Did you hear her today at all?'

'No,' the lady replied. 'But then I've been at my daughter's for the last few days. That's why I need to get to the shop. I'm out of milk.'

Phillips smiled. 'Well, don't let us keep you.'

'It's pension day, too,' the neighbour added before shuffling towards the end of the short path and onto the pavement.

'Mind how you go,' said Jones.

The old lady raised her left hand before continuing slowly up the street.

'Sweet little thing,' said Jones. 'Reminds me of my mum.'

'Yeah,' replied Phillips absent-mindedly as she pulled her phone from her pocket before dialling Entwistle.

He answered after a few rings. 'Hi, boss.'

'We're getting no answer at Paula's house, and I'm wondering if she's at work. Can you call Busy Bees and see if she's supposed to be working today, and if so where?'

'I'll do it now,' he replied.

Phillips ended the call and moved back onto the pavement to take in the house once more, noting it was not dissimilar to the property she'd lived in before buying a home with Adam. After a few moments, she turned to Jones. 'Houses like this usually have access to the rear. Come on, let's have a look.'

Walking down the road adjacent to the house, they soon came across a narrow cobbled alley that ran parallel to Paula's property, which did indeed have a back gate. Frustratingly, it was locked shut with an industrial-sized padlock, but they could at least see the rear of the house. As had been the case at the front, all the windows were obscured by either blinds downstairs or curtains on the first floor.

'Looks like she's keen on maintaining her privacy,' noted Jones.

Just then Entwistle called back.

'Any luck?' she asked as she flicked on the speaker function so Jones could hear.

'Her boss said she called in sick this morning, guv.'

'Really?' Phillips turned her attention back to the rear of the house. 'How easy would it be for Digital Forensics to the locate her phone right now?'

'If they have access to her network provider, not long at all.'

'In that case, let's see if they can do that. Her house is locked up tight, and without a search warrant, we'll need to know she's inside before we start breaking down doors.'

'I'll speak to them and call you straight back.' Entwistle hung up for a second time.

'If she *is* inside' – she turned to Jones – 'then judging by the state of the house, and considering her potential state of mind given what we suspect she did to Callus and Mahoney – I'd say she's high risk in terms of self-harming.'

'You think she's suicidal?' he asked.

'It's certainly possible. She's had a lot to deal with in the last few weeks, not to mention the effects of the abuse she's had to carry around over the years.'

At that moment, her phone began to vibrate in her hand. Once again she switched it to speaker. 'Did they find her?'

'Not quite, but they have managed to triangulate her phone to an address near where you are right now. It was last located there at around midnight last night. The house belongs to a Lesley Wood.'

'Paula's sister is called Lesley, isn't she?' Jones cut in.

Phillips nodded. 'Do we have an exact address?'

'Not from forensics, but I checked the voting register, and I've found one. She's at 49 Chassen Lane. I'm texting you the postcode as we speak.'

A message appeared on Phillips's screen a second later. 'Good work, Whistler.'

'My pleasure, boss. Anything else I can do to help?'

'Not this second, but stand by just in case we need you.'

'Will do,' he said before ringing off.

THE HOME of Lesley Wood was just a five-minute drive from Paula's, a semi-detached house set back from the road on a quiet, tree-lined street.

As Phillips strode up the path towards the house, she noted the large, dry patch on the driveway where a car appeared to have been parked until very recently. As had been the case at Paula's place, every window at the front of the property was protected by either curtains or blinds.

After pushing the doorbell fixed to the wall to the side of the front door, she took a step back and waited. When nobody answered, Phillips tried again, and a minute or so later, she spotted the curtain twitch slightly in the front window to their right.

'Did you see that?' asked Jones, obviously having seen it too.

'Yeah,' replied Phillips, pressing the bell for a third

time now. 'And I'm going to keep on ringing this bloody doorbell until they show themselves.'

A few more minutes passed before the door opened tentatively on the chain, and a woman – in either her late thirties or early forties – peered out through the gap. 'Who is it?' Her voice was barely a whisper.

Phillips pushed her ID closer to the door so the woman could clearly see it. 'DCI Phillips and DI Jones from the Major Crimes Unit. Are you Lesley Wood?'

'Yes.'

'Is Paula Thomas your sister?'

'She is.' Lesley's voice increased in volume now and was laced with panic. 'Has something happened to her?'

That simple question caused Phillips's heart to sink. 'Are you telling us she's not here?'

'No. She left hours ago.'

'Could we ask you a few questions inside, please?' Phillips said.

'Is this about the stalking?'

Phillips glanced at Jones, then back to Lesley. 'Why don't we come in, and we can have a proper chat about everything.'

The door closed, and a second later reopened, allowing them to see Lesley properly for the first time. She was petite, her stooped posture appearing almost apologetic, and her red eyes betrayed the fact she'd either been crying or not sleeping. Looking at her now, Phillips suspected it was probably both.

'Please come in,' she said, her voice timid.

Phillips and Jones followed Lesley down the narrow, darkened hallway to the rear of the house into an equally dark living room, a pair of full-length blackout curtains protecting the interior from the world beyond. The decor within the room was conservative and a little dated, more suited to someone much older than the woman standing opposite them.

'Have you caught him?' Lesley asked, her voice tense.

Phillips did a slight double take. 'Caught who?'

'My stalker.'

'Why don't you take a seat, and we can talk properly,' replied Phillips.

Lesley nodded, then dropped gently into the armchair nearest the large, antiquated television set.

Phillips and Jones sat down next to each other on the adjacent sofa.

With no time to waste, Phillips got straight to the point. 'Do you have any idea where Paula might be right now?'

'I thought you were here to talk about Albert?'

'As in your dad Albert?' said Phillips.

'Yes. He's been stalking me. Didn't Paula tell you about him?'

'We haven't spoken to Paula,' Phillips replied. 'We were hoping *you* might be able to tell us where she is.'

Lesley's bottom lip began to tremble. 'She *promised* me she was going to sort it all out.'

'Sort what out?'

'Albert and the stalking.'

Phillips sat forward on the sofa. 'Paula told you she was going to sort Albert out?'

Lesley nodded as a tear streaked down her cheek. 'He's been terrorising me ever since he got out. I've not slept since Sergeant Price told me he'd been released.'

Phillips paused. 'Are you talking about Lionel Price? From the sex crimes team?'

'Yes. Do you know him?'

'Only by reputation,' said Phillips.

'I know Lionel,' Jones cut in. 'I worked with him back in uniform.'

Phillips felt her brow furrow. 'But how come Sergeant Price told you about Albert? I thought he was retired.'

'He is,' Lesley replied. 'But he's stayed in touch over the years. He came round as soon as he heard about Albert getting out.'

Phillips turned her attention to Jones. 'How would Price know Albert had been released?'

'I dunno.'

'I think one of his former colleagues told him,' Lesley ventured before catching herself. 'Oh dear. I hope I haven't got him in trouble.'

'Not at all.' Phillips waved her away, keen to return to the matter in hand and finding Paula. 'So when did you last see your sister?'

'This morning, when she left for work.'

'What time was that?'

Lesley shrugged. 'I don't remember exactly, but probably around half-seven, eight o'clock.'

Phillips shifted in her seat. 'We spoke to her boss about twenty minutes ago, and he told us that Paula called in sick.'

Lesley's face wrinkled. 'Paula did?'

'Yes. Just after eight o'clock.'

'That can't be right,' said Lesley. 'I mean, I did ask her to call in sick, but she said she had too many clients and that her boss would go mad if she cancelled.'

Phillips's mind was drawn back to the dry driveway at the front of the house. 'Does Paula have a car?'

'No.'

'So whose car was parked on the drive overnight?'

'That's mine.'

'And where is it now?' Phillips asked.

'Paula has it. She asked to borrow it this morning.'

'Did she tell you why she needed it?'

'She said she was using it to get to work.'

'And does she borrow it often?'

'Look, why is my car so important?' Lesley protested.

With the potential risk that Lesley might speak to Paula and alert her before they could track her down, Phillips chose to skirt around the edges of the truth. 'Your sister may have important information that could really help us with one of our ongoing investigations.'

'Is this to do with her client who died?' asked Lesley.

'You know about that?'

'Paula told me what had happened. It came as quite a shock when she found out he'd died.'

'I can imagine.' Phillips was doing her best to hide her growing impatience. 'Look, it would really help if you can think of where she might be going in your car.'

'Like I said, she told me she wanted it for work. She normally gets the train, but apparently they've not been very reliable of late.'

'Could we get the registration?' Jones cut in.

'Er, sure, it's MJ67-UAT.'

Jones made a note in his pad. 'And what kind of car is it?'

'A VW Polo.'

'Colour?'

'Black.'

'Thank you.' Jones scribbled down the details.

Phillips took the lead once more. 'Do you know if Paula uses the Find My feature on her phone?'

'We both do. Ever since Sergeant Price told us about Albert getting out, we've both been tracking each other.'

'Could you check where she is now?'

'I guess so.' Lesley appeared deep in thought for a moment. 'If I can find my own phone, that is. I think it's in the kitchen,' she said before stepping up and heading out of the room.

Phillips locked eyes with Jones, silently mouthing the words, 'For fuck's sake.'

He chuckled as he shook his head.

Lesley returned a minute later, phone in hand. 'That's odd,' she said, retaking her seat.

'What is?' asked Phillips.

'It's saying the last place it was tracked was here, five hours ago.'

'Which means it's probably switched off now,' Jones added.

Phillips sat forward again. 'Would you mind calling her for us?'

Lesley did as instructed and held the phone to her ear for a long moment before shaking her head. 'It's going straight to voicemail. That's not like her at all – she always answers. Especially with everything that's going on just now.'

Phillips and Jones exchanged knowing glances. As they were both aware, Paula had turned her phone off after both the Callus and Mahoney murders. Considering she'd promised Lesley she was going to 'sort Albert out', the fact it had been switched off again after lying to her sister about what she was doing today didn't bode well. They needed to find her urgently, and sitting here discussing Lesley's concerns about her stalker wasn't helping. It was time to go.

Handing across her business card, Phillips pointed to the mobile number at the bottom.

'If Paula comes back, could you tell her to call me as soon as she can. Like I say, we urgently need to speak to her about our investigation.'

Lesley took the card and stared down at the details printed on the front. 'And can I call you if *he* comes back?'

Phillips took a beat to process the question. 'If who comes back?'

'Albert.'

'Absolutely,' said Phillips firmly. 'If you get so much of a whiff of him anywhere near this place, call me, day or night. I'll have a uniform team here in a matter of minutes.'

Lesley's posture visibly softened as she swatted away another tear from her cheek. 'Thanks, Chief Inspector.'

Phillips stood up from the chair, with Jones matching her a second later. 'We'll see ourselves out.'

As soon as they were back on the driveway, she called Entwistle and asked him to run a check on Lesley's car. As ever, he promised to get straight onto it and call her right back.

'So when Paula she said she was going to sort out Albert,' said Jones, 'do we think she's talking about killing him?'

'Given her recent track record, I worry that's *exactly* what she's talking about.'

'Let's hope Whistler can find that car, then.'

'Yeah.' Phillips's mind was racing as she tried to process the conversation they'd just had. 'You said in there that you know Lionel Price.'

'Yeah. We go way back. He's a good bloke.'

'When did you last speak to him?'

Jones blew his lips. 'It must be a while now, I reckon. A few years at least.'

'You have his mobile number?'

'I have *a* number, but I'm not sure if he's still on it.'

'Pull it up on your phone, will you?'

Jones took a moment to find it, then presented her with the handset.

She pressed dial, and a second later it began to ring at the other end. Placing it to her ear, she waited.

'Jonesy! Well, this is a surprise, mate,' came the jovial voice at the other end as it was answered.

'Sergeant Price, this is DCI Phillips on Jonesy's phone. I need to talk to you about Paula Thomas and Albert Stone.'

41

The sun was already threatening to set as she parked the VW in the retail car park and made her way inside in search of a phone shop, looking for an unregistered and untraceable handset.

Pulling her collar up in an attempt to fend off the cold February weather, she kept her head down as she made her way across the windswept car park and soon found herself in the small shopping centre, wandering along the main mall in search of her quarry. Thankfully, it didn't take long to find what she was looking for, a small independent retailer whose window signage promised the best deals in town on 'previously loved handsets' as well as phone screen repairs, handset cases and pay-as-you-go mobiles.

With little desire to strike up any form of conversation with the shop assistants, she made a beeline for the off-the-shelf phones located on a stand next to the sales counter. Knowing she would have no use for the device after today, she picked the cheapest and simplest-looking model she could find, retailing at just over £10, and was relieved to see it came charged and ready to use. And so, after handing over the cash, she headed out of the store and set off back towards the car.

As she dropped back into the driver's seat a few minutes later, she checked the time: 2.55 p.m. She was fully aware of the risks involved in acting out her plan to deal with Albert and decided that working under the cover of darkness once the evening rush hour had passed would give her the best chance of pulling it off. With that in mind, she decided it would be best to wait for at least another hour before messaging him. Switching on the phone to ensure the promise of being ready to use was indeed true, she was relieved to see the screen illuminate and the battery icon declare itself full and fit for purpose. 'That's good,' she whispered before placing the handset into the cup holder located in the centre console.

Sitting in the slowly warming car, her recent insomnia came back to bite her and as the heat of the confined space began to engulf her, sheer exhaustion took hold, causing her to slump sideways soon after as she drifted off to sleep.

She woke with a start sometime later to the sound of a loud banging noise nearby, and her heart raced as she tried desperately to orientate herself in the darkness that surrounded her. Glancing at the clock on the dash, she could see she'd been asleep for almost three quarters of an hour, as the time approached 3.35 p.m.

Looking out through the driver-side window, she located the source of the banging and what appeared to be a mother knocking on the window of the car next to her as she attempted to get the attention of the teenage girl sitting inside – a large pair of headphones evidently rendering her temporarily hard of hearing.

Straightening up in the seat, she wiped the saliva from the side of her chin and took a moment to refocus her mind on what lay ahead. After switching on her own phone, she pulled her recently purchased handset from the centre console and keyed in Albert's number before ensuring her own phone was once again turned off. Then, after taking a deep breath to steady her nerves, she began typing out the details of this evening's meet. A moment later, with her finger hovering over the send button, she was suddenly filled with a sense of doubt and foreboding; was she doing the right thing? Should she just go to the police and let them deal with him instead of trying to sort things out herself?

Glancing out the window once more, she locked eyes on the teenage girl, who had remained sitting in the adjacent car. In spite of the fact she was wearing headphones, she could see enough of the young girl's face to spot the fact she was a young teenager – about the same age she and Lesley had been when each of their nightmares at the hands of Albert had begun. Staring at the young girl now – oblivious to the fact she was being watched – she was reminded of the innocence that had been stolen from her, from Lesley, and from all the other children her father had abused, and she was in no doubt what she had to do. Albert would never knowingly stop, the reason being simply because he didn't want to. He was an evil man who cared for nothing but his own sick perversions. Perversions that could no longer be allowed to continue. With another breath taken in and then loudly exhaled, she slammed her finger down on the green phone icon and watched as the message on-screen declared it sent.

No more than a few seconds later, a loud beep indicated she had received a reply. Opening the message, she read it aloud, '"I'll be there",' she muttered, and nodded. 'But not for long – if I have anything to do with it.'

42

'Do we really think Paula would try anything here?' said Jones as they walked towards the entrance to Harry Gregg House. 'I mean, there's CCTV all over the front of the building.'

'Maybe not, but she went out of her way to find out where Albert was living, so there's a good chance she may be preparing to pay him a visit.' Phillips stopped outside the front door and pressed the buzzer on the intercom.

A few seconds later a man's voice chimed through the small speaker, the accent thick Liverpudlian. 'Can I help?'

'DCI Phillips and DI Jones from the Major Crimes Unit. We need to speak to one of your residents.'

'Push the door.'

There was a loud buzz as the magnetic lock was released.

A moment later they stepped into the main reception area of the building to be greeted by a short, pot-bellied man with a shaven head – likely in his early thirties –

wearing a blue Everton football top, standing behind the reception desk.

Phillips pulled out her ID and, as they approached, glanced down at the man's security lanyard. 'Neil, is it?'

The man nodded.

'Is Albert Stone in the building?'

Neil shrugged. 'I've just come on shift, so your guess is as good as mine.'

Phillips felt her jaw clench. If there was one thing she detested in life, it was people being deliberately obtuse. 'Well, is there any chance you might be able to check for us?'

Neil sniffed heavily, as if in protest, then turned and disappeared through a door marked Office.

'Lovely to see people so happy in their work.' Jones kept his voice low, his tone sarcastic.

'Lazy bastard, more like,' added Phillips.

A minute or so later, Neil returned. 'There's no answer on his flat phone.'

'Does he have a mobile?'

'I don't know. There might be one on file.'

Jones stepped in now. 'Well, why don't you check for us, hey?' he said. 'There's a good lad.'

As Neil disappeared back into the office, Phillips shook her head in disbelief. 'Unbelievable.'

Neil was back a couple of minutes later. 'Sorry. There's nothing on file,' he said flatly.

Phillips took a silent breath as she attempted to keep her temper in check. 'In that case we'll need you to let us into his flat.'

'Have you got a warrant for that?' Neil asked. 'He has rights, you know.'

'This isn't the movies, son,' scoffed Jones.

'Look, Neil.' Phillips stepped forward with purpose. 'You might not know this, but Albert Stone is on the sex offenders register after serving seventeen years for multiple counts of abusing children over the age of thirteen. Now, we have good reason to believe he recently made contact with one of those victims, which constitutes a breach of his bail conditions and means we don't need a warrant. So unless you want to be arrested for obstruction, you need to give us access to his flat right now.'

Neil stared back defiantly.

'*Right now*,' she repeated.

'I'll do it,' said Neil. 'But I want my protest noted.'

Jones shook his head. 'I think you've been watching too much *Law and Order*, mate.'

A few minutes later they arrived outside flat 17, which was located on the third floor of the building.

As Phillips and Jones pulled on latex gloves, Neil unlocked the door and let them in.

'Wait here,' she said. 'We may need you.'

Inside, the small flat was quite unremarkable. Aside from the strong stench of stale tobacco, it appeared to be well maintained, clean and tidy. The small open-plan kitchen connected to an equally compact living-room space, which featured an old armchair and matching sofa but, quite unusually, no TV. Moving through to the only bedroom, they were presented with an equally sparse space comprising of a well-made double bed complete with a bedside table.

'It's almost as if he's never been here,' said Jones.

'Yeah.' Phillips moved across to the bedside table and pulled open the top drawer. 'Well, well, well.' She bent forward to get a closer look at the contents. 'Will you look at this.'

Jones stepped to her shoulder. 'What is it?'

Reaching inside, Phillips fished out something that resembled an oversized wristwatch. 'If I'm not mistaken, this would be Albert Stone's location tag.'

'Which is supposed to be locked around his ankle twenty-four seven.'

'Yeah, it bloody well is.'

'Sodding G-SEC,' said Jones. 'I've heard this has been happening quite a bit since they took on the government contract for tagging. Cheap Chinese manufacturing that can be tampered with if you know your way round a toolbox.'

Phillips examined the ankle bracelet for a moment before marching back out of the flat to find Neil had remained standing in the hallway as instructed. 'Do you guys keep a log of visitors for the residents?'

He nodded. 'The visitors book. We make a note of everyone who comes into the building based on who they say they are when they buzz through for access.'

'And where's the log kept?'

'In the office.'

'Show me.'

A few minutes later and now inside the inner sanctum of the support team office, Phillips watched on as Neil riffled through a thick A4 notepad in search of the most recent entries. Once he'd found what he was looking for, he passed it across. 'This is today's log, and it works backwards into previous days and weeks.'

Phillips scanned the entries for today, then turned to Jones. 'It says here Albert received a visitor at 10.30 this morning. Someone called Lina.'

'Shorthand for Paulina?' asked Jones.

'It has to be.' She turned her attention back to Neil.

'Can you access the CCTV cameras on the front of the building from here?'

'Yeah. It's in a shared folder on the central drive.'

'We need to try to figure out who this Lina person is who came to see Albert.'

Neil took one of the seats on a bank of desks connected to the longest wall of the office, and after taking a few seconds to log in to the middle computer of three identical PCs, went in search of the timeframe they were looking for. It took a couple of minutes for him to find it. Clicking on the file now, black-and-white footage suddenly appeared on the screen.

Phillips and Jones moved to stand on either side of his shoulders as the video played.

After watching for a short time without seeing anyone entering or leaving the building, Phillips suggested he fast-forward.

Neil followed the instruction, and a second or two later the footage played out at three times the speed.

As the timestamp reached 10.37 a.m., a woman walked into the shot. 'Stop it there,' demanded Phillips, her pulse quickening as she stared at the screen. 'Gotcha!'

Standing in the middle of the frozen shot was Paula Thomas.

'So she *was* here,' said Jones.

Phillips nodded. 'Let the video play, will you? So we can see what happens next.'

Neil once again acquiesced, and as the footage rolled on, Paula could be seen entering the building for just a few minutes before leaving soon after with Albert following closely behind.

'What are you two up to?' muttered Phillips as the video continued to play.

Five more minutes passed before Albert could be seen walking back into the building alone.

'So where's Paula?' Jones asked.

'That's the million-dollar question.' Phillips placed a hand on Neil's shoulder. 'Is there any way to know what time he left the building after this?'

'We keep a log of when the residents come in, and when they go out.' Neil reached across the bank of desks and pulled across another A4 pad. Once again, he took a moment to find the latest entries before presenting it to Phillips. 'Says here he left around 4 p.m.'

'You have a log?' she asked, yanking the book out of his hands. 'Why didn't you tell us this when we first arrived?'

Neil swallowed hard, evidently aware of his error. 'Sorry, I never thought.'

Phillips examined the entry, which had been made by the duty warden going by the name of John G. 'Is there any chance Albert would have told this John G where he was going?'

Neil shrugged. 'Depends if the office door was open when he left, and also what John was doing at the time. If he wasn't busy and free to talk, then maybe.'

'Can you call John for us and ask?'

'I can do, but he's off shift now for a few days. I don't think he'll be very happy about it.'

'Well, considering how urgent this is.' She glared at him now. 'And given the fact we've already wasted enough time, I really don't care *how* he feels. So do us all a favour and call him, will you?'

'Yeah. OK,' replied Neil before picking up the landline phone located on the desk. And after taking a second to scan the contact list on the wall, he keyed in the number for John G.

As the phone began to ring, Phillips leant forward and flicked on the speaker function. 'Now we can all hear.'

'There had better be a fucking fire, Neil!' came the camp and acidic tone on the other end of the line as it was answered.

'Sorry to call you off shift, John, but the police are here, and they've been asking questions about Albert Stone.'

Phillips stepped forward now. 'John, Detective Chief Inspector Phillips from the Major Crimes Unit.'

'Oh. Hello,' he replied, his tone instantly warmer.

'We urgently need to track down Albert Stone, who you logged out of the scheme around four o'clock today. I don't suppose he told you where he was going, did he?'

'Not exactly, no. But he did ask me to google a Metrolink timetable for him.'

'He was planning on using the tram?'

'Yeah. Wanted times from Piccadilly out to Radcliffe. I gave him a few options, and he left.'

'What the hell is in Radcliffe?' said Jones under his breath.

Phillips continued, 'I don't suppose he told you *why* he wanted to go there, did he?'

'I did ask, as it seemed a strange place to be going, but he just said he was meeting an old friend.'

'Male or female?'

'He didn't say, and I didn't ask, to be honest.'

'Did he say anything else that might give us an idea of where he might be going?'

'No. Nothing. Sorry,' said John. 'Is he in trouble?'

'That's what we're trying to find out,' she replied. 'Listen, we won't take up any more of your time. Thanks for your help, John.'

'No bother,' he replied.

Leaning forward, she ended the call, then turned her attention to Jones. 'Looks like we're going to Radcliffe, then.'

Soon after, as they jumped into the squad car and Jones fired the engine, her phone began to ring through the centre console. It was Entwistle. 'Whistler, what have you got?'

'I've been checking ANPR, boss, and I've been able to track the VW Polo from around 10 a.m. this morning when it registered on a camera on the main road that runs adjacent to Harry Gregg House.'

'We've just been looking at CCTV footage of Paula meeting with Albert,' said Phillips. 'Where did she go after that?'

'It was flagged on Moorside Road in Irlam just after midday.'

'Maybe she was going home?' ventured Jones.

'Yeah, and if she was, it looks like we just missed her.'

Entwistle continued, 'The most recent entry was on the A665, Radcliffe New Road.'

'Radcliffe?' Phillips asked.

'Is that important, boss?'

'Albert left the scheme at around four, and we believe he was heading *towards* Radcliffe. Has the car been spotted anywhere since?'

'No. Like I say, the camera on Radcliffe New Road was the most recent entry. I can check the logs again in the next half an hour once they're updated and see if it was picked up anywhere else.'

'Do that, and let us know if anything changes. And while you're at it, get an alert put out on the car Paula's driving. I want every uniformed team in the city looking for it.'

'Will do.'

'In the meantime we're going to head over to Radcliffe ourselves. You never know, we might get lucky and spot one of them.'

'Well, good luck with that, boss. It's a big place.'

'I'm not familiar with it,' she replied. 'What's out that way?'

'Quite a lot of houses and a decent-sized retail park, from memory. If you give me a second, I'll google it and see.'

Phillips and Jones sat in silence for a short time as they waited for him to return to the call.

'Looks like there's a large ASDA, a Lidl, a Dunelm, and a McDonald's,' he said eventually. 'Right on the edge of the River Irwell.'

'And how far away is the Metrolink station from there?'

There was silence on the other end again as Entwistle went in search of the answer. 'About ten minutes on foot if you take the main road – or fifteen if you go via the Outwood Trail.'

'*Outwood?*' Phillips flinched. 'Is that anywhere near Outwood Viaduct?'

'Hang on a sec.' He paused. 'Yeah, looks like the trail runs parallel to the viaduct.'

'Shit.' Phillips locked eyes with Jones. 'Price told me Albert abused most of his victims at Outwood Viaduct. She has to be meeting him there.'

Jones didn't need telling twice as he slammed the car into gear, and a second later they screeched away from the kerb.

About ten minutes from Radcliffe retail park, Entwistle's name appeared on the centre console once more as another call came through.

'A uniform team have spotted her car in the car park just outside the ASDA, guv.'

'Is she in it?'

'No. Apparently not,' he replied. 'What do you want them to do?'

'Keep an eye on it from a distance, but under no circumstances should they approach her. I don't want her spooked. If she comes back to it, they need to tell us immediately. We'll liaise with them as soon as we arrive in about ten minutes.'

'I'll let them know.'

'Thanks, Whistler.' Phillips rang off.

'What do you think she's planning?' asked Jones.

'I honestly have no idea, but given the fact she's potentially meeting him at the scene of his crimes, my guts telling me whatever it is, it ain't good.'

'Yeah. I get the same feeling.'

Ten minutes later, Jones pulled the car into the ASDA car park and circled round until he spotted the patrol car parked up in a far corner, out of sight of most of the shoppers and facing outwards so they could see the majority of the car park.

After pulling in next to it, Phillips deployed her electric window as the officer in the passenger seat did the same.

'Still no sign of her, ma'am,' he said.

'Where's the car?'

'Just over there. We've got a clear view of it.'

Phillips nodded. 'How long have you been here?'

'Just over twenty minutes.'

'OK.' Phillips passed over her business card. 'We may have an idea where she's headed, so we're going to head over there and check it out. In the meantime, if you spot her, call me immediately.'

'Yes, ma'am.'

Phillips continued, 'This woman is a suspect in two homicides and may well be armed in some way, so this is a watching brief. No heroics, OK?'

'Understood,' said the officer.

Phillips closed her window as Jones began to reverse out of the space.

'According to Google Maps, there's a car park at this side of the viaduct. Let's head over there and see if there's any sign of her.'

'Sounds like a plan,' replied Jones as he manoeuvred the car towards the exit.

43

The contents of the bag were surprisingly heavy. She'd never had any reason to handle it until today; Des's pride and joy since buying it a couple of years ago. As such, he'd kept it under lock and key in a specially made box stored in the garage, and he'd never have let her near it had he been at home. In all honesty, she'd completely forgotten it was there until this morning when she spotted the key to the lock box on his bunch of keys. A lucky coincidence or divine intervention, she wondered.

Just as she had hoped, it was mercifully dark now the winter sun had fully set, but the full moon at least allowed her to see where she was going as she moved through the shadows.

Ten minutes later, and feeling distinctly out of breath, she reached her final destination and for the first time in twenty years gazed out across Outwood Viaduct, the scene of so many of her childhood nightmares. Standing here now was suddenly incredibly triggering, making her feel sick to her stomach. Her natural instinct was to run away and hide, just as she had tried to do as a child, but to no avail. No matter where she ran, Albert would always find her. And the same was true today, even after all these years. Unless she took control of the situation, he would haunt her and Lesley for the rest of their lives.

She took a deep breath to steady herself before making her way to the spot near the edge that she figured would be the best place to activate her plan. Scanning her surroundings she felt confident she was very much alone in that moment, and after dropping the bag to ground, she crouched down and unzipped it, checking inside to make sure all was as it should be. Happy everything was ready, she stood up and waited.

It wasn't long before the sickly smell of her father's tobacco wafted through the night air, and she turned to see him walking awkwardly towards her, his limping gait visible in the moonlight, the rolled-up cigarette between his lips glowing in the darkness as he took another drag.

'Hello, Lina,' he said, exhaling smoke. 'Nice night for it, isn't it?'

She swallowed hard as her heart pounded in her chest.

Albert took another long drag before casting his butt end to the ground. 'So where is she, then?'

'Not far,' she said, attempting to keep her voice level. 'I'll bring her out in a minute.'

'This is all very cloak and dagger, isn't it?' He chuckled. 'But then you always did have a flair for the dramatic.'

She didn't respond and instead stared back at him.

'I must admit, I was surprised when you suggested this as the location of our rendezvous.' He flashed a wicked grin. 'I guess this place means something to you two girls after all.'

'I brought you here for the same reason you did all those years ago,' she bit back. 'Because it's so isolated.'

'Oh really?' His smile was visible even in the darkness. 'What did you have in mind?'

She had to fight the urge to vomit, listening to his vile patter. 'Why did you do it, Albert?'

'Do what?'

'Rape your own daughters?' It was the question that had plagued her her entire life, and now she was finally ready to hear the answer.

'It wasn't rape,' he said nonchalantly. 'It was lovemaking.'

'Lovemaking?' She found herself shaking her head. 'You're sick.'

'It's society that's sick. Not me.'

'And how do you work that out?'

'Because if I were a tribesman in certain parts of the world, it would be expected – as the alpha male – that I would show love to my offspring in the way I did to you and Lesley. And as a man of distinction, a doctor no less, it would be my duty to sow my seed with as many young women in the tribe as possible.'

She was incredulous now. 'We weren't women, we were *children*.'

'Mere semantics, Lina.'

'Semantics?'

'The only reason you were classed as children is because, over time, society has changed its view on what is deemed an acceptable age for procreation. I mean, it wasn't that long ago – as recently as the reign of Queen Victoria in fact – that it was commonplace for girls in their early teens to have children with much older men. In truth, the only real crime here was that I was born into the wrong era based on the age of the women I'm attracted to.'

'You really believe that, don't you?'

'It's true. I had a lot of time to study in prison, and it's all there in the history books.'

'And what was all that crap this morning, then, about it being a disease, and that you're not like that anymore?'

'A well-rehearsed line I used on the parole board,' he said with a smirk.

'More lies.'

'Plus I told you what you wanted to hear.' He waved her away. 'I knew you'd never let me near Lesley otherwise.'

Her jaw clenched so tightly now she thought her teeth might crack. 'Have you any idea what you did to us? Of what you *took* from us?'

'Whatever you feel was lost or taken from you is society's fault, not mine. All those social workers and police officers polluted your mind. If they'd left you well alone, in time you'd have grown to appreciate – even cherish – the love I showed you. Just like your sister did.'

'What the hell are you talking about?'

'Lesley understood my love for her, and that's why she didn't testify against me.'

'Are you for real?' she raged. 'She was fucking terrified of you. That's why she didn't testify – and that's why she's not slept for three weeks since she heard you got out of prison.'

'That's nonsense. She loved me as much as I loved her. Bring her out, and she can tell you herself.'

Shaking her head, she let out an ironic chuckle. 'You didn't *really* think I was going to bring her here, did you? Subject her to a monster like you again.'

'What are you talking about?' Albert's posture visibly stiffened. 'Where is she?'

'Safe from you and a *long* way from here.'

'Don't lie to me, girl,' he growled.

'I'm not lying, Albert. Tonight is just about me and you.'

'So what the fuck did you bring me all the way out here for?'

'To make sure you never bother her – or any other young girl for that matter – ever again.'

He laughed loudly now. 'Oh really? And how do you propose to do that?'

In one fluid movement she bent down and pulled out the shotgun from the large sports bag before training it on his chest.

He instinctively raised his hands in surrender. 'What the hell is that for?'

'Let's call it a bit of encouragement,' she replied. 'Now, walk over to the edge.'

44

Phillips held her phone in her hand as she used the torch feature to guide their way along the darkened path to the viaduct located about five hundred metres ahead of them. After so much rain lately and with the temperature dropping rapidly, it seemed the ground beneath their feet was becoming more slippery with every step.

'I don't think I'm wearing the right shoes for this,' said Jones, taking tentative steps alongside her.

'Me either,' she replied just as her phone began to vibrate in her hand. Glancing at the screen, she could see that Bovalino was calling. After hitting the green phone icon, she activated the speaker function. 'Bov?'

'Guv, I've found something on the system I thought you'd want to know about.'

'Go on.'

'I was going back through one of the domestic incident reports involving Paula, and I noticed her husband, Des, has a firearms licence.'

'Firearms?' Jones was incredulous. 'That information wasn't flagged when I did her background check.'

'This particular report was saved as a draft and not published,' Bovalino replied. 'So it wouldn't have come up automatically when you keyed her name in.'

'So what kind of firearms are we talking about?' Phillips asked.

'A shotgun and a rifle.'

'And are the licences active?'

'The rifle has expired, but the shotgun one is, guv.'

'Jesus,' Phillips muttered. 'We're going to need the Tactical Firearms Unit down here ASAP.'

'I can sort that,' said the big man. 'Where exactly do you want them?'

'Outwood Viaduct,' she replied. 'We don't actually know for sure that she's in this exact location, but we do believe she's somewhere in the vicinity. And if there's chance she has a shotgun we'd better hang back until the firearms unit gets here.'

'I'll call them right now,' said Bovalino.

A split second later, a thunderous bang filled the air in the distance, stopping Phillips and Jones in their tracks. It had come from the viaduct, and it was a sound she was, sadly, only too familiar with as she locked eyes with Jones. 'Did that sound like a shotgun to you?'

He nodded as he swallowed hard. 'Yeah, it did.'

'Shit. There's no time to wait.' Phillips set off running in the direction that the shot had come from. 'We need the TFU here now, Bov!' she yelled into the phone before ending the call.

'Bollocks,' said Jones as he set off running after her.

AFTER FIRING the warning shot in the air above Albert's head, Paula trained the smoking gun on his chest once more. 'I won't miss next time. So do as you're told, and move to the edge.'

Albert's arms remained raised in surrender as he took a couple of steps backwards. 'We both know you won't shoot me, Lina. You won't hurt your dad.'

The hatred she felt as she stared at him was like a living thing, eating away at her insides. Stepping forward, she kept the gun pointed at his chest. 'You're not my dad. You ceased being that the moment you took away my innocence. You're nothing but a sick, deluded pervert, and the world will be a much better place without you in it.'

'That's a lot of big talk for a weak little woman,' he spat back.

She let out an ironic chuckle. 'You think I'm weak, do you?'

'You're not a killer, Lina. We both know that.'

'Really?' She took another step closer. 'Well, how come I've killed two people in the last month?'

'Pah,' he scoffed. 'What utter nonsense. Who did you ever kill?'

'Charlie Callus for a start.' Her spine tingled as she admitted her guilt out loud.

'The car salesman they found in Salford? You saw that on the news, just like everybody else.'

'Oh, no. It was me. *I* killed him.'

'How? How did you kill him?'

'I pushed him down the stairs,' she replied calmly. 'I was his cleaner, you see. Privy to some of his biggest secrets, and like you – and just like that good-for-nothing husband of mine, Des – Charlie was an abuser. So when I saw his poor wife, blood pouring from her mouth after he'd given her a backhander, well, I just lost it. I hit him with my broom, and he fell backwards down the stairs. Smashed his skull in. I didn't mean to kill him, but I'm not sorry that I did. He got what was coming to him, and now his wife is free.' She tightened her grip on the shotgun. 'And then there was the pervert on the train. Getting away with abusing women day after day. It was only a matter of time before he escalated and raped some teenage girl – yet, no one was willing to do anything about it. Not even the police. So when I saw him bearing down on that poor young girl, and the train coming into the station, I decided it was up to me to step up and take that responsibility. *I would stop him.* And so I did. One big shove in the back and that was the end of him. The end of his abuse.'

Albert shook his head vigorously. 'This is bullshit. None of this happened, Lina. You're imagining it, having a breakdown.'

She rubbed the trigger of the shotgun with her index finger. 'I am *not* having a breakdown,' she growled. 'Far from it. My mind is clearer than it's ever been.'

'You might think that, Lina, but believe me, this has all the signs of a breakdown,' he replied. 'You're suffering with delusional fantasies that feel like real life. But they aren't. Put the gun down, and let me help you.'

'Enough!' she screamed. 'I've heard all your psycho-babble bullshit before. You can't help me. You're incapable of helping anyone. You're the one who's delusional. Acting as if child rape is some kind of noble blessing you bestowed on your victims.' She prodded him with the barrel of the gun once more, pushing him further back.

A moment later he stopped in his tracks as he came up against the waist-high railings that acted as a barrier between the edge and the seventy-foot drop to the river below.

Her pulse quickened and her adrenaline spiked as she pressed the gun against his chest and stared deep into his black eyes. 'Now jump.'

Glancing over his shoulder, he took a moment to survey the drop, then turned back to face her. 'No fucking way, Lina.'

'Jump!' she yelled, shoving the end of the gun against him.

In that instant, Albert grabbed the barrel with both hands and in one fluid movement pushed the shotgun away.

The action caused Paula's finger to pull hard against the trigger, and a second deafening shot rang out across the night sky.

'You're out of cartridges,' he hissed before slamming his left fist into her right temple.

She stumbled backwards, the gun still in her hands, her world spinning as she struggled to stay upright.

He continued his assault, smashing his right hand into the bridge of her nose with a sickening crack as it broke on impact.

As blood poured from her nostrils, she instinctively dropped the gun and raised her arms in a vain attempt to protect herself, but it was no use as he struck her a third time, knocking her clean off her feet before she fell to the cold hard ground in a heap.

'You should have let me help you when you had the chance,' he growled before slamming his heavy boot onto the side of her head.

A split second later, her world went black.

IN THE GLARE from the moonlight, Phillips could see what appeared to be a man attempting to lift something heavy up and over the railings up ahead, and as they drew closer, it became clear the man was Albert Stone, and the heavy object was Paula Thomas.

'Stop right there!' she demanded as they came within twenty feet of them both. Paula's head and torso were already hanging over the railings face down as she let out a series of moans. Evidently she'd been beaten almost unconscious.

Albert stopped what he was doing and turned to face them, staring at them in silence.

Even in the moonlight, Phillips could see his black, soulless eyes dancing in his head, and a chill ran down her spine as she sensed the evil that was trapped within him.

With Jones at her back, she raised her hands in surrender as she took a gentle step closer. 'Albert, I need you to stop what you're doing *right now*.'

He shook his head as he adjusted his grip on Paula, hoisting more of her body over the railings as he did. 'I can't do that. This little bitch has to pay for what she did to me. She tried to kill me, you see.'

'I know, Albert. And *I'll* make sure she faces justice for that – *not you*.'

'No,' he said flatly. 'This is a family matter.'

'That's right,' she shot back, quick as a flash. 'It is a family affair. Paula's your daughter. You don't want to kill her.'

He was holding her in such a way now that the only thing stopping her from tumbling to the water below was his grip on her thighs. 'I only have *one* daughter, and that's my Lesley. This wretched little bastard means nothing to me.'

Phillips moved within just a couple of feet of him as he continued to hold Paula's thighs in his grip. Her moans were growing in volume now as she began to come round.

'Think very carefully about what you're doing, Albert. If you drop her over the edge, you'll spend the rest of your days in prison. Is that what you want?'

'I've no doubt you want to send me back there anyway. I may as well clear out the trash before I do.'

'It'll be murder, Albert,' said Phillips, moving to within touching distance of him now. 'And at your age, that means you'll die in prison.'

He shrugged. 'Everyone's gotta die somewhere.' A split second later he bent almost double as he grabbed Paula round the shins and flipped her over the railings, only to stop a split second later as her Dr Martens boot snagged on the upright post of the railing. Suddenly fully conscious, her screams filled the air as she hung seventy feet above the blackness of the water below.

Acting on instinct alone, Phillips lurched forward and thrust out a hand as she hooked her fingers into the laces of Paula's boot as she attempted to get a grip on her.

Jones was by her side in a flash.

'Where's Albert?' Phillips asked as she locked her left hand onto Paula's ankle.

'He's legged it,' Jones said as he reached over the railings and grabbed Paula's other leg before her boot ripped open and she fell to her death. 'She's too heavy. I don't think we can hold her.'

'Get your handcuffs out,' said Phillips.

'I don't want to let go,' he growled as Paula begged for them to save her.

'Just do it; otherwise she's a goner.'

Reluctantly, Jones released his grip and swiftly pulled out his handcuffs.

'Put one end around her ankle and the other around my wrist,' she instructed. 'Quickly.'

Jones was on his knees in an instant, leaning through the railings, and a moment later, Phillips felt the thick metal bracelet lock onto her wrist before he fixed the other end around Paula's left ankle.

A sudden searing pain shot through her shoulder as Paula's weight bore down through the handcuff, causing her to cry out.

'Are you OK, guv?' Jones asked in a panic as he stood back up.

'Forget about me, just get her up.'

Jones didn't hesitate leaning dangerously far over the edge of the railings now as he attempted to pull her up.

The pain Phillips felt through her arm and shoulder now was like nothing she'd ever known. She took a deep breath in an attempt to block it out. 'On three…'

Jones nodded as he secured his grip on Paula's right leg.

'One, two, three.'

They both heaved with all their might, and mercifully, they managed to lift Paula far enough upwards so Jones could get a grip on her thigh.

Paula continued to scream hysterically.

With Phillips's wrist still connected to Paula's ankle, she was forced to take a step backwards. 'And again,' she said. 'On three.'

Repeating the process a couple more times, they inched Paula upwards far enough to dislodge her boot and for Jones to latch onto her arms. Then, with one final gargantuan effort, they hauled her up and over the railings. As they did so, Phillips heard a loud pop and felt the pain in her right shoulder intensify as the three of them fell heavily into a heap on the ground, causing her to cry out in agony for a second time.

'What's happened? Where does it hurt, guv?' Jones asked.

Her shoulder was not the priority right now. 'Get Stone,' she managed to mutter through gritted teeth. 'Don't let him get away.'

Jones nodded before jumping to his feet and, after taking a moment to release Phillips and Paula from the handcuffs, set off running into the darkness.

With an ungodly pain surging through her shoulder, Phillips managed to sit upright next to Paula, who was lying on the ground next to her, breathing heavily and sobbing like a child.

It was the last thing Phillips wanted to do given what the poor woman had just been through, but she was duty-bound to do it. Inching painfully closer to her now, she clicked one end of the handcuff onto Paula's wrist and the other onto the metal shaft that a moment ago had supported her boot and inadvertently saved her life. 'Paula Thomas, I'm arresting you for the murders of Charlie Callus and Patrick Mahoney. You do not have to say anything, but it may harm your defence if you do not mention when questioned something which you later rely on in court. Anything you do say may be given in evidence.'

THE GROUND WAS EVEN MORE slippery now as the temperature continued to drop.

Up ahead, Jones could just about make out Albert

hobbling at pace under the glare of the full moon, back towards the retail park.

'Stop!' Jones shouted after him.

Albert didn't flinch and instead continued unabated.

Despite the slippery conditions, Jones began to gain on him, and just a few minutes later as the lights of the busy shopping area came into view, Albert was less than a hundred feet in front of him.

Pulling his phone from his pocket, Jones dialled Bov.

'Firearms are five minutes out,' said the big man as soon as he answered.

'I don't have time to explain but I'm in pursuit of Albert Stone on foot,' he shouted between breaths. 'Tell the uniform team at the retail park he's heading their way. And get an ambulance out here for the guv and Paula.'

'Are they OK?'

'I think so, yeah, but I'm pretty sure they've both sustained injuries.'

'What should I tell the TFU?'

'Anything you like, the priority is the uniform team and that ambulance.'

'You got it,' said Bovalino before ringing off.

Slipping the phone back into his pocket, Jones continued to chase down his target.

As he reached the edge of the retail park he took a moment to locate the uniform team, who had jumped out of their vehicle and were now looking in his direction. He pointed to Albert, who was now limping across the car park, shuffling between cars as he attempted to evade capture. 'That's him!' he shouted at the top of his voice.

Albert stopped in his tracks and turned first to Jones and, after following his line of sight, cast his gaze towards the two uniformed officers looking in his direction. A split second later and without hesitation, he turned and set off at pace again.

Jones had never been known for his fitness, but he wasn't about to let Albert get away, and it was with a renewed determination that he made his way carefully down the now slippery grass bank and gave chase across the car park.

The place was teaming with cars and people moving in all directions, but Jones kept his eyes locked on the prize ahead as he found himself gaining on him with every step.

With the uniform team closing in from the right, and Jones at his back, Albert began glancing over his shoulder with every few steps taken until he reached the busy junction that connected the retail park to the main road ahead. Unable to move forward momentarily as he attempted to find a break in the traffic, he hopped from foot to foot, his eyes darting between Jones and the uniformed team as they closed in on him.

'It's no use, Albert,' shouted Jones as he approached. 'We've got you surrounded.'

Albert locked eyes with him, then looked across at the two officers moving ever closer, before glancing at the traffic streaming behind him at speed.

'I'm not going back to prison,' he said firmly.

'That's *exactly* where you're going, mate,' said Jones, moving to within a few feet of him now. 'It's over. Time to give yourself up.'

Albert flashed a knowing smile. 'I won't be caged again,' he said before turning and stepping off the kerb.

A sickening thud, followed by the screeching sound of hydraulic brakes activating filled the cold night air as

Albert Stone's miserable life was finally extinguished – his evil tenure on earth brought to a close under the front wheels of a fast-moving articulated delivery lorry.

45

TWO DAYS LATER

Carter arrived at Phillips's door just as Jones was placing a steaming cup of coffee on her desk.
'Do you want one, sir?' asked Jones.
'No, thanks,' Carter replied with a soft smile. 'I've just put one out.'
'My first of the day,' said Phillips, wincing slightly as she picked up the cup in her left hand, her right arm locked in a blue fabric sling.
Carter shook his head as he placed his hands in his trouser pockets. 'You know, you really should be at home, Jane.'
'That's what I keep telling her,' said Jones as he took the seat opposite her desk.
'Don't you two start as well,' she grumbled. 'I've had enough of that from Adam.'
'Well, he is a doctor,' said Carter. 'You might want to think about listening to his advice.'
Phillips took a sip of her coffee. 'I'd only be sitting at

home worrying about the IPCC investigation, so I'm better off at work. At least I've got plenty of distractions here.'

'Like the Paula Thomas case?' ventured Carter.

'Exactly,' she replied.

'So what's the latest with that one?'

Phillips nodded to Jones. 'Can you fetch the file?'

After placing his mug on Phillips's desk, Jones jumped up from the chair and headed out to the office, returning a moment later with a thick file in his hand. After opening it up, he pulled out a single sheet of printed paper, which he handed to Carter.

'That's the prepared statement her solicitor has come up with,' said Phillips. As Carter scanned the page, she continued, 'They're going for diminished responsibility in the cases of Callus and Mahoney. They claim after suffering years of domestic abuse at the hands of her husband, Paula was triggered by the release of her sexually abusive father into committing the acts that led to both deaths. They're saying the same on the additional charge of the attempted murder of Albert Stone, too.'

Carter nodded. 'Makes sense. A good KC will no doubt paint the picture of a diminished and emotionally damaged woman systematically driven to breaking point.' He handed the paper back to Jones. 'And what about the attack on her husband. Does that come into play?'

'Not really, but as we already know, she was claiming self-defence on that one based on the fact he had a history of knocking her about. He finally came out of his coma last night, so no doubt the Domestic team will be talking to him to get his version of events.'

'Well, I'm not surprised they've gone down the diminished responsibility and self-defence routes,' said Carter.

'Most juries would lap that up given what she's been through over the years.'

'You sound like you almost feel sorry for her, sir,' said Phillips.

'Not sorry, no, but I can perhaps understand why she reacted the way she did.'

Phillips nodded. 'I have to say I'm a bit conflicted myself. On one hand, I'm sympathetic to her as a woman who suffered years of abuse throughout her life. But on the other hand, she also murdered two people and planned to kill a third. And no matter how she tries to justify it, she can't be allowed to walk away from that.'

'Well, whatever happens to her,' added Jones, 'at least she doesn't have to worry about Stone terrorising her or her sister anymore.'

Phillips nodded. 'He did everyone a favour when he stepped off that kerb.'

Just then Carter's phone began to ring. Pulling it from his pocket, his shoulders sagged as he glanced down at the screen. 'It's Brown,' he said before stepping out the door to answer it.

Phillips glanced at Jones, who gave her a knowing look as she took another sip of her coffee.

Carter stepped back in a moment later. 'Brown wants to see us in his office right away.'

'*Us?*' Her heart sank. 'That's all I need right now.'

'I know, but he said it's urgent.'

'It always is with him.' She winced as she pushed her chair back and stood up.

Jones matched her. 'I'd best be getting back to work, boss.'

Phillips nodded, then slowly followed Carter out.

FIVE MINUTES later they were being ushered into Brown's office by his ever-enthusiastic PA, Viv.

Once inside, they found Brown standing with his back to them at the far side of the room, looking out the window.

Phillips was once again struck by how small he looked in his official police uniform.

Carter cleared his throat to announce their arrival.

Brown turned, his expression grave. 'Ah. Thank you for coming so promptly.' He gestured to the two chairs in front of his desk. 'Please take a seat.'

As Phillips painfully took her position next to Carter, her stomach churned in anticipation of what was to come.

Brown sat forward in his oversized leather chair and linked his fingers together on the desk.

'I believe congratulations are in order on the Callus and Mahoney cases,' said Brown without feeling.

'Yes, sir,' replied Carter enthusiastically. 'DCI Phillips and the team did a great job in tracking down Paula Thomas.'

'It would appear so, although it looks like you came off a little worse for wear, Chief Inspector.'

Phillips forced a smile. 'I'll be all right. Just a ruptured rotator cuff.'

Brown couldn't have seemed less interested as he sat forward. 'Anyway, those investigations are not the reason why I wanted to speak to you.'

Phillips's mouth dried instantly.

Brown continued, 'I wanted to give you both an update on the state of play with the IPCC investigation.'

'Really, sir?' Carter replied. 'What's happened?'

Phillips swallowed the dry lump in her throat.

'Er, well...erm.' Brown appeared to be searching for the right words. 'Things have changed, and the investigation has gone in a different direction.'

Carter frowned. 'Sorry, sir. I'm not following you.'

Brown shifted in his seat. 'The decision has been made to pause the investigation for the time being.'

Phillips felt herself do a slight double take. 'It's been paused, sir?'

'Yes.' Brown sniffed with disdain. 'It seems the higher-ups believe that another internal investigation – especially coming so soon after the revelations around Fox – could be damaging to the force as a whole.'

'Higher-ups, sir?' asked Phillips. 'Who exactly are we talking about here?'

Brown cleared his throat before replying, 'The Home Secretary.'

Phillips tried to hide the shock she felt in that moment. The Home Secretary had intervened? My God. This was big news.

Brown continued, 'It seems that the Police and Crimes Commissioner shared the fact that the investigation was taking place with the Home Secretary, and having considered all the options, she felt it was not in the best interest of the GMP to continue with it at the present time.'

'Wow.' Carter turned to Phillips. 'Looks like MCU has a new ally in Whitehall.'

'Well, let's not congratulate ourselves *too* quickly,' Brown cut in. 'As I say, the investigation has been paused as opposed to closed. And that means it can be reinstated at any point should the conduct of DCI Phillips – or anyone else in MCU for that matter – come under scrutiny in the future. Is that understood?'

'Oh, of course, sir,' Carter shot back enthusiastically.

Phillips, though, wasn't about to let him off the hook *quite* so easily. 'So does this mean you no longer want me to take early retirement, sir?'

'Not at this moment in time. No.'

'Looks like it's good news all round, then, doesn't it?' she said, trying hard to keep the smile from her face.

Brown stared back in silence for a long moment, his jaw clenching slightly. 'Right, well, I've got a lot on today,' he said finally. 'So don't let me keep you.'

A minute later, out in the corridor and well out of earshot, Phillips and Carter debriefed.

'Well, that's a result,' he said with a wide grin.

Phillips let out a loud sigh of relief. 'I can't believe it.'

'The Home Secretary stepped in?' said Carter. 'That's *insane*.'

Her head was spinning as she attempted to process what had just happened.

'Not a bad person to have in your corner,' he added. 'You must be relieved.'

'Like you wouldn't believe.' She shook her head. 'I don't think it's sunk in yet.'

'Well, let it. You're free and clear.'

'Yeah.' She nodded lightly. 'I wonder if this will have any impact on Brown's plans to merge the teams?'

'Who knows,' said Carter. 'But let's not worry about that today, hey? Let's just celebrate this win. *Your* win.'

Phillips blew her lips. 'Yeah. I honestly can't believe it. The *Home Secretary*.'

'I know. Brilliant, isn't it? And this time she's stepped in to save someone who actually deserves her help.'

Phillips let out an ironic chuckle. 'Just when I think this job couldn't get any stranger…'

'We should celebrate,' said Carter. 'Can I buy you a drink after work?'

Suddenly in that exact moment, she felt a wave of fatigue crash over her and was acutely aware of the pain in her shoulder. 'Actually, sir, can we take a rain check? If you don't mind, I'd quite like to take you up on that offer to go home.'

He smiled softly. 'A very sensible idea indeed.'

'Thank you, sir. I suddenly feel absolutely knackered.'

'I'm not surprised. It's been a tough couple of weeks.'

'It really has,' she replied.

'Take as long as you need, and when you're feeling up to it, you must let me buy you that drink to celebrate.'

'I'll look forward to it.'

'Would you like me to give the team the good news?' he asked.

'No. I'd like to tell them if that's ok?',

'Of course.'

'And then if it's all right with you, I'll get off home.'

'Absolutely.'

She locked eyes with him now. 'Thanks for all your support on this, sir. I know my actions have caused you a lot of unnecessary stress over the last few weeks.'

There was a glint in his eyes now. 'I'm sure I don't know what you mean, Jane.'

She nodded as she let out an ironic chuckle.

'Go on,' urged Carter. 'You get yourself away.'

'I will. Thank you,' she said before turning and heading back towards the lifts.

Soon after, as she stepped into the elevator, the enormity of what had just happened began to dawn on her. She – a lowly DCI – had been given a get-out-of-jail-free card by one of the most powerful women in government – the

Home Secretary. Not only that, she knew the decision to save her had been taken well over Brown's head, something he would have absolutely detested. As the door closed, she allowed herself a wry smile. Carter was right; it seemed she now had a very powerful ally in Whitehall, something that would come in very handy in future when it came to keeping Brown in his tiny box.

ACKNOWLEDGMENTS

This book would not have been possible without a host of amazing people.

First and always foremost, my wife, Kim, who is my biggest cheerleader and my greatest advocate.

My lush little boy, Vaughan, who makes me smile every day with his stories and complete obsession with everything Newcastle United and football.

Carole Lawford, ex-CPS Prosecutor, and retired police officer, Bryn Jones; your guidance on British Law was as robust as ever.

My coaches, Dr Donna Elliott and Cheryl Reid, from 'Now Is Your Time'. Your faith and unwavering support inspire me every day.

Thanks to my publishing team of Jan, Brian, Garret, Stephen, Claire, Alice and Lizzie. I couldn't do this without you.

And finally, thank you to my readers for reading *Deadly Fury*. If you could spend a moment to write an honest review, no matter how short, I would be extremely grateful. They really do help readers discover my books.

www.omjryan.com

ALSO BY OMJ RYAN

The DCI Jane Phillips Crime Thriller Series
(Books listed in order)
DEADLY SECRETS (a series prequel)
DEADLY SILENCE
DEADLY WATERS
DEADLY VENGEANCE
DEADLY BETRAYAL
DEADLY OBSESSION
DEADLY CALLER
DEADLY NIGHT
DEADLY CRAVING
DEADLY JUSTICE
DEADLY VEIL
DEADLY INFERNO
DEADLY FURY

DCI JANE PHILLIPS BOX SET
(Books 1-4 in the series)

Printed in Great Britain
by Amazon